I0653476

SAVAGE RENDEZVOUS

The Nickie Savage Series
Book Two

◆ • ◆ • ◆

R.T. Wolfe

Photography by SL Jones Photography

Cover and Book design by eBook Prep www.ebookprep.com

First Edition, August 2014
ISBN: 978-1-61417-644-2

ePublishing Works!
www.epublishingworks.com

CHAPTER 1

Fist cocked, Nickie bolted upright. Her chest rose and fell like she'd just run down a perp. Although her eyes were opened wide, everything was blurry as hell.

No. This wasn't real. There was no Jun Zheng. No danger.

Soft, warm sheets. They lay over her legs and waist. Darting her gaze to the side, she spotted Duncan's easels, the stool he used and her cello.

Oh no. Duncan.

Blinking rapidly in the silence, she forced her eyes to find him. He sat next to her, fully dressed, his arm lifted in a traditional high block. The scenario was becoming all too common. He didn't speak. Wasn't much of a talker. His eyes said enough. Pity and pain.

"Oh, Duncan." She lifted both arms in surrender. "Why do we keep doing this?" Taking his flexed forearm, she lowered it carefully as she watched his deep chocolate eyes turn from the two Ps to the two Cs, cold and calculated.

He pushed away the hair from her sweaty forehead and tucked it behind her ear. The lines in his jaw were tight and familiar. She didn't allow herself the luxury of touching them. Standing, he gestured to the wet bar. "There is fresh yogurt and orange juice in the fridge. The Diet Coke is in the back."

As she took one last deep breath, her heart rate slowed to almost normal. Brilliant rays beat down from the sunlit windows in the ceiling onto the spotless bedroom floor. His briefcase stood open on his desk.

She should use her head. Yell at him and tell him to stop stocking his fridge with food only she would eat. Stop asking her to stay the night when they both knew he could end up with a black eye. Instead, she spoke from her heart. "Thanks. I'm going to hit the pool before I leave. You look ready to go. Don't wait up."

"You might want to skip the workout this morning." He nodded to the grandfather clock that stood centered along the far wall. Stoic. Beautiful. Too classy for her. Was she internally describing the clock or Duncan?

"Seven-frigging-thirty?" Her heart went back to racing as she whipped the covers from her waist. The burst of cool air created goose bumps along her arms and legs and helped her escape the dream. The thought of being late for work made her forget it altogether. "What the hell? Why didn't you wake me?"

"Because you just went to sleep four hours ago," he said as he closed his briefcase.

The hair that nearly matched the deep color of his eyes, curled slightly over his shirt collar, the way it did when it was almost dry from his shower. He already had on his suit jacket, but it couldn't hide his physique. Lanky and toned.

"That's your fault," she complained with an evil grin.

The sexy smile that spread across his face changed

her mind about the workout. "I can catch some zzzs at the station." She stood and looked around. "Where's my—"

Duncan reached out his arm, laced his rough fingertips across her cheek, then into her hair. His subtle scent of earthy cologne reminded her of the woods mixed with a clean art canvass. This time, the rise in her heart rate was for a completely different reason. Glancing down, she realized she was butt naked. The palm of his hand was warm and rested on the curve of her hip. He pulled her in and kissed her once, twice. The taste of him made everything else disappear.

"It snowed last night," he said. "I cleared the drive, and the plows have already made a pass on the highway. Will I see you tonight?"

She nodded helplessly as her phone rang. It was Eddy's ringtone. Duncan's expression turned…expressionless.

"I gotta get that." It was silly, she knew, but she threw on underwear and her bra before answering. "Savage," she said, setting it on speaker as she finished dressing.

"Late night, Nick? You gonna show up anytime today?"

"Shut up, asshole. What do you want?"

"We've got a stiff. Found in the alley behind the Noble Strip Mall by a garbage truck driver. You think you can make it? Or do you have to ask Pretty Boy permission to leave?"

She glanced at Duncan. His jaw muscles flexed and released.

"I'm on my way," she said, then clicked off.

"He needs to be pummeled," Duncan growled.

As she tugged on yesterday's slacks, she tried to temper him. "You two already did that. All shows of testosterone settled and complete."

"He crosses the line and—"

"I know, I know. I can take care of it." She had never been good at this side of men.

Crime tape closed off both ends of the alley behind Northridge's stuffiest strip mall. From what Nickie could tell at this end, there were four black and whites and an ambulance. She guessed that meant no possibility of a heart attack victim.

She double-parked her beloved tank and left it unlocked. "Morning, Parker," she said to her favorite beat cop as she pulled on her leather gloves. How much snow could come down in one winter, she wondered as she watched her breath in front of her. Parker stood as crowd control and nodded to her in return. "Lighten up some, Parker. It's a sunny day."

"Yes, ma—Yes, Detective," he corrected. Smart guy. He lifted the yellow tape for her. As she reached Eddy, she spotted the ME's car. Shit. When was the last time she was so late to a crime scene that the medical examiner beat her there? Next, she noticed the odor. Sheesh. It wasn't the unmistakable stench of a rotting corpse or even the copper scent of blood, but the smell of ripe garbage.

A garbage truck was close to the back door of an espresso shop with a dumpster turned upside down and hovering over the open compactor.

"Morning, Savage." Eddy Lynx was a good detective and an all right friend. She may not be any good at shows of testosterone, but she knew how to keep a man from crossing the line. It wouldn't be like him to razz her about being late in front of the other uniforms. "Garbage dude found him," he said. "He's the one puking in a bag." He pointed at a man who sat on the bumper of the ambulance. Great.

Eddy finished briefing her. "He was in a body bag of all things. Garbage guy says he picks up once a week. Pretty clean place," he said, looking around the alley.

Newer brick buildings lined the wide alley. Other than an occasional dumpster, it was spotless.

"He must not have been lying here long, or someone would have noticed. Then again, he was tucked beneath the dumpster." Eddy shrugged a shoulder before continuing. "Doesn't look that stiff anyway. Rickard is checking him out now."

After stepping over to the ME, Nickie leaned by Rickard's head as the she dipped uncomfortably close to the corpse. The stiff looked fresh enough. She had the guy's shirt open, examining some abrasions on the chest mixed with a handful of gunshots. Sloppy shots. That, plus some random dark red circles said it wasn't a professional hit. She wished she'd gotten to the vic before the ME but kept a respectful distance while Rickard worked.

As Nickie waited, she walked the scene. The plows hadn't been through yet, likely were turned away by Parker or the beat cop at the other end of the alley. Her boots crunched over the fresh snow as she took note of the evenly spaced brown doors on each side of the alley. They were the back doors to the strip mall shops and eateries. Only a few had nameplates identifying what was on the other side.

Clearly, the guy wasn't dropped from the roof, but she looked up anyway. Both buildings were single story. A body bag? That was weird. The driver was still sheet white, but at least he wasn't puking anymore. She pulled out her ancient recorder before she approached him so she wouldn't have to shake his hand.

"Good morning. I'm Detective Savage." His

forearms rested on his thighs, so she squatted down to his level. "I need to ask you some questions."

"More questions?"

She understood the guy was likely just minding his own business, out doing his crap job on an early Wednesday morning, but it still rubbed her wrong. "I know." She did her best at sounding sympathetic. "This death stuff takes a long time." Hopefully, he didn't catch her sarcasm. "I'm going to record this, okay?"

He nodded.

She rattled off the date and brought the recorder closer to him. "Could you answer for the recorder, please? Are you giving me, Detective Nickie Savage, permission to record this conversation?"

"Yes."

"Thank you. Name?"

He sighed. "Terry Moore."

"In your own words, Mr. Moore, tell me what happened."

Straightening, he took a sip from the bottle of water that dangled from his fingers. He was a large man. Long brown hair slipped from the back of his cap. Maybe between twenty-five and thirty.

"I was emptying the dumpsters in the alley. That one—" He gestured to the one hanging upside down over his truck. "- -was my fourth. As I used the lift to raise it over the back of the truck, I noticed the black bag on the ground and shut her down. I walked over and—" He lifted the back of his hand to his mouth. "I thought someone must have tossed it out and missed the dumpster. I tried to move it, and I could tell...I called 9-1-1."

"Was there anything out of place when you were emptying the other dumpsters? You said this was your fourth."

"No."

"Anyone in the alley? Any doors open to businesses?"

"No. Was he murdered?"

It was a fair question. "We won't know for some time," she lied. "Thank you for your help. We may be in touch." She patted his shoulder and turned to check on Rickard.

"Preliminary assessment says he's been dead between three to five hours." No greeting or pleasantries from someone like Leslie Rickard. "His pockets were empty. Could be a robbery gone wrong, but I guess that's up to you to decide." It was a good thing she was the medical examiner and not the detective. If the dude was robbed, the perp wouldn't have been carrying around a body bag for cleanup.

Rickard was all business, and since she didn't bother to turn and look at Nickie, must have ID'd her by her boots. "He's cold but not stiff. It's what, twenty degrees out this morning? I'm going to say he died from the gunshots, but I'll have something more conclusive when I get him on a table." She finished writing in her notebook, took off her gloves, stood and stretched like she'd been squatting in the cold for an hour. Nickie guessed it was because she'd been squatting in the cold for an hour. "All yours, Detective. Good morning."

Nickie jutted up her chin once in acknowledgement, then squatted down, taking Rickard's spot. She judged the man to be forty to forty-five years old. Caucasian. She pulled on a pair of gloves from her holster, then started digging in pockets. "You find anything on him?" she called to Eddy.

"You'd kick my ass if I touched him."

He lowered next to her, his proximity making her jump, his grin making her think of what Duncan said.

"Rickard didn't find anything," she said as she rotated the guy's arm. Yep. Still soft. Mostly. She pulled his wrist closer. His cuff links had three Js on them. Three Js. Why was that ringing a bell? Squinting, she looked down, to the side, then up at Eddy. "Let's take a walk." Raising her voice, she gestured to Rickard. "Don't move him yet. We'll be back."

She led Eddy to the longer end of the alley, checking around the ground and the doorways as they went. The place was cleaner than her living room.

"He kept shit from you. Now, he's making you late for work. You were crying in my arms, because he kept shit from you. Now, it's just…fine?"

She sighed. This was why she didn't like working with Eddy. It was always something. She'd already explained about the photos and leads Duncan hadn't shared with her. So Duncan had taken her aversion to hunches overboard? They had moved on from that. No need to live it over again.

She certainly wasn't about to tell Eddy the reason she was late. Deciding less was more, she didn't answer.

They came around the front of the strip mall. Cars were already parked in front of the classy espresso shop. The classy restaurant wasn't open yet. Bridal gown store. Hurry past that. Classy liquor store…and Jackson & Juracek Jewelers. She smacked Eddy's shoulder. He looked over, and she pointed at the gold-plated, wooden sign. "J & JJ."

CHAPTER 2

Duncan stood with one leg braced behind him. He squinted down the scope of his Remington 700. Today, he wanted distance and kick. *Bam.* The recoil against his shoulder was satisfying. The headphones did little to muffle the echoes of his stint in the Middle East. But today, he was here for Nickie.

Jun Zheng. *Bam.* Duncan knew it was he who haunted her dreams. *Bam.* They'd taken down Zheng's child trafficking ring. *Bam.* Every single girl saved. *Bam, bam, bam.* Every perp arrested. *Bam.*

Everyone except Zheng. Duncan lowered his gun. His aim was spot on. Of course it was. Serving as an explosions expert on the front line provided him excellent aim. Watching as all but two of his platoon died in a bloody death gave him the vivid memories. The smell of gunpowder threatened to take him back. The images. As one of the two who survived, he never completely sorted out whether that was a good thing or not.

Zheng had been within Duncan's reach. Twice. If Duncan had bothered to share that with Nickie, he would have known who Zheng was. He could have throttled him with his hands. The tightness in his shoulders from the recoil was replaced with the burden that lay there.

With the dismantling of Zheng's trafficking operation, Duncan had a new list of girls and perpetrators' histories to search. Maybe he would get lucky and find a piece of information somehow connected. A picture, a reference to an Asian man with short, black hair. Five-foot-ten. Between the ages of thirty-five and fifty. He'd just described a few hundred thousand U.S. residents. It didn't matter. He had plenty of picture-perfect images burned into his photographic memory. It was one more thing he hadn't sorted out as good or bad.

He would find him. He had a handful of pictures. He would find more. Find a trail, a trace he could follow. He'd already put in a solid workday at his office, checking on real estate possibilities in the Ozarks and meeting with a few potential buyers. Not yet ready to sit at his easel, he decided to swing by the station.

Signaling to the lookout, Duncan let him know he was finished and headed to the checkout window. He'd built his new house with intentions to have his own, personal and highly illegal shooting range in the basement. Then, he had to go and fall in love with a cop. Give and take. He lifted a corner of his mouth.

She was unlike any other woman he'd been involved with. Temperamental, dedicated, moody, real. And she was his.

Almost.

He told himself for months Nickie's aversion to anything that hinted at commitment was fine with him. The aversion to accepting a key to his house, the way she insisted on bringing an overnight bag when she stayed instead of simply keeping some things at his home. Although he may recognize her motives for continually keeping him an arm's length away, it simply wasn't fine with him anymore.

Sliding his hand into the pocket of his pants, he traced the edges of the tiny velvet pouch he carried with him. The *almost* needed to be eradicated and soon.

Nickie's desk was clear of everything except the stack of financials from Jackson & Juracek Jewelers. Looking over her reading glasses, she realized it was the only clean spot in her office. Someday she was going to be a neat person. For today, she needed to figure out who killed William Juracek.

They'd searched the store and found the scene of the shooting. No forced entry. No sign of struggle. He'd been shot in an office in the back of the place. So far, nothing seemed to be missing.

One bullet was retrieved from a large wooden desk. Rickard found the other two in Juracek.

He may have been white as a sheet and lying in an alley, but Nickie easily made a match to a picture on the office wall. In it, he stood next to his father-in-law, Gerald Jackson.

Still, procedure made it necessary for the widow to come in and make a positive ID. Mrs. Juracek had brought her twelve-year-old daughter for the identification. Not that Nickie knew a damned thing about raising kids, but seriously? The girl's whimpers were a sound that was too familiar for Nickie. The mom insisted, citing some shrink who said the sooner the closure the better. It was damned cold.

Her eyes wanted to cross at the piles of paperwork she'd gone through in the past five hours. The ME already confirmed that Juracek did, indeed, die of a gunshot wound to the chest. One went in and out, grazing the side of the lowest rib. It was the bullet lodged in the desk. Another stuck in his shoulder and bounced around some. The one that did him in was one that nicked his heart before bouncing throughout the guy's left lung. She shook her head. What a way to go.

She focused on the next few papers as she went over the evidence in her head. No defensive wounds. No skin under his nails. The body bag was what stuck in Nickie's head. It screamed premeditation. No one could figure out the circular bruises on his chest. There were three of them, just like the three gunshots.

Wait a minute. She stopped and went back to the previous page of the bank statement she'd been combing. A payout entry to an SS8? That didn't sound like a jeweler. Five thousand dollars. It wasn't an odd check amount for a jewelry business, but it still didn't sit well with her.

Waking her desk computer, she searched SS8. Nothing. She dug a little deeper and found the account number of the bank the check went into.

SS8. No physical address. No phone number. Deposits from the Cayman Islands, L.A., Chicago, and as far away as India. All from ordinary names. John Smiths and Jane Does. Not very creative, people.

She punched in Eddy's intercom number on her elderly desk unit.

"Lynx," he answered.

"I think I've got something."

He must have stopped what he was doing, because he came in almost immediately. He glanced at the guest chairs full of files, then to the side of her desk that had three Styrofoam soda empties. He moved behind her. She pointed out the J & JJ check in question, then showed him the SS8 bank records.

"You thinking money laundering? Maybe Juracek

was dipping into something?"

She shrugged. "It's time to visit the missus." She rose and they stood nose to nose. He didn't move.

"Oh," he said and sidestepped out of the way.

Duncan's voice echoed in her mind. 'He needs to be pummeled.' She grabbed her jacket on the way out.

Duncan turned onto the gravel side of the Northridge Police Department staff parking. He noticed her car in the space she deemed her own. Pulling over near a row of parked cars, he took his cell and punched in her number. Before he hit send, he spotted her. Her thigh-length black jacket tied at the waist and gave her female shape an extra punch. She hadn't noticed him yet, and he made no attempt to signal her. He'd seen her use her female shape to her benefit in a plethora of situations. To distract a man assaulting her, give the wrong impression during interrogation, make Duncan insane. She was a complicated mess, and he wanted the whole package. It was a problem.

He recognized the moment her eyes found him. She paused as her expression changed from intense thought to a mixture of contentment and endearment. He opened his door and headed toward her car.

"You're here," she called over to him and started walking again.

He didn't answer, beating her to her car and leaning back against the cold metal.

"It's late. I still have a stop to make and paperwork after that." Her firm body pressed into him. "Can I take a rain check for tonight?"

Her warmth made him forget about the cold metal of her rusty oversized town car on his backside. "Come late." He pulled off a single glove and ran the backs of his fingers down her cheek. "You have a key."

At the mention of the key, she stiffened beneath his hands. He masked the pain it caused him. They'd had this discussion a dozen times and this wasn't the place to have another.

"I've got a case. A murder. I'll be crazy late."

"You're welcome to do the paperwork in front of a fire with Chomsky playing in the background."

Her eyes sparkled as she squinted. "That's what you say when you want me to pose for a painting."

Footsteps clicked along the concrete part of the lot, then crunched when they hit the gravel. He recognized them as belonging to Eddy Lynx. Duncan wished he could forget what they sounded like, but he was never going to forget what anything sounded like. Not in this lifetime.

"Pretty Boy," Lynx called as he swaggered toward Nickie's car.

"Loser." Duncan nodded.

Nickie shook her head and blew out a steamy breath in the cold, the steel gray in her eyes turning sharp. Lynx strutted as he stepped past them and waited by the passenger side of her car.

"I have a stop to make with Eddy," she amended in a low whisper.

Duncan accepted her role as a cop; it didn't mean he had to like each part of it. "He wants you."

"He's harmless."

"Hardly."

"Okay, how about I'll show up tonight if at all possible? I'm in love with you," she whispered in his ear, then kissed him on the cheek. She headed to the driver's side, her eyes moving between Lynx and him.

"I'll take good care of her," Lynx taunted as he opened the door.

* * *

"Thirty-six Mulberry," Eddy said as he fooled with his smartphone. "I'll put it in my GPS."

Nickie flipped on the radio and turned it up so they wouldn't have to talk. She didn't need to talk; she needed to think. Paperwork in her cramped office at the station, or in the master bedroom at Duncan's house? She knew which she preferred, but it seemed too intimate and she didn't do that kind of intimate.

The Juracek house was in the nicest neighborhood in Northridge. Her car stuck out and made her think she should have taken Duncan's Audi. She parked away from the front door and left it unlocked. The path to the house was long and shoveled precisely.

"What are we looking for, Nick?"

"I'm not sure. Something doesn't smell right." She dipped her head around the sides of the enormous door. "Where is the bell?"

Eddy found a button in the knocker. It worked, so Nickie straightened.

A man who looked to be in his early twenties answered. He wore a blue button-down shirt, jeans and sneakers. She leaned back to recheck the engraved address on the brick before introducing herself.

"I'm Detective Savage," she said. "This is Detective Lynx. We're here to see Mrs. Juracek. Is she available?"

The man nodded, walked away and left the door open. She and Eddy entered a giant foyer and shut the door behind them. A white, winding staircase climbed the side of the area and led up to a long second-floor landing. Other than the just-vacuumed smell, it made her think she'd stepped into a scene from *Gone With the Wind*. Mrs. Juracek came from where the man had disappeared. She wore a dressy coral pantsuit but was pale with puffy, red eyes.

"I'm Detective Savage," Nickie repeated. "We met briefly at the station when you came to view your husband's body. This is Detective Lynx. May we have a minute of your time?"

The woman dipped her chin and led them to a small living room off the foyer. Nickie and Eddy sat in the loveseat that faced a large picture window, overlooking the snow-covered front yard. Lights glowed beneath the piled snow still hanging onto mature bushes and trees after some melting from the above average temperatures that day.

The missus seemed to be in shock. Nickie hated this part of her job. Did this woman truly deserve a shoulder to cry on? Or was she a great actress who needed forty-five to life?

"We are sorry for your loss, Mrs. Juracek. You understand we need to ask you some questions. We're going to do everything we can to find the person who did this to your late husband." She meant every word whether or not she was staring at the person responsible for his death.

Mrs. Juracek pulled a tissue from her pocket, resting it beneath her nose.

"Do you mind if I record our conversation?"

"No, and please call me Sylvia."

Nickie pressed play on her ancient device, compliments of the ancient NPD. "Sylvia Juracek. Do you give me, Detective Nickie Savage, and Detective Eddy Lynx permission to record this conversation?"

She nodded.

"If you could answer aloud, please. For the recorder."

"Yes, I give permission."

Unfortunately, it helped to judge how much people squirmed at having to recite their name into a recorder. It could be telling. Mrs. Juracek didn't wring her hands, turn red or seem to have discomfort with giving her name, which put her either in the grieving wife camp or the cold-hearted nut job camp. Shoulder to cry on or forty-five to life.

"Do you know of anyone who would want to hurt your husband? Does he have any enemies?"

Mrs. Juracek shook her head. "No. No one. We're just a small town jeweler."

Nickie couldn't help it. She glanced around their home. It was bigger than Duncan's and stuffy. White painted everything. Tall pillars. Marble floors. This is what you get from a small town jewelry store?

"And the business was co-owned by your late husband and your father?"

"Yes. My maiden name is Jackson. Jackson & Juracek Jewelers."

Nickie already knew all of this.

"Do you recognize the name of a business called SS8?"

Oops. There it was.

Mrs. Juracek's eyes darted to hers. "No." She answered a little too quickly.

Nickie didn't do hunches but was smart enough to bank the reaction in a corner of her mind.

"Who takes over the Juracek half of the business at your husband's departure?"

The woman's brows sank as she moved her gaze from Nickie to Eddy and back again. "What are you saying? That I could have had something to do with this?"

That wasn't what Nickie was saying.

"These are all routine questions, ma'am. We would ask them under any circumstances."

"Oh, of course. I'm so sorry. I have a son from a

previous marriage. Tommy. You met him when he answered the door. William and my father were discussing leaving our half to him, but I don't know how far my father and he had gotten with the idea."

Nickie started to ask the following question, then stopped as it looked like Mrs. Juracek was considering her next thought.

"I haven't worked at the shop since our daughter was born."

Nickie looked through her notes. "Is that Renee?"

Mrs. Juracek nodded. "Yes. She's the child William and I had together. She's twelve years old." Mrs. Juracek looked to a bookcase that held some photos. In it was a picture of the missus, little Renee and the late Mr. Juracek.

"How old is your son?"

"He's twenty-five. I had him very young."

"Do you know why your husband was out in the early morning hours last night?" Eddy asked. "He was fully dressed in a suit jacket and tie."

Tears trickled over Mrs. Juracek's pale eyelids. "No," she wailed. "I didn't even know he was gone. We don't share a bedroom. He is restless when he…" Her eyes slid to Nickie's. "We don't have anything to hide."

Nickie always thought people who didn't have anything to hide didn't need to say so.

"You can look through the house if you want. His office is back there." She shook her finger toward a hallway.

Nickie stood and Eddy followed. "Thank you for your cooperation. We'll take a look."

The room fit the aura of the home. Big, white painted wood. A large picture window with a view to the spacious backyard.

The electronics were password protected, of course.

She would have liked to bring them downtown to IT, but it wasn't time to push a warrant, yet.

"Nick. Take a look at this."

She walked over to the small closet where Eddy stood. It wasn't used for clothing. Shelves held neatly labeled boxes. One was wooden with three Js on the top. He made sure to point out the monogram before opening the lid. In it were stacks of large bills. Several, thick stacks. A velvet bag was opened at the top. Inside were dozens of glittering diamonds.

"Money *and* diamond laundering," he whispered.

CHAPTER 3

The partially completed painting of Sophia Colour waited impatiently for Duncan. He was set to fly out first thing Monday morning and deliver it personally. While he was out there, she asked if he would serve as her date for a charity event. He'd done so many times before with several different clients. It gave him the reputation of arm candy and a local title of 'The Taste of L.A.' The title may have been well-deserved at one time in his life, but now...

He would stay a few days in order to create the beginning sketches of the other paintings she ordered. He needed to solidify a few appointments before he could answer her yet about the charity event. Who was he kidding? None of his other appointments would be on a Monday night at nine.

Instead of sitting at his easel, he found himself at the wraparound desk his uncle had made for him. He had three computers up and running. His desk unit sat in the middle, with a laptop to one side and his tablet on the other. The aroma from the black coffee that rested between his forearms helped streamline his thoughts. Unfortunately, it didn't streamline his painting. As he dipped his head closer to the mug, he flicked his gaze to the flaming tattoo that crawled up his arm. The flames flicked as anxiously as his mood.

The names of exactly nineteen victims, twenty-nine johns and fifteen perpetrators lay neatly next to his tablet. The paper list wasn't necessary. The names of those involved in the child trafficking he and Nickie discovered would live in his memory for the rest of his life. Still, he preferred having the physical copy next to him as if he were a regular person doing research.

He'd already done an image and general search on all of the victims. No Zheng. Each girl was average, abducted in a variety of methods—from their homes, bus stops, only one had been homeless, the rest were sheltered innocents. Duncan turned his head and ground his teeth together. That was what the johns wanted. It was what Zheng wanted. That's what Nickie was. He clenched and released his hands before continuing.

The searches on the johns were different. So far, they had either police records or shady connections. Some were judges, politicians, the wealthy. He isolated on each, one at a time, searching for a shot of Zheng in the background of an image, possibly finding some reference to an Asian man.

He took his pencil and made a check mark on his list next to the name of each john as he worked. They would serve as a physical reminder of what was etched in his memory. The check marks were increasing. His hits on Zheng were not.

The perpetrators would be a different story. The men who served as guards over the girls. Thugs who supervised and organized the trafficking. The ones who catered to the men who got off on abusing children.

Were they, also, sexually interested in the young teens? Or were they only interested in making a dime? He pounded the side of his fist on the top of the desk a half-dozen times, each hit harder than the last, nearly spilling coffee over his keyboard. His detective. He rubbed his hands over his face and through his hair. She'd been put through this for eighteen months of her life when she should have been wearing braces and going to school dances.

Pushing away from the desk, he stood and paced. He gave in and allowed the images to run through his mind like a slide show. The night Nickie risked her badge and broke into the governor's assistant's property. The girls they saved in the cold. As he and Nickie hid them, one at a time, in Duncan's SUV. Naked, drugged, frightened. Just as Nickie was sixteen years ago.

Inside the SUV, Nickie had covered the girls in blankets. He shook his head as if the scenario didn't make sense. Why would they need blankets in the blazing heat? Would they serve as cover from the sand as it whipped around in the chopper?

Cries rang out as they were hit. Blood covered every inch of metal as the Chinook twirled toward the ground, the vast sea of light-colored desert approaching fast. "How many girls are dead?" his commander yelled through the sound of the wind and fire. Duncan looked around at the bodies of his platoon. "All of them," he said.

Grabbing the back of the closest chair, he dipped his head and sucked air. A line of sweat trickled down the fire tattoo on his forearm. Nickie. He went to the window and looked out at his drive. His were the only tire tracks. "Okay," he said. "Okay." Stepping away from the window, he ran his hands through his sweaty hair. A swim. The constant rush of water over his ears and the unmoving straight lines at the bottom of his pool would help muffle the sounds and sights pounding his head.

Nickie wasn't about to park in the garage. No more snow was forecasted for the next few days, so there was no reason. She tapped her thumb on the steering wheel and sighed. Parking in your boyfriend's garage was creepy. Flopping the back of her neck against her seat, she stared at the roof. What a head case.

Lowering her gaze, she slammed the heel of her hand on the steering wheel and looked around. Taking a deep breath, she shook her head clear and got out of the damned car. It was well past midnight. She welcomed the first deep breath of crisp air as it burnt her lungs.

The moonlight and the snow lit the area almost as much as the porch light he'd left on for her. Nearly subconsciously, she stopped in front of the granite steps that seemed to go for miles up to his house.

She'd let him give her a drawer, hadn't she? Hung clothes in his closet and had his key hanging from her key ring. Figuratively, she patted herself on the back.

Something took a step in the woods to the west side of the house. She jerked her head in the direction of the movement, then let out a breath that was half-laugh and half-huff. It was late. With the four hours of sleep she'd had the night before, she was letting herself freak over wildlife in the trees.

"I should have gone home," she mumbled and pulled her overnight bag over her shoulder. She climbed the steps, letting the steam from her breath lead the way. The steps were one of the few things that survived the fire. The fire that burned Duncan's first home to the ground. The fire that was set for her alone. What was she doing? she asked herself as she unlocked the door.

She walked directly to the alarm. She never wanted to experience Duncan's alarm. As she punched in the code to tell it she was friend and not foe, she spotted a note in his artist's handwriting. *Gone for a swim.*

He knew to leave it at the front door alarm and not the one inside the door leading from the garage. Good. He needs to know they should have boundaries.

The place was immaculate as usual. No coats hanging on the banister or magazines left on tables. His extra set of house keys hung neatly on one of the key hooks. The hardwood floors didn't have drips from snowy boots or dust at the edges. A swim would do her good, she decided. Shrugging, she plopped her bag at the bottom of the stairs and headed for the basement.

The water always took out tension and loosened her joints. She stopped at the top of the stairs leading down and considered. It was much more than that to him. The water drowned out the sights and sounds that cluttered his eidetic memory. It was hard for her to wrap her head around the idea of thirty-three years of images, sounds and smells, all whirling through his mind 24-7.

He was the best thing that had been given to her. She smacked her forehead against the stairwell wall. What would she do when they were over? With a defiant sniff, she lifted her shoulders and jogged down the stairs, through the boy room, she liked to call it. Big screen TV, leather armchairs, pool table, wet bar, and a large table designed for playing cards.

She found him still going full throttle. Forgetting all about her swim, she leaned against the jamb of the door and watched. The water slid like liquid ice over his chocolate hair and down the lanky muscles of his back. He used his arms like he hadn't been shot in the shoulder a few short weeks before. The strokes were long and smooth, his hips hardly rotating as he kicked. Reaching for the end of the pool, he flipped quick as an otter, turned over and came out barely tilting his head as he took a short breath.

When he reached the other end, he stopped and rose. Of course he knew she was there. He never missed anything. His eyes were a mixture of relief and warmth. "There you are," he mouthed as he rubbed the gunshot wound scar on his shoulder.

They were the three words they shared between each other and only at the most intimate of moments. Her heart melted into a puddle of mush enough to gag any rational person.

When he pulled himself out of the water, she nearly choked. His golden skin sparkled as the water dripped over him. The tattoo of Black Creek lay over his pectoral and below his fresh, circular scar. Both dripped with water, making it look like a storm was coming. Her feet were magnets, leading the way to her hard, golden creature with the deep brown eyes.

Their lips met in a meeting of hearts and minds as they worked together to rid her of the layers of clothing that kept flesh from flesh. His skin was wet and cool from the water, his lips warm and exploring. They trailed icy lines over her neck, her shoulders, her collarbone. She was naked and pinned to the nearest wall in seconds.

Flesh. Glorious flesh covered her as she let her tongue taste the water and the man. She assaulted him with lips and hands. There was never enough of him. Of his skin or his love.

"Duncan," she cried as he adjusted her legs and cupped her. Both threatened to fail her. He lifted one and draped it over his forearm, pressing her harder into the wall and allowing her to lean into him. In how

many ways did he take the weight from her? Too
many to count.

She turned into a useless pawn. He took her up,
turning her arms and legs into noodles. Her head
turned from side to side as he gave.

"There you are," he repeated, making the rush take
her higher than the moon that lit the snow. Euphoria
seared through her veins, lifted her arms in triumph
and shook her core. He knew her, knew exactly how
long to keep her there and how to lead her on the slow
journey down. It was the perfect harmony with just
the right amount of melody.

The sound of his Nickie's magical voice purred his
name and sent a sense of urgency deep within
Duncan. Her body's reactions were like his most
treasured paints. He knew them well, yet the response
to his touch intoxicated him. He pressed against her,
using his weight to keep her grounded as he brought
her down from her high.

She should be exhausted after her last few days. He
should have been able to lead her back up that hill of
sensation, but he didn't have the chance. The steel
gray of her eyes opened with determination, the slight
scent of lavender permeated his mind. Slithering
down, she took him in. His hands smacked the wall,
fingers spread and elbows braced. The air left his
lungs as if he'd had the wind knocked out of him.

Her lips, her hands. She would be his undoing. His
Nickie. Just before it was too late, she knew. Knew
him as well as he did her. His body shook as her
tongue drew a lazy line up his chest.

"Take me," she purred, the invitation making his
vision blur.

His body responded long before his head. He
grabbed her muscled thighs, and pushed into her.
Groaning, he clenched his teeth and lifted his eyes to

her. "Look at me," he demanded as they moved together.

She did, even as her head fell back against the wall and deep catlike growls came from within her. He pressed his forehead to hers and the air left his lungs. His legs nearly betrayed him, but they kept moving, kept climbing. That last ounce, that last push. He could tell the moment she was ready. Limbs trembling in his arms and beneath him, she arched, held for what seemed like eternity, then pushed again.

The calm after the storm was long and slow. Her legs twined lazily around his back, the backs of her feet locked together. Her arms fell over his shoulders, and she rested her soft cheek against him.

Why hadn't he installed an elevator? Could he make it up the stairs? "I'm in love with you," he said into the long locks of her honey-wheat hair. She responded with a tiny croon that gave him the energy to try.

He cupped her backside and linked his fingers together. She must have sensed what he was doing, because she pulled back her head. "Three flights? I'm not a small woman, Duncan." Her smile was too composed considering what they'd just done. She unlocked her feet, slid to the ground and headed for the bathroom. Pulling on his robe, he sat on the nearest wicker chair. He ran his hands through his hair and let himself have a moment to be relieved he didn't have to carry her up three flights after his swim workout and his *workout*. And a moment to inhale the relief that she chose to come home to him.

She came out with a towel wrapped around her in all the wrong places. "You were going to carry me upstairs," she accused as she pulled her hair over her shoulder. "You told me you love me *after* sex and were going to carry me upstairs. Your brother would call you whipped."

"That's not exactly how the saying goes." He stood and took her hand.

"I was being a lady." She left her clothes on the pool deck. It made the corner of his mouth lift.

It wasn't time. But soon.

CHAPTER 4

Nickie had no leads, no weapon and a caffeine headache. Pushing away from her desk, she stood and stretched. Her joints were still slightly unhinged from the night before. A wicked smile threatened to escape her lips as she headed for the pop machine. The Diet Coke was sold out. She could kick someone's ass.

A twenty-ounce bottle came from behind her and hung in front of her nose. Eddy. She grabbed it and turned. "I could kiss you." The words came out before she had time to take them back. Back pedal? Explain? Apologize? Ignore. She liked the last option and walked with him to the break room table.

Good ole police department break rooms. She'd been in enough of them. The academy, Liberty, Vegas. And as a victim, getting her first real meal in over a year. They might be ritzier in some places than others, but they always had a few things in common. Dirty microwaves, the smell of burnt coffee and a large table surrounded by a handful of chairs. "I haven't had a bite on this case in hours. I feel bad since the captain took us off everything else." She twisted her cap halfway, letting the sound of the sizzle wet her lips.

"Me either," he said. "What's with the Jane Does and the John Smiths? This SS8 must think no one's going to look too close at its records."

She huffed and set her boots on a nearby chair, one then the other. "Or that whoever does is stupid." She took a long swig, letting the burn of the first drink wake her senses, then set her bottle on the table. Jane Doe. John Smith.

Joe Johnson. She'd seen that one in more places than SS8. Slinging her legs to the floor, she grabbed her soda and headed for her office. "See ya later, Lynx."

He must have recognized her epiphany because he said, "I don't think so," and followed.

She unburied William Juracek's date book from the middle of her pile and started flipping through pages.

It wasn't long ago. A week? A few days? "There," she said. She leaned back in her chair so Eddy could see. "Juracek had a meeting with a Joe Johnson at the Seneca Hotel and Casino last week."

"You gonna let me in on where you're going with this any time soon, Nick?"

She pulled the SS8 bank records from the top of the pile. There was a five-thousand dollar deposit from a Joe Johnson. She put her finger on the entry, letting Eddy get a look. Of course, he dipped closer to her than he needed to. Men.

"Diamonds and money laundering at a casino?"

She shrugged. "Maybe. Let's see if we can find out."

Grabbing her coat with one hand, she shut down her computer with the other. "I'm taking a trip to the casino."

He picked up her Diet Coke, making her auto-defense go on high alert.

"You might need backup."

She didn't. But it was okay, she convinced herself. She could always turn up the radio.

The Seneca Hotel and Casino wasn't a place of great memories for Nickie. It was under new management since the former owner was doing time in the big house for aiding and abetting. The place seemed the same to her. Marble this and marble that. Shiny floors. Loud noises. Wall-to-wall people leaving the unmistakable scent of bodies and stale cigarettes that no amount of air freshener could mask. Those weren't even the bad memories.

Eddy took point as they approached reception. "Hello, miss." He pulled out his badge but from the look on the gal's face, he probably could have just asked. "I'm Detective Eddy Lynx. I need some information on a Joe Johnson. We believe he was a visitor at your fine establishment. Could you check and see if you have records on him..." He leaned over to see her name tag around her computer screen. "Louisa?"

The girl adjusted the collar of her uniform. Nickie would choke herself if she had to wear a suit vest and skirt as a uniform. How would she sling her boot over her knee when she needed to make an impression? Not a hair was out of place from Miss Louisa's smooth ponytail, but she still ran a hand over it like she was making sure.

"I'm really supposed to get my manager for things like this." In a tone that sounded like it should come from a small child, Louisa giggled and moved her eyes from one side to the other. "But since you're a detective and all, I'm sure it's okay."

Louisa pretended to lean over and check Eddy's badge, her cleavage nearly falling out onto the counter. Nickie almost puked.

"Yes, sir, Detective. We had a Joe Johnson stay last Sunday in our Sweethearts Fox River Suite. Shall I print a copy of the record for you?"

"That's it?" Nickie never could keep quiet when it was Eddy's turn to lead. "One night?"

The girl looked at Nickie like she was a fly in her non-fat latte. Turning her eyes to Eddy, Nickie attempted to silently apologize.

"The printout would be helpful," he said, ignoring Nickie. "Thank you."

"Ask her if he has any reservations," Nickie whispered to Eddy loud enough for the girl to hear.

Louisa huffed and pounded away at her keyboard. "He has a room reserved for this Tuesday." She squinted her eyes and looked closer at the monitor. "The same suite actually."

"Is there anyone in that room today?" Eddy asked. "We'd like to take a look."

Sighing, Louisa confessed, "For that I really had better call my manager."

It was Nickie's turn to sigh.

They waited a few minutes. It gave Nickie time to assess. Sweethearts Fox River Suite? It was an odd choice as a place to exchange diamonds or discuss money laundering, but stranger things happen. What kind of people came to a place like this to have sex with a man when they're married to a woman? It made her smile. Now, *she* was making assumptions. "Keep an open mind," she randomly reminded Eddy.

He scowled at her as a short man in a tailored suit approached them. "Hello, I'm Mr. Edwin McGowan. Welcome to the Seneca Hotel and Casino." He held out his arms like he was the owner. "What can I do for you, this afternoon, Miss…?"

Nickie stepped forward and smiled wide. "Detective

Savage. This is Detective Lynx, Mr. McGowan." She emphasized the mister. "We need to take a look in your Fox River Suite."

McGowan smiled condescendingly and steepled his fingertips to his lips. "Do you have a warrant, Miss Savage?"

She stepped forward and stood nose-to-nose with the little dweeb. Or, at least, nose-to-forehead.

"Oh, boy," she heard Eddy huff.

"Listen, Mr. *I-have-short-man's-complex.*" She smiled as she cocked her head from side to side. "I took point at the operation that took place in this casino about a year ago." She pulled out her phone and pretended to look at the date. "Just about exactly one year ago." She stepped forward as the little prick stepped back. "I'm worried some of the same trysts could be continuing. Right here. Under your supervision. Do I need to call in the feds? 'Cause I have them on speed dial."

"Ha," McGowan breathed. "N-no need. I believe that room is empty for the next few days. Louisa!" he called over his shoulder. "Get these officers a key to the Sweethearts Fox River Suite."

"Detectives," Nickie spat.

"Picky," Eddy mumbled in her ear.

Nickie glanced to him and grinned. "You're just mad because Louisa's going to want in my pants now instead of yours."

Eddy took the key card from Louisa, then they made their way to the elevator. He pulled a handkerchief from the inside pocket of his coat. It shouldn't annoy her, and yet. "We have a handy latex gloves compartment on our gun belts."

"Free country," he said as they approached the suite. He used it to turn the knob on the door. "Wow," Eddy said as he opened it. "Think of the broads you could get for the price of this room."

He wasn't wrong. It reminded her of the suite she and Duncan stayed in while in Vegas. She wasn't about to mention that to Eddy. She could use Duncan right about now. "They reserved this room for both nights. Could be a sex thing but look around for bugs."

It was a nice enough place. The places she'd been forced to turn tricks were generally single rooms with no connecting bathrooms. Fancy beds and satin sheets, but certainly none of these fresh flowers in vases or chocolates on the pillows.

Nothing in the ceiling lights. Phones looked good. Lamps, desk hook-ups. They looked around for a good hour and came up empty. It was beginning to be a habit.

"Come back next Tuesday?" Eddy suggested.

Nickie nodded as she took one last look.

When you're dating Duncan Reed, you learn to keep a change of dress clothes in your locker. She was done for the night and tomorrow was Saturday. Unless the ME came up with something profound, she was on-call until Monday. The lack of leads in the case was making her crazy. She'd planned to go in the next day regardless, but it was satisfying to know she didn't have to if she didn't want to.

He took her to Rossetti's. Romantic. Intimate. She would have to do an extra mile in the pool to burn off the calories, but the food would be worth it. The company very worth it. Sweet, but she drew the line at leaving her car at the station. Boundaries were necessary.

It was dark and the tablecloths were, well, cloth. Real candles and a waiter who actually held a towel thing over his forearm. He brought a silver bowl full of bread so fresh, she could smell it before he set it on the table.

Duncan ordered food she couldn't pronounce but knew she would love. He chose the wine, but she decided on a single glass since she planned to get in some hours on the case bright and early.

"Abigail is restless," he said, running a thumb over her knuckles as he watched the string quartet. His horse. Abigail preferred Nickie over Duncan, but that was their little secret.

"I haven't seen Rose in days either." Sliding her hand from underneath Duncan's, she pulled out her phone and texted her, 'you free tomorrow night?'

"Are you texting on our date?" A rare smile took his lips. It may have been slight, but it made her lose her breath anyway.

"She's your relative, so it doesn't count." Her phone vibrated and lit up. Yikes. She turned down the brightness to its lowest setting before reading. 'let's kick up some dust, friend'

Nickie was terrible with women. Other than her foster family, she didn't have a single girlfriend. Other than Rose, that is. 'you got it. cheap drinks and slutty men?'

'ha. i'll get andy to watch the baby.'

"The deed is set," she said and lifted her eyes to him. He wasn't smiling anymore, his eyes penetrated into her. Did she have something on her face? If she could only dig into that eidetic mind of his at times like this.

The string quartet changed to the music of the Trecento. It distracted her, making her yearn for her cello. Closing her eyes, she let herself imagine it resting between her legs as her hand danced over the neck and her bow teased the strings.

He must have noted her shift in attention, because

he covered her hand with his. "Will you play for me tonight?"

"My cello? I shouldn't." She wrinkled her nose. "I stayed at your place the last two nights. I'm going to crash at my town house."

"Alone." He said it as a statement and pulled his hand away. He used a tone she didn't recognize, and she was sure she'd heard every tone he had.

"Of course, alone. We're exclusive. Why did you say that?"

The following length of silence unsettled her, the sound of the string quartet seemingly disappearing.

When he spoke, his voice was nearly a whisper. "I can't do this anymore."

Like she'd jumped into icy water, the muscles in her body tensed.

His eyes turned defeated. "I know what you're doing, why you push us away."

Which was fine except *she* didn't know what she was doing.

"You know how it hurts me the times you throw up your wall between us. You're afraid." He leaned in, his tortured eyes boring holes into her, making her tremble and reflexively lean away.

"I'm asking you to trust me," he said. "I'm asking you to stay."

"I'm not afraid. It's just not a good idea." The pain that grew in his eyes frightened her.

"After all we've been through?" He waved his hand back and forth between the two of them, then covered hers with it. "You know this is right."

It was her turn to pull her hand away.

He took a sip of his wine, then wiped his mouth with his napkin. "I've understood your insecurities and your aversion to moving forward." His tone turned defensive. "I've accepted what comes with dating a cop. I've loved each part of you."

Was this supposed to make her feel better?

"The reason you're not staying with me tonight is because you did last night?" he said with the first raise in his voice she could ever remember him using with her.

"The last two nights," she corrected before she realized that was probably the wrong thing to say.

The look he gave her was one she'd only seen him use with other people. Never her. And he was speaking in past tense. The room became hot, her breath quickened.

"This is all I have to give." It sounded too much like pleading. "I've always been honest with you about that," she said more forcefully.

"You have, yes." He nodded as he tossed his napkin on the table. "This is my honesty. You're either going to be mine, or you're not. Don't answer me now."

"Answer what?" She didn't care how it looked. She grasped the edges of the table with her hands until the tips of her fingers turned white.

"Marriage." He nearly barked it before his pained eyes drilled holes into her. "I'm not willing to continue to fear your reactions if I buy you Diet Coke for my refrigerator. That you might push me away if I install a hook in my bathroom for your hairdryer. Marriage. That's what I'm putting on the table. We're either taking this to the next level, or you're going to keep your town house so you don't have to be with me more than two nights in a row."

Marriage? He wanted to marry her?

The next length of silence paralyzed her. "I thought silence may be your answer." He shook his head as he finally looked away. "I'll put your things in your place tomorrow while you're at work." The sound of his voice turned weak and low. "I'll lock up on my way out."

He stood as she sat, still clenching the table. Reaching in the pocket of his suit jacket, he took out his wallet. "You know where to find me if you change your mind. Leave my key on the table in your hallway. It will lighten the load of your key chain." A few hundred-dollar bills fell onto the table.

Marriage? she repeated somewhere in her head.

CHAPTER 5

Nickie dragged her tired legs back and forth in front of the door to her town house. She was fully dressed—coat, boots, scarf. She'd told her captain she would be in for a few hours that morning, but not this early. She might be gone by the time he arrived, but that wasn't what was keeping her from walking out the door.

Stopping her feet, she dipped her hand into the pocket of her slacks. She'd gone as far as to remove the key from her ring. Wrapping her fingers around it, she squeezed. It was warm from resting next to her thigh through the hours of her sleepless night. Her eyes betrayed her and traveled to the small, glass table that sat empty in the tiny foyer.

Another tear escaped. How many more of these things could a body have? It ran down her chapped cheek. It was what her feet wanted to do. Run. Run to the next state and apply for a job. It's what she did. Ran. Ran as a child to the horse stables when she couldn't handle her parents anymore. Ran from her captors. Ran from foster family after foster family. Ran from her first job the minute she got an offer as detective at the Northridge Police Department. What a fool she'd been.

Her feet started pacing again. Her mind became a swirling mass of confusion. Lifting her gaze, she looked around her town house as she paced, still clenching Duncan's key. It was spotless. Not a single shoe or magazine left out anywhere. Sleep hadn't come and that gave her time to clean around every outlet cover, dust the cords to the lamps and even vacuum the crumbs from her kitchen drawers.

Forcing her feet to stop, she jerked her shoulders and stood tall. Using her knuckles, she craned her jaw to one side, cracking her neck before doing it again the other way. She took the key and slammed it onto the table hard enough to leave a scratch in the glass. But her fingers wouldn't let go. She stood, fighting herself for the longest damned time.

Grabbing it, she sank to the floor, pulling her legs close and wrapping her arms around them. Stupid, stupid girl. Her torso rocked forward, then back. She knew better than to let it get this far. It was never going to work. He was Duncan Reed. The man on the cover of how many tabloids? Proper grammar, good taste, smart, sexy, collected. How could she keep hold of something like that?

But he wanted to marry her. He said that, didn't he? In the sternest tone she could remember him using with her, he nearly barked it down her throat. What had she done? Was he really that angry because she wanted to sleep apart? Didn't want him to wake with a black eye, because the woman he was sleeping with couldn't get it together enough to wake up like a normal person?

Her physical reaction to the idea of marriage was nearly unbearable. The uncertainty. The risk. Giving herself to another person like that? As soon as she let her mind entertain the idea, her body began to react. Small tremors that weren't from the cold. They mixed with the beads of sweat that lined her hairline and upper lip, shutting down coherent thought. Then, the tears. Surely she had cried before, maybe as a child. She had no memories of crying, but now, tears. Buckets of them ran over her cheeks that were already chapped from the buckets that fell throughout the night. They made her mind clouded and useless. She expected him to leave her someday, not want to marry her.

"Ah!" she yelled and bolted upright. This is why she wasn't cut out for relationships. Her mind didn't work that way. From the day she turned eighteen, she'd been in charge of her path. Her. No one else. It was what kept her feet moving forward. Or was it? Shaking her head, she realized she had no clue what was what. This was why she wanted to keep things the way they were. Didn't he see that? What they had was good. It was perfect. Why couldn't he just be happy with safe?

She was Nickie Savage. She changed her name for a reason. She was smart, independent and had a fucking murder case to solve. Flipping up the hood on her jacket, she stuffed the key in her pocket and stormed out the front door, barely remembering to lock it behind her.

Duncan sat at his aunt and uncle's enormous kitchen table. Red rested at Duncan's feet, on them actually. As Duncan rubbed circles around Red's furry ears, Nathan talked in circles about a sleigh bed he was making out of mahogany.

Their house smelled like wood and plants, like home. He revered his aunt and uncle for taking him and his brother into their lives and raising them as their own. The love was there, and it was thick. It just wasn't the kind he needed at that moment.

Brie was eerily quiet as she set plates and butter on the table. Her focus was clearly on him and not morning coffee cake. Since she'd been able to see through him since he was eight years old, it was disconcerting. "Mother." He lifted from his chair. "Let me get that for you."

She nodded and slid into her seat. Her actions were as bad of a sign as the ill focus.

"Mostly straight lines with slightly arched head and footboards," Nathan continued as he poured a cup of coffee for Brie, then himself. "You need a warmer, Duncan?"

"No, thank you," he said and brought over the coffee cake from its cooling rack.

His aunt placed a hand on his uncle's forearm. Nathan seemed to take the hint as they both turned their attention on Duncan. "What's new with you?" Nathan left the topic of the mahogany bed.

So, she could tell something was different. He wasn't in the mood to talk about it. Instead, he smiled as the front door opened. They heard cries from baby Andrew before it closed.

"Oh, Andy," Brie called to the front of the house as she got up from her chair. "What have you done to my grandbaby? Let me have him."

Duncan's brother didn't remember their biological parents...the ones who would be the actual grandparents. Of course, Duncan remembered them. Like normal people, those with eidetic memories didn't remember their younger years as well as the rest of their lives, but Duncan was four when his parents died. Which was old enough for him to remember them as if they sat next to him at the table.

"If you're going to make him a junior, he should be

Sylvester Jr." Duncan reminded Andy, hoping to make Brie forget what she'd noticed from Duncan.

"As you keep reminding me," Andy said and hung up their coats.

Brie and Nathan not only earned the title of grandparents, but also mom, dad, advisor and good friend. He could hear Brie cooing as her heels clicked along the hardwood floor.

"Duncan Reed." It was Rose. "What did you do?"

Uh-oh. He looked to Brie who seemed to be paying attention to Andrew Jr.

Rose marched in with a diaper bag draped over her shoulder. Sitting across from him, she poured a cup of coffee from the carafe. "Nickie canceled on me last night. We were supposed to drink shots and get in a pub fight. Instead, she called to tell me she had a cold. It sounded more like a stuffy nose from crying rather than some cold."

Nickie didn't cry. "I'm sure it's a cold."

"Ah ha. So, you don't even know whether she's sick or not. I repeat, what did you do to her?"

He shook his head. The look on his face must have made an impression, because Rose leaned back in her chair and suddenly became interested in her mug.

Brie sat, holding a bottle for the baby. Her expression almost broke him. It was like the whole damned place morphed into a funeral home.

"Well." Rose cleared her throat. "If you speak with her soon, please tell her she was greatly missed."

If he spoke to her again. They knew. They all knew. And yes, she was greatly missed.

Nathan changed the subject to fishing when the lake thawed and described how the water still trickled into Black Creek, even in the exceptionally cold winter they were having. Andy briefed them all on his latest development project and Rose on her promotion to director at the Birds of Prey Research and Action Center. Brie remained quiet. The whites in her eyes turned pink.

"I'd like to take Abigail out for a ride, Andy. Maybe Wednesday or Thursday? I leave for L.A. first thing in the morning, but I should be back by then."

"Do you have any red carpet events with hot women?" Andy asked.

Rose smacked Andy soundly on the arm. As a matter of fact, he did, but since it was purely platonic, he saw no reason to share.

Nickie should have left the car running. Her gloved fingers were getting stiff, but the discomfort was oddly welcome. Her foster mother's drive was shoveled of every last speck of snow, yet Nickie sat parked in front of the mailbox. Cars lined both sides of the street. No one was bold enough to be the one who parked in the drive on Sunday dinner night.

He wanted to marry her. Her forehead dropped to the cold steering wheel. She closed her eyes and let the burn take her. His tone still reverberated throughout every inch of her. He tossed his napkin. Such a small, small, incredibly huge thing. It wasn't like him. She rocked her forehead from side to side along the wheel as she tried to make sense of his demands when someone rapped on the passenger window. It should have made her jump. Instead, she kept her forehead glued to the wheel and rotated it in the direction of the noise. It was Gloria.

Quickly, she pulled back to a sitting position, then opened her door. A gust of cold brushed across her wet face as she stood and peered over the roof of her car.

"Why do you do this, child? I have to get you from your car again?"

Nickie only remembered one other time this happened but would never argue with Gloria.

"You must be cold," Nickie said as she came around the front of the town car. Gloria wore no coat, and her boots hadn't been laced.

"That is right. I am cold. Come." Gloria gestured with her hand. Of course, Nickie would follow. She owed her life to this woman. A debt she carried gladly.

The driveway was short and the walk to the front door shorter. She could hear the crowd long before she entered. The smell of spices and sugar from a dinner soon to be served permeated the air. It was all familiar and surprisingly comfortable. Gil's twin girls ran to greet her first, each wrapping a warm arm around her waist. They were followed by their dad. He kissed Nickie on the cheek, whispering in her ear as he hugged her, "I have a favor, big sister."

He called her 'big sister.' That meant it was a big favor. She didn't think she had anything in her to give. The only reason she showed up tonight was because it wouldn't have been worth it to face Gloria's phone calls if she hadn't.

One of the twins pulled on her shirt. She looked down at the glossy black hair, pulled in a ponytail that framed a most beautifully caramel-colored face.

"Where's Uncle Duncan?" little Neva asked in her thick, Latino accent.

Gil turned his head out the front window. "Yeah, what did you do with him?" He laughed and added, "You didn't shoot him, did you?" His face fell as soon as his eyes landed on hers. "Go find your mother," he said to his girls. They took the hint and slinked away with little pouting.

"You didn't have to do that." Nickie didn't want pity, and she didn't want to talk about it. She wanted to get through dinner so she could go home.

Go home to what? A bag she refused to open that sat in her foyer? Her beloved cello she couldn't bear to take out of its case? She slipped a hand into the pocket of her pants and wrapped her fingers around Duncan's key. "I'm going to see if Gloria needs help," she said, then headed for the kitchen.

"Take these." Gloria offered no small talk and handed Nickie two large bowls of seasoned rice.

Working on autopilot, Nickie placed the bigger one on the dining table that comfortably sat twelve. She offered polite greetings to her foster brothers and sisters, and Gloria's extended family. It was like a beehive, and she was able to ignore most of the rest. The smaller bowl went on the table in the kitchen addition.

"Teresa," Gloria called out to Gil's wife in the busy living room. "Gather everyone for dinner."

Nickie finished passing out large serving trays of amazing food that she had no intention of eating. The buzz of activity was pleasantly deafening. It brought her back to a time she felt the first hint of hope she had in many years. She understood most of what was spoken but wasn't anywhere near ready to speak the language. It had been a many years since her foster family politely spoke only English around her. She'd been one of them for too long. No one asked her to give more of herself than she could give. This was a safe place.

Gil leaned over as he reached for more sauce. "We have a gig at The Pub on Friday night, and Neva has a peewee basketball game."

The favor. "I can't." There was no way she could sing in front of a bar full of people. "I'm in the middle of a case." She'd never turned him down before. She'd had to cancel at the last minute before but never a flat 'no.' "It's turning high profile," she amended, hoping it would satisfy him.

He looked like she'd just run over his cat.

"S'okay." He shrugged. "I'll ask Ma if she can take Neva to the game so Teresa can sing."

With a deep sigh, Nickie pushed away from the table, stood and started clearing the dishes. No one entered the kitchen while she was in there. She was like a plague. A house full of nearly thirty people and Gloria was the only one who was with her in the kitchen. Gloria, who didn't speak.

"He wants to marry me."

Gloria paused only for a moment as she lit the stove and set a teapot full of water on the flames. It wasn't like her to make tea before the dishes were done, so Nickie plopped some of them into the soapy water and rolled up her sleeves. "He gave me an ultimatum." She scrubbed circles around plates as Gloria took a single mug from one of the hooks beneath the cabinets. The water felt good on her arms, sending currents of warmth over her shoulders and down her back. "It was more like a threat."

She loaded the dish rack until it was full, then changed to drying. Gloria prepared dessert at the small, wooden table that served as her island. When the teapot sang, Gloria turned off the heat and poured the water into the mug.

"Sit, child," Gloria ordered as if there wasn't a house full of people in the adjoining rooms waiting for their dessert.

Nickie wanted to argue, to tell her to finish preparing dessert as she worked on the dishes, but the string that seemed to pull her butt to the old chair next to the wooden table was stronger than her reluctant legs.

Gloria opened the fridge with her free hand and

came to Nickie with a can of Diet Coke. She placed both drinks on the table and sat. Her long, shiny hair was pulled in a low tail. The streaks of gray made her look as wise as she was.

She pushed the can across the table, then rested her hand on the back of Nickie's.

Nickie looked down. Gloria's skin was smoother than it should be at her age. Dark and warm, her hand gripped the top of Nickie's. Nickie's eyes closed tightly.

"How can I be a wife, Gloria? The things I've done." Her shoulders became like lead. Tears slipped between her defeated lids, down her face and dripped on the table.

"You were captive, my child. You survived."

She opened her eyes and looked into the nearly onyx ones that stared back at her. A large tear threatened to fall from Gloria's lid, too.

"I can stuff it all, focus on the job. Take it out on perpetrators for the sake of the victims. But his need for commitment. And now marriage? He is Duncan Reed," Nickie whispered as her breath began to speed and her heart to panic. "He is making me remember. To think about it. I am not worthy."

Tears fell freely now. So many parts of her were numb.

"Has he ever done or said any—"

"No," Nickie interrupted. "This is on me. I have scars. I am confused and moody. I can be heartless and selfish."

A tear dripped down Gloria's wonderful face. "You have made me proud to call you daughter."

CHAPTER 6

"Are you sure you don't want to come?"

Duncan shook his head. "You go. I'm going to get started on your next painting."

He lifted his arm as Sophia Colour's limousine drove away, then turned to greet the doorman at the Hotel Grande. The paparazzi's flashing lights still burned holes in his vision. They'd nearly thrown him into a flashback right there on the red carpet.

"Good evening," he said and held out his hand to the doorman. The gentleman opened the door and dipped his head toward Duncan, almost missing Duncan's outstretched hand.

Startled, the man straightened. "Oh, thank you, sir." He took Duncan's hand and shook. "And you as well, sir."

Duncan slipped him a healthy tip before taking hold of the door himself. He loosened the tie from his tuxedo. "Warm evening. I hope it cools off for you."

"Thank you, yes. Thank you, sir."

Duncan's heels clicked on the marble floor as he made his way to the elevator. Digging in the pocket of his jacket, he searched for the key card to the penthouse suite and found the small velvet bag. Grinding his teeth together, he took out the card and started the long trip to the top. He rode alone, pulling the tie from his neck and winding it around his knuckles. The door opened to his room, and he did as he always did when he came into a new place. He checked his surroundings, memorizing every detail. Habitually, he pulled the jacket from his arms and carefully hung it on the freestanding coat rack.

He looked at it, hanging there, for a long moment before taking it and tossing it on the floor along with the tie. He went straight for his travel easel and collapsible swivel stool. As usual, he picked a spot by the window, although the lights of the city wouldn't provide proper lighting. He set up a makeshift studio, including his paints and the canvas from his oversized portfolio. Unbuttoning the top button of his shirt, he rolled his sleeves as he considered.

The velvet bag.

He turned and had to force his feet to walk at a normal pace over to the jacket he'd thrown on the floor, then dug through the pocket. Taking out the small bag, he stuck it in his pants pocket without opening it. Before he took his seat on his swivel stool, he pulled out a pad of practice paper and laid it over the canvas. He had no idea what he was doing and decided on chalks.

Closing his eyes, he did something he rarely did, yet seemed to be doing more often as of late. He allowed images to run freely over the backs of his eyelids. Years of them. Images of his aunt attacked at the spot along Black Creek that was tattooed on his chest. His stint in the Middle East. The scars on Nickie's back. The remnants of the paintings he'd drawn of her, burned to ashes in the fire that was meant to draw him away from his Nickie.

He started with larger lines using his blackest chalk. He copied one of the paintings he'd already drawn of her. The one that had been for his eyes only. The lines of her curves as she lay on his walnut settee. She'd been flushed from a lengthy tryst in his bed. No, he recalled. They hadn't made it to his bed. Rarely had they made it to any bed. He let the lines flow as his head pounded.

In a corner of the paper, he drew a small sketch of her scars. They were like a map to him. Six lines, straight and deep. Three circular cigarette burns. In the opposite corner, he drew him. Jun Zheng. The time Duncan saw him at the casino in Vegas. The images of him he and his brother had found on the Internet.

He stood, his chest pumping and knocked over the easel, letting it slide across the floor. He walked to the shiny oak desk, locking his elbows and dropping his head between his arms. He'd made the right decision. He was sure of it. Then, why did it cut so deeply?

He pulled his tablet from his briefcase and placed it on the slippery desk. He decided to check on his house alarm system via remote. Maybe she had come home. He wrung his hands as he waited impatiently for his tablet to power up, for Wi-Fi to connect.

The alarm hadn't been disengaged or tripped. The doors were locked, and the timed lights were all in working order. No sign of her. He switched to the perimeter. It had rained since he'd left. Clusters of small puddles created bare spots in the snow between the trees. The camera switched screens. The garage door was shut and sealed.

He went back to the previous image. The bare spots looked too uniform. It could be a pattern created from the melting snow, but the few depressions looked like footprints. He took out his phone and texted his brother.

'have you checked on my house?'

He tapped his fingers for a few minutes before he took his phone into one of the bedroom suites. He placed the velvet bag on the side dresser, then started to undress, purposely tossing one article of clothing after another half-heartedly onto the Victorian dresser near the bed. His phone vibrated on the glass top.

'no. was i supposed to?'

Duncan considered. Wearing his boxer briefs, he walked back to his tablet, checked the stills again, and copied and saved them this time. Snow doesn't melt in a walking pattern.

'if you were thinking of it, don't'

'like hell. sup?'

'i mean it, little brother. stay away. i'll call the captain and have him check it out.'

'don't give me that little brother shit. check what the hell out?'

'it's nothing'

'i'll just go up and see'

'i think i see footprints. it's probably nothing. if it's not nothing, it's bad. stay away'

Nickie dressed casually. No one was going to peg her as a cop in her taller heeled boots, tight black slacks and a sweater that hung like loose curtains over her shoulders. It was the one that concealed her holster well. Her hair was down and in long waves. She wore her makeup thicker than usual.

Eddy, on the other hand, was a beacon. His clothes screamed unmarked uniform, his haircut status quo.

Captain Nolan made her take backup. She would have preferred Parker. If she was going to take someone who looked like a cop, at least he was in full blues and didn't talk her ear off.

Regardless, work was good for her. It was right. She'd been able to spend the day assisting with checking video records on a robbery as well as doubling back over the SS8 records.

This time, she came to the hotel with a warrant. These places never seemed to slow down, not even on a Tuesday night. Same smell. Check. Same people. Check. And here came *Mr.* Edwin the wannabe. He was practically waiting for them, although minus the outstretched arms this time.

"Detective Savage." He nodded in her direction. "Detective Lynx. I have a key card for each of you. No one has inquired about the room as of yet."

Had Joe Johnson read the paper? Learned his lover was murdered? Was it he who did it? Most police work was chasing tails. This would likely be the same.

She took the key and slid it into the back pocket of her pants. "No activity from a Joe Johnson anywhere?"

"No. I have each outlet keeping an eye open for any transactions or reservations made with that name, just as you requested." The sarcasm in his voice was oddly comfortable.

"Keep your cameras rolling, Ed. We'll be upstairs."

Eddy shook his head as they rode the elevator to the floor with the Fox River Suite. "The thought of picking up a hooker always gives me the creeps. Don't they know where that thing's been?"

Nickie didn't have it in her to retort.

"What's up with you today?"

Still nothing.

"Is it Pretty Boy again? Did he—?"

"Fuck you, Lynx."

He held up both hands, palms out. Asshole.

Eddy took out his handkerchief, but Nickie shoved her shoulder in front of him. "Let me," she whispered when they got to the room. She knocked three times softly. "Room service."

No one called out or opened the door, so she used her key and cracked it. Without a handkerchief. She couldn't hear anything. Stepping inside, the room looked like it hadn't been inhabited since the last time they were there. Rustic wood trim, earth-toned couches. The stools at the wet bar looked like half-sawed logs. Not a single footprint crossed the pattern left from the lines of the vacuum. It was chilly. Was that different from last time? Fresh flowers. Chocolates on the pillows. Blah, blah, blah.

Like good little cops, Eddy took the bedrooms and she checked the bathroom and closets. They'd kept the door cracked, and she heard footsteps.

"Get a load of—"

She held up a finger to quiet Eddy as the footsteps stopped in front of the cracked door. A short woman with asymmetrically cut jet-black hair leaned in.

"Hello? Oh—" She pulled her head back and checked the number on the door. "Wrong room. I'm sorry."

Short cocktail dress with matching pumps in fuck-me red. "Joe Johnson." Nickie said it like she was sure, which she wasn't.

The pause was slight, but it was enough to answer her question.

The woman turned and hightailed it toward the elevator. "Shall we talk to you here or at the station, Ms. Johnson?" Nickie called before she had to run after her.

Nickie swore the woman was about to stomp the floor like a toddler, the way her body language flipped. "I didn't *do* anything." Turning to face

Nickie, Miss Joe Johnson crossed her skinny, white arms.

Nickie glanced from one end of the hallway to the other. "Are we talking out here? Or should we make use of your kick ass suite? It's very pretty."

Slinging her purse over her shoulder, Johnson strutted back to the room and plopped on the wooden bench in the foyer.

"We're not here to discuss your work, Miss…?"

"Wendy. You can call me Wendy."

"Right. Well then, Wendy." Nickie didn't bother sitting but pulled out her recorder. "Do you mind if I record this?"

"Of course I mind the freaking hell if you tape me."

Nickie lifted her brows.

"Fine. I agree," Wendy-Joe Johnson amended.

Nickie wasn't going to push stating her name verbally with this one. The woman was a cute little thing. She didn't show any outward emotional or physical signs of captivity. Nickie would never understand how so many striking women voluntarily let men do this to their bodies and wondered if the gal fell into that category.

"What can you tell me about SS8?"

Wendy's head remained tight, but her gaze turned to Nickie. "I've never seen any of them."

She seemed to have her alibi prepared. "Of course you haven't. A woman in your position would never do anything illegal."

"I mean it's all done electronically. Mostly phone calls."

"I'd like that number."

"Okay, but it's a prepaid phone and changes almost daily."

"Give me what you've got, *Wendy*. How many

times have you met with William Juracek?" And how could she have missed that he was dead? Nickie made sure to keep that question to herself.

"Just one other time. And I don't know about the other girls. We don't talk about this shit. Is he a cop?" Reluctantly, Wendy handed her a business card. A hooker with a business card. Nickie thought it was a sign of the apocalypse. On it, there was a phone number. Nickie didn't imagine she had a new business card each day to go with a daily changing prepaid cell number.

Hookers who don't talk to each other? This, Nickie personally knew was a crock. "Lucky you. No, he's not a cop. Write down your name. Your real name. And your personal address and phone."

Wendy-Joe Johnson didn't look too pleased.

"Give me false information—" Nickie sat next to her and dipped her face to within inches of the woman's. "—and I'll hunt you down like a stray dog in the woods."

Unlocking the door, Nickie checked her surroundings and stepped in. The bag and her cello case were still there, untouched. Not that he was coming back to get them. He'd placed this in her lap.

The ache to play her cello finally became stronger than the fear she had of touching the things Duncan left in her foyer. Standing just inside the door, she gathered the nerve. She was going to man up and empty the damned bag. She imagined each of her articles of clothing, the ones she'd accumulated at his place over the past year, each cleaned and folded neatly.

First, a glass of dry red. Keeping her feet planted, she looked around her town house. Not a scrap of newspaper or clothing anywhere. The tops of the coffee table and end tables were wiped clean with single candles centered on each. Her coats were hung, her boots in a line at the bottom of the coat closet.

"It looks like we have a new murder suspect," she said, contemplating Sherie Douglas, alias Wendy-Joe-Johnson, as she took off her boots. In her closet, she had a pair of house shoes waiting side by side in the spot where her boots went. She traded the two, slipped on the furry, moccasin house shoes, then hung up her coat.

Mrs. Juracek hadn't mentioned an escort service. Surely, she knew. The look on her face when Nickie mentioned SS8. The night he was murdered, he'd been out in the middle of the night dressed to kill. Or be killed.

She unbuckled her holster and hung it neatly on her standing coat rack in the foyer.

As she made her way into her bedroom, her feet stopped before the rest of her. Instinctively, she backed up slowly, searching the area with her eyes. Foyer, living room, hallway. She slid her gun from the holster and took it off safety all in one, quick movement. Stepping back against the nearest wall, she listened. Someone had secured a set of handcuffs to each of her four bedposts. It was a message, and it was for her.

CHAPTER 7

Come on, baby. Show yourself. Nickie crept along the carpet, thankful she was in her quiet house shoes. Slipping back into her room, she checked the mirror. No one in the bathroom. She pushed open the door with the back of her hand to check behind the door anyway. Like a cat, she dipped low, checking under the bed before moving to the closet.

The cuffs. They were arranged the same way Zheng held the girls when he did his *training*. It was the word he used for drugging and beating early teens until they did what he wanted. She was never smart enough to quit fighting. Instead, she earned the name Savage and was given to men who liked it.

She hated checking around clothes in a closet. Too many places to hide. She did it anyway. Her hand ached to reach for her phone. It wasn't to call the captain, or even Eddy. She didn't want to think of the man whose number she wanted to call.

She continued until she'd searched every inch of her house. She found an unlocked window that was still cracked. Securing it, she noted that she hadn't left it unlocked in the first place.

It was Zheng. He'd either been in her town house or had someone to do it for him. Was he grooming her for what was to come? Because she was too far gone to let this shit scare her. He'd made her savage enough that she legally applied for a name change the day she turned eighteen. She didn't do it for him. She did it for the girls. The ones she didn't go back for.

Looking out into the ink black, she decided to play her cello after all, just in case he was out there. He would listen to her play like she would any other night. Her days of being scared of Jun Zheng were over.

It was the crack of dawn, and Nickie stood at Sylvia Juracek's home, pressing the nifty ringer in the middle of the enormous door. Technically, she'd ditched Eddy but still planned to give him shit about getting in too late that morning to tag along.

Mrs. Juracek had recognized SS8. William Juracek had been having an affair with an SS8 employee, and she didn't know a thing about it? Even when her husband, who doesn't sleep in the same room with her, leaves the house in the middle of the night dressed in a suit and tie? Mrs. Juracek earned herself a ticket to the top of the suspect list.

It was cold as hell and icy from the melting that happened the day before. She rang the bell another time for good measure. Her breath made a small cloud around her before someone finally opened the door. It wasn't Mrs. Juracek, nor was it her twenty-something son or her daughter. Gerald Jackson stood wearing a royal blue robe and matching slippers. She went from haughty cop to schmuck in three seconds flat.

To make things worse, he was nice about it. "Good morning, Detective. Do you have news? Did you find who killed William?" As if he suddenly realized he was the one with bad manners, he stepped aside. "Please come in. Did you come out here at this hour alone?" He glanced down the walk before shutting the door.

"Yes." Nickie squirmed as she stepped inside and wiped her feet.

He gestured for her to follow as he limped to the kitchen.

Great, Nickie. You woke up an elderly *handicapped* man so you could get some satisfaction in giving shit to his daughter.

"Can I get you something to drink? Cranberry juice? Coffee?"

Twist the knife in her back, why doesn't he? "No, thank you. Is Mrs. Juracek home?"

He paused. The look on his face was pained. "She'll be asleep for hours yet. Depression medicine. Little Renee, too. Well, not the pills." He grinned as he opened the fridge. "She's going to be a teenager soon. She sleeps until noon any chance she gets."

"And Tommy?" Nickie asked.

The man was an open book. His expression went from pained at the mention of his daughter to endearment at the mention of his granddaughter to content at the mention of his grandson. Tommy Marino. No blood relation to William Juracek, yet this elderly man and Juracek had been considering leaving Juracek's half of the business to him.

"He's not quite home yet."

Ah. "Was he out the night William was killed?"

The man sighed. "No. He was home before midnight that evening."

Right. Because you were up at midnight waiting for him.

"Is that why you're here?" he asked. "If you don't mind me asking." He moved his arm as an invitation for her to sit at the table in their kitchen nook that faced the immense patio and backyard.

"No, of course you can ask." She sat in a cushioned chair and pondered the vast sea of ice-glazed white. Not a single footprint, animal or human, tainted the snow. Somehow, she thought this was sad. "And I'm sorry, but I don't know who killed your son-in-law yet. I have a few questions. In searching through the business records, I noticed the name of a business that didn't seem to fit. SS8."

He turned his gaze to her as if he was considering, then gingerly lowered himself to the seat across from her. "Yes. Yes, that rings a bell. William mentioned the name a few weeks ago." He sighed and gazed at the floor before turning his eyes to her. "I can't remember the context of our conversation. I think it was as we discussed credits and liabilities."

"Can you think a little harder?" She hated to press. "It might help us."

"SS8. SS8. I'm just not sure, Detective. It's not any jeweler or name of a supply company I recognize, but it does ring a bell. I'll certainly call you if I remember anything."

"I'm afraid I need to ask you where you were the night William died. It's routine, you understand." He'd already been asked, but she wanted to see his reaction for herself. Which made her the biggest schmuck of them all.

It was more than Jackson's age that seemed to make him smart. Business savvy? Able to be woken at dawn by a head-case detective?

"I understand, yes. I was home all night, as were Sylvia and Renee."

All four of them, than? Convenient.

Duncan's canvases, easel and folding stool were

packed and waiting by the door to the suite next to his personal bags. His pilot waited in the small plane terminal at LAX.

Sophia Colour was happy with the first of the three paintings she'd requisitioned. The next two were well on their way. She appreciated the use of his arm at the charity event and helped land him another job with a new and upcoming country singer.

He should be in the limousine Sophia arranged for him in front of the Hotel Grande. Just one last search first.

His list of victims, johns and perpetrators sat next to him at the desk in his suite. All but two perpetrators were marked off. He wanted to get through this first, legal, Internet search before he returned to Northridge.

He leaned back in the hotel swivel chair and checked his pocket. The velvet bag was still here with him, but she was not. No phone call. No messages.

He ran a hand over his face and looked down at the monitor on his tablet. Two more thugs. He would do a thorough search to see if Zheng was connected to any picture or public record of these two before he left for the airport. When he returned to Northridge, he would get Andy to help him dig deeper, using means less ethical.

His attention distracted to his little brother. Duncan appreciated that Andy agreed to buy a portion of the forty acres Duncan had purchased. What would he have done with forty acres? Now, he had a place to keep his horse. Rose took excellent care of her. It was nice having them down the hill. Except when Duncan had a feeling someone was watching his house.

Was he paranoid? Having a home burnt to the ground could do that to anyone, especially when convinced the woman you love was still inside. A decoy. A ruse. Those responsible sat in separate federal prisons at this moment, yet still, it made him cautious.

He opened a new tab and connected to his security system by remote access. The lights scheduled to turn on at that time of day were on, doors secured, pool at an even seventy-five degrees Fahrenheit.

Changing to the outdoor cameras, he noted that a fresh layer of snow had fallen. Upstate New York was truly as pretty as a picture. Fresh footprints. It was unmistakable. Larger, must be male. Duncan's heart sped as he spotted a man walking around the back corner of his house. He scooted to the front of the hotel desk chair as if that would get him closer to the man. Quickly, he hurried to switch cameras. Damn, he ended up back inside.

Forcing himself to find control, he chose the correct link to the back corner of his house and rotated the camera manually. It would make a noise if the intruder was close by, but it was necessary. There. The camera focused and Duncan zoomed in.

His brother turned toward the noise just as the camera found him. He waved his gloved hand, then turned around and dropped his pants. Duncan told him to stay away. He would kick his ass when he got home. Right after he made Andy agree to travel out of town to one of their preferred public spots and hack into a federal database.

"I'm not asking."

Not now, Nickie thought. There was no way for the captain to know what she was going through, but her patience was threadbare. To crank the wrench a little farther, it was Valentine's Day. She'd just lost the only other person in this world she could carry on an actual conversation with, and her boss wanted her to make nice? With a stranger?

"I don't play well with others, Captain." In order to make sure she kept the look on her face respectful, she allowed herself to sling a boot over her knee and slouch in his guest chair.

"I'm still not asking."

"Especially women," she pleaded. It was true. Other than Gloria, who didn't count because she was more like a mother, what one woman did Nickie have as a friend or colleague?

Rose.

She'd backed out on her for their night of shots and potential bar fights. Rose may have been the mother of a new baby, but she was wicked quick, and Nickie would trust her to have her back in any alley anywhere. Since she also happened to be the captain's stepdaughter, Nickie decided to keep that to herself.

"Nick?"

What? Oh. "You're the boss."

He sighed and gave her that father-figure look that made her feel like shit. The gray that laced his hair sat like quotation marks around his crow's feet. It made him look smart. And, unfortunately, like the boss. "I take Lynx with me all the time. Isn't that good enough? Now you want me to work with the A.D.A.?"

"Lynx is called backup. We do that in police work." He sat up now. "And you're going to work with the A.D.A. like every other detective whether she's a man or a woman or a cat or dog. I'm not sure what's going on with you and Duncan, but keep it out of the station."

Her eyes darted to his. That was crossing the line. The look on his face said he realized it, too. And he was right, damn it. Pinching the spot on her nose between her eyes, she squinted. "I'll meet with her. I'll play nice. Right now, the wife is the top suspect, followed loosely by a prostitute the deceased met at the Seneca Hotel and Casino. It's all circumstantial at this time."

The captain leaned over and punched some buttons on his ancient intercom. "Miranda. She's ready. My office."

She's ready? Now? Nickie looked around like she just realized where she was. Here? Sitting up, she craned her neck and looked between the slats in the captain's blinds. Parker sat at the edge of one of the desks in the common area. Now there was a good cop. Easy. Smooth. Confident. By the book. Why couldn't the captain want her to get advice from Parker?

Smooth, confident Parker stood like he'd just burned his ass on the desk, spilling a mug of coffee down the side of it. His face turned three shades of red as the new assistant district attorney, Miranda Vaughn, walked past and smiled at him. Well, Dale Parker, you cougar-loving slick. Vaughn must have ten years on him.

Slouching farther in the captain's guest chair, she got rid of the respectful face.

Vaughn waltzed into Captain Nolan's office in her skirt, suit jacket and shiny pumps. Her hair was pulled back in a tight ponytail like the squeaky receptionist from the casino. "Good day, Captain." She held out her manicured hand. He took it and shook. Traitor. Then, left his office? For Vaughn? Spineless traitor.

Nickie slid her boot along her leg so the side of her foot rested on her knee. Draping one arm across the back of her chair, she sat still, waiting.

"Detective Savage." Vaughn held out her hand. It wasn't like they'd never met before. Nickie tilted her head up as a greeting and ignored the hand.

"I see," Vaughn said and leaned back against the captain's desk. "Why don't you tell me what you've got thus far, and I'll see if there is any advice I can offer."

Why? Because she just said, 'advice?' No one wanted her *advice*. Keeping her eyes glued on the A.D.A., Nickie opened her mouth. "Time of death was estimated between three and four a.m. He was found in the alley behind his business with two bullets in him, one lodged in his clavicle, the other in his left lung. A third grazed a rib and exited the right side. The murder took place in the business of the deceased, where we found the missing bullet. The wife inherits her late husband's half of the business equity upon his death. Three hundred and fifty thousand in cash and a bagful of diamonds appraised at over a mil were found at the home. The deceased had at least two dates with a professional prostitute with a company that calls itself SS8. The wife claims to have no knowledge of it. Business partner and father-in-law says stepson, preteen daughter and Mrs. Juracek were all home by midnight the night of the murder."

"Convenient," Vaughn mumbled.

Hey, that was what she'd said.

"Possible money laundering," she mumbled some more. "Crime of passion?" Vaughn nodded her head like she was actually considering it. "All of this is circumstantial."

Enough pleasant formality. "No shit, Sherlock."

Her eyes moved to Nickie's. Too bad. She'd earned it.

Vaughn sighed and ran a hand over the top of her black, glossy ponytail. "What does your gut tell you, Detective? What are you feeling?"

Hunch? Feelings? Was she freaking serious? "I don't do hunches." And she tried not to have feelings. They screwed everything up.

"Okay." Vaughn moved her hand from her ponytail to the back of her neck and squeezed. "Who is at the top of your suspect list?"

"My list of suspects include, in no particular order," she lied, "the deceased's wife, prostitute, father-in-law, and stepson."

Wasting more of Nickie's time, Vaughn pushed away from the captain's desk and paced. "In no particular order," she repeated under her breath. If she mumbled one more time, Nickie was going to kick her neatly pressed ass all the way back to wherever she came from.

"What if I got you clearance on a bug for the phones over at this SS8 place?"

She could do that?

"I can have it set up by the end of tomorrow. Will that help, Detective?"

"Maybe." Was she going to have to owe her for this?

CHAPTER 8

Duncan ran Abigail's brush along the smooth brown of her back. She was doing her best to ignore him, pointing her snout as far away as possible.

He took a deep breath, letting the aroma of fresh hay and crisp winter wash into his lungs. "Yes, girl. I know. I came alone." She preferred Nickie. So did he.

If he stopped brushing, she rotated her head, considering him with pleading eyes. As soon as the brush touched her back, she turned away again as if he wasn't there. So, he continued. He brushed her with long, smooth strokes. Her ears and tail slowly relaxed. He was honored to have such an amazing animal and fortunate that Rose provided a home for her. Her mane and tail were last. The mane was nearly the color of Nickie's hair, just a shade darker. Her tail and single front leg a pearly white.

He placed the brush back in the wooden box Andy had made for it on the wall. The area was cleaner than Nickie's town house. Each stall had a set of stairs leading to the hayloft. Hooks for bridles and saddles, cubbies for the brushes, blankets and nail files. Even in this weather, Rose kept the floors free of old hay and manure.

He brought bribery with him this time. Nickie generally carried the contraband. Since he could think of nothing else but every part of her, he remembered the carrots.

Perching on the side of the stall, he pulled one out and held it low. Abigail's golden brown head perked; her pretty nose twitched, letting out streams of warm breath in the cool air. He didn't hold it out to her and gave her time to consider. She picked up a mouthful of the fresh hay he'd tossed for her, chewed it thoughtfully, then let her feet take a step in his direction.

She walked as if she was window-shopping—nothing special. It must have been the smell, because she suddenly stepped forward and grabbed it with her teeth. "No, you don't, you gorgeous thief." He only let her bite off half as he rubbed the palm of his hands over the white spots between her eyes. In order to keep his fingers safely connected, he opened his hand flat before letting her take the rest.

"There's more where that came from," he said as he slid to the ground. He took the blankets from their perch, shook them clean and made sure they were folded neatly with no creases. Taking another carrot, he broke it in half and palmed it, letting her take it before he placed the blankets carefully on her back. Another carrot, the saddle. Before Nickie came along, he didn't need to bribe his horse before saddling her.

Abigail adored Nickie. Nickie had been raised around horses. The years of English riding her parents put her through didn't seem to stick. Nickie preferred bare back, and the only jumps she did were over fallen logs on the trails behind Andy's home.

Had he lost her forever? He led his horse down the corridor of the rows of stalls and out to the snowy trails. Abigail was tall; a good fit for a five-foot-ten woman. Or for himself, he supposed. As he placed a foot in the first stirrup, she snorted. He pulled another carrot from his pocket, then reached around to give it to her. Placing his weight in the stirrup, he lifted and swung his other leg over her muscled back.

He stroked her neck as he adjusted in the seat. It was the first solo ride he'd taken with her in nearly a year. They passed Andy's handful of oversized earth-moving equipment that made Duncan feel incredibly small.

The trails were clearly marked and a little muddy from the melting snow and horses that had used them in the past several days. Lines of snow hung to evergreens, falling in wet clumps every so often. It was the only sound other than Abigail's snorts and her hooves as they crunched in the snow.

He'd certainly planned on a different marriage proposal, something meaningful. Nothing public. Possibly out here, just the two of them.

Definitely not in a booth at Rossetti's.

He practically yelled it at her—marriage. He knew her aversion to commitment. The content was necessary, but his delivery? He'd never lost his temper with her before. Around her, yes. But toward her?

The rhythmic clop of Abigail's feet both soothed and confused. An occasional squirrel darted around a tree trunk to investigate the large beast and the man in black who rode on her back. Abigail seemed to become lost in the ride, as well. Her breaths were strong and even, her feet sure and light. The crisp air comforted his lungs. He was bundled warmly enough to ride all day if he wanted.

Pulling the glove from his right hand, he held onto the reins with his left as he checked his pocket for the velvet bag. Would she come back to him? It had been over a week since he left her things and her cello in the foyer of her town house. His key had not been waiting for him on the tiny table near the entrance. The rush of hope at the sight of the empty glass top was nearly his undoing.

The beauty of this land was meant to be experienced. Hundreds of towering evergreen trees flanked both sides of him as they rode between them. A blanket of white that traveled miles was littered with the footprints of life and survival. This beauty was meant to be respected and shared.

The pain he carried now was profound. It wasn't like the pain when he witnessed the attack on his aunt. Not the barrel of the gun when Brie's childhood nemesis pressed it to his young head. Not even from the flashbacks of his time in the Middle East.

It was his heart. He would never find another Nickie. Smooth, quick, smart-as-hell, and all woman. Brazen, tough, a survivor. He wanted every part of her.

And there was their problem.

"I appreciate you taking your afternoon for me. I know you have work." Duncan drove his Barracuda, not willing to let Andy be seen in one of his Reed Builder's vehicles.

"Then why are you acting like an ass?"

Brothers. "Because you searched my property when I told you not to. You have a wife and a baby. My place was burnt to the ground last year with yours just down the hill. Now, it might be under surveillance." It appeared he was more upset about it than he'd realized.

"I'm not stupid."

"I can't call you stupid when you're spending the

afternoon illegally hacking with me, but if the shoe fits…"

"You're making shit up, anyway. No one's been around your house. You've been dating a cop too long."

He still hadn't heard from her. His fingers clutched the steering wheel as he drove through the snow packed Rochester roads. He was sure he had done the right thing with Nickie. Maybe. He turned onto the last road. Small strip mall, just inside town.

The silence must have gone on for too long.

"Everything okay with you, man?"

"Yes." He was just taking his little brother, the one with the wife and baby, out to illegally search for information that might help his ex-girlfriend, who hadn't responded to his miserable proposal.

There were a number of spots in Rochester they could use anonymously and confuse the hell out of anyone who tried to trace them. They pulled in front of a café that wouldn't have surveillance but would have Wi-Fi. He chose a spot away from the windows and the coffee stand.

Andy was neurotic with safety—creating false trails, traveling through enough countries to keep anyone that might want to track them guessing long after their trail split, then ran dry. Duncan could memorize the longest, most complicated IDs and passwords. For as many years as necessary. They were a damned good team and had been since high school.

They each came with their laptops and tablets. They were the ones they'd purchased with cash and used solely for hacking. Duncan ordered coffee from the counter as Andy did his thing. He always went first using dummy desktops and anonymously logging into Internet cafés around the globe. One machine linked through the Dominican Republic to Oklahoma and supposedly resided in Toronto. His went through Ghana and landed in Puerto Rico.

His end goal was CODIS, NCIC and any other federal database where he could dig into the protected files of the johns and thugs he had already researched legally. They would also comb through the files of the victims. It may be wrong but would be necessary. They might find a shot as Zheng staked out one of them, grooming her or whatever they called that demented shit. This was going to take time and would have taken even more time if they hadn't done this sort of thing a dozen times before. "Two coffees." He set them on the table away from their machines. "One black and leaded and one frappe thing for the Reed who needs to learn to drink like a man."

"I've got the new security down. We just need to wait now. Give me my frappe, mother fucker."

It was Duncan's turn. He watched and waited for someone to enter a user name and password. He would be able to break down the binary code into letters and numbers, memorizing each.

"It's none of my business, but you rode Abigail without Nickie."

He could feel his face wince as if he'd been sucker punched. He didn't answer.

"And that's the face you make each time I mention her name."

"Stop looking at my face and watch the screens. I can't scan all four at once." Nickie called his eidetic memory a super power. When would time start to heal?

"Rose said she answers her texts."

What? He turned to look at Andy.

"Ah. I knew that would get you."

"You're lying?"

"No. She does answer, but Rose says they are short

and off. Talk to me, dude."

He turned his focus back to his tablet. "Shit, Andy. I missed one." He got the password, but not the ID.

"Brother." Andy put his hand over Duncan's screen. "Talk to me."

"What do you want me to say? She kept me an arm's length away for a year. It worked for a while, and although I understand why she does it, I'm not willing to be that anymore. I asked her to marry me."

"You what? Why the hell didn't you tell me? What did she say?"

What *did* she say? "I don't think she said anything."

"What do you mean you don't *think* she said anything? You never forget anything."

He had never told Andy about his...memory. Did he know? Surely, he didn't know. "I sort of barked it at her. We were arguing. Or, I was arguing. She sat there."

"Did you have a ring? What has she said since? How do you bark a proposal?"

"I haven't talked to or seen her since. It's up to her now."

"You dumb ass. Call her. What the hell's the matter with you? She's the best thing that's ever happened to you. She gets your crazy brain." Andy flicked him on the side of the head.

Duncan's eyes left the screen again, this time as a defense. If he weren't in such shock over the comment about his brain, he would bend Andy's flicking fingers back until they cracked. He'd never told anyone about his eidetic memory. Although, their hacking would lead one to believe...

It was more of a freakish circus act in Duncan's opinion. After a few years as a child, their aunt figured it out. After two weeks, Nickie figured it out. He missed her more each waking minute, but he wasn't going to call her.

"This is about your life, man."

Duncan closed his eyes. His shoulders became as heavy as his heart. "You're right, Andy. Everything you're saying is right. And it's why I have to stick with my decision. She wants halfway, and I can't do halfway anymore."

Andy bumped his shoulder in time for Duncan to open his eyes to the employee ID as it was typed in. All Andy would see was the binary code. Duncan knew how to break it down. Their system didn't provide for case sensitive. It took several dozen trial and error attempts to test which letters were caps and which weren't, but in twenty minutes time, they were in.

It wasn't a good idea to stay in one café too long. They weren't college boys anymore. Two adult males sitting with coffee for too long would draw attention, so they took their user names and passcodes and hauled their machines down the street to a chain coffee store.

Duncan worked on his fourth cup of java as Andy re-created his complicated maze of a trail. It gave him time to think. Too much time to think. He and Andy's last efforts at hacking. Discovering Nickie's parents—her own flesh and blood—had illegally concealed the crime scene file containing the details of her abduction. She'd had more people deceive her in her short lifetime than most experienced throughout eternity.

Andy connected their machines to the link they'd saved, then started surfing through the files of each person, innocent and guilty, from the sex trafficking ring Duncan and Nickie had helped take down. They searched in silence for four hours, much longer than Duncan had asked of Andy. His brother was like that.

Together, they found a total of six additional pictures of Zheng.

Duncan's teeth ground as he copied and studied the date stamps. Three of them coincided with dates and locations of where Nickie had been. Add those to the time Duncan spotted him at the casino in Vegas nearly a year ago, and he could hardly keep himself in his seat.

His proposal didn't matter. Nothing mattered. Zheng was close. He'd been keeping tabs on her. It wasn't the first time Duncan had discovered someone, somewhere had put a tail on her. The personal assistant to the governor, the former captain at the NPD. Duncan pulled out his phone. Slowly, Andy put his hand over it. Their eyes met and Duncan read what was his brother was thinking. If Zheng was this close, he could be tracing Duncan's calls.

CHAPTER 9

She wasn't going home. Not again. Not to the bag
that sat in her foyer. Nickie had placed some of those
bar things people put in their windows to keep people
out. Not that Zheng couldn't bust through the glass if
he really wanted to. But she would hear that. Or see it.
And she wasn't a little girl anymore. She was a cop.
She had a gun and could kick the ass of some forty-
five-ish-year-old scumbag who got his kicks from
using and abusing young teens.

But the bag. The handcuffs by Zheng or whoever
were nothing compared to facing the bag. She stepped
into the shower at the station and turned the water to
blistering. Closing her eyes, she turned her face to the
nozzle and let the water beat down her cheeks, her
forehead. She would stay there until she could think
straight again or until she became a prune, whichever
happened first.

It wasn't getting better. Tremors shook her head, her
heart. Could she do it? Could she give herself to him?
Entirely? It would be like a dream. How could she
deserve that? She was a bitch. She was a head case
bitch who woke up swinging when her past came to

haunt her. Or when it left handcuffs attached to the four corners of her bed. But he knew all the parts of her, good and bad. And he asked her anyway. Or did he? Was it something he threw out in the heat of a moment? She lathered her hair and ran the lavender suds quickly over her body.

Turning, she let the water beat at the scars, then craned her head and let it turn her hair into silky threads that brushed the middle of her back. This was insane. She was off her game, couldn't wrap her head around her case. There was shit she didn't know. It had been a week since the A.D.A. had authorized the bug on SS8.

SS8.

Shit. The backs of the checks. Way off her game. Turning off the water, she grabbed a towel. Barely dry, she held her phone between her shoulder and her ear as she pulled on her slacks. "Lynx?"

"You're calling me?"

"Yeah, we have work to do."

"Aren't you here?"

"I'm in the shower."

"Yum."

"Shut up, dickhead. Meet me—"

"I'll be right there."

"Forget it. I don't need you." She heard him apologizing as she hung up and realized he should have been home for the day by this time.

A quick braid and she was good enough. She wasn't a prune and couldn't nearly say she could think straight, but she had something to occupy her time that didn't involve going home.

He was in her office when she got there. Sitting in her chair. His feet were propped on her desk. "You don't have on any makeup."

She was too psyched to worry about it.

"I've never seen you without makeup. You don't need any."

"Get out of my chair, Lynx."

"I'm here for the work we have to do."

She had a good feeling about this, a hunch if she had to admit it, although she never would out loud.

"Take these," she said, handing him a stack of the paper copies of J & JJ canceled checks. "Go through the backs. Who signed them? How were they signed?" Why hadn't she done this already?

Three Diet Cokes later, she was still stuck at square one. Police work could be boring as shit. She loved it.

"It's been two weeks," he said. She barely heard him.

"Hmm?" Most of the checks were stamped 'J & JJ/For Deposit Only.' Standard.

"It's been two weeks since you talked about him."

He didn't refer to Duncan as Pretty Boy. Not a good sign. "I never talk about him." The printouts of the fronts and backs of the checks were hard to read. It was late, and her eyes were tiring. She looked up at the clock. Close to midnight. She stopped and leaned back. "What are you still doing here?"

"You asked for my help." He leaned into her and took her hand between both of his. They were warm. Or else her hands were cold. The station turned the heat down at night. Standing, she headed for her coat.

"And you're right. You don't talk about him, but I can tell. What's going on, Nick? I'm here for you."

He was. She had to give him that. "I didn't realize it was so late. I asked for your help. But I…What were you even doing here when I called? You should go home." She draped the coat over her shoulders, plopped in her chair and started thumbing through checks.

"Home to what?"

"Yeah. Two peas, huh?" She never answered him about Duncan.

"Bam," Nickie said and flicked the paper in front of her. "A check written for six thousand, five hundred. Made out to The Guest House."

"Not so weird. Are you reaching here, Nick?"

She turned over the copy of the check and held it out to him. On the back it read, 'Pay to the order of SS8.'

"What the hell is The Guest House?"

Good question. The deposit was local. She thought she knew every local spot within a thirty-mile radius. But she did know who to ask.

It was late, so Duncan drove to her town house before dropping off his brother. "Wait here."

Andy scoffed and got out of the Barracuda, following him to the front door.

Duncan rang and waited, then rang again. Why did he give back that damned key? He tried to look between her drawn mini-blinds. "What the fuck? She installed locking bars." His chest started to heave.

"Let's check for her car," Andy said.

"Good idea." Why hadn't he thought of that? What was the matter with him? They hurried to the few parking spaces next to her unit. Her town car wasn't there.

"I'm going to try the station. I'll take you home first."

Andy scoffed again.

"She's okay, brother," Andy said as Duncan sped toward NPD, the engine of his Barracuda loud enough to hear halfway across town. They only called each other brother if they were giving each other shit, or if they were dead serious. Andy was not giving him shit, so Duncan slowed down. It wasn't going to do them any good if they crashed.

His heart sank as he found her spot empty. "Come on," Andy suggested. "Let's take a drive through the parking deck just in case."

It was useless, Duncan knew. Never, in the year he'd known Nickie, had she parked anywhere but in the gravel section of staff parking. But it couldn't hurt so he drove as carefully as his lead foot would take him.

As they exited the deck, Andy spoke up again. "Call her from my landline. The chances of Zheng tracing it are practically nil."

Duncan let his eyes wander as he considered. "But I'd be calling Nickie and her phone would be his first target."

"Maybe you can be covert. Lie or something. Tell her you've changed your mind?"

It would be worth it. "Good idea. I'll use my landline. I haven't used it in months. I can make it sound authentic in case he's got it tapped. You're a good man, Andy."

Duncan dropped him off to his wife and baby before he climbed the hill to his house. As he did, he forced himself to take cleansing breaths. He wouldn't have Andy to help him think clearly. His Nickie. If Zheng laid a single finger on her, he would crush him with his hands and watch as he choked on his spit.

He parked in front of his steps. It was faster. He took the stairs two at a time, unlocked the oak door and almost forgot to disengage the alarm as he stepped inside. His landline was in the far back of his home. He ran to it. The woods were black behind his house. They appeared glossy through the large picture window.

Picking up his phone, he set it down. He had no idea what to say. Slowly, he picked it up again and held the traditional unit to his ear. He dialed her number. It seemed to ring in slow motion.

"Detective Savage. Leave a message." The sound of her voice, alto and smooth. He ached to call back just to hear it again.

"Nickie. It's me. I've had some time to think, and I'd like you to call me as soon as you get this message. I mean, please call me. I've…got some things to do tonight and—So, call me now. Okay?"

Nickie parked between Slippery Jimbo's two favorite T & A bars, one of which was named T & A's. She brought Parker with her. Since Eddy had tomorrow off, she would take whatever shit he gave her about it on Monday. It had been past time for him to go home but she didn't want to face the bag in her foyer yet. Parker was on graveyard. He was the logical choice. As if she'd made a single logical choice in the past two weeks, she thought sarcastically.

Glancing in her passenger seat, she couldn't help but stare. She planned to have him wait in the car. Lookout or backup or whatever. He would stick out like a sore cop thumb, right? Nope. He used some hair product thing to spike his blond locks. She could only see the ones over his forehead since he wore an Under Armor hoodie flipped up over the rest. His pants sagged so low, his bright green boxers peeked out between the hoodie and his torn blue jeans. He was young enough to pull it off and had the best undercover getup she'd seen in all her days in police work.

It was well past midnight. She would sit and watch for Jimbo for twenty or so, then stop in his favorite joints, letting Parker keep her car running. It was too cold for smokers to hang out by the entrances. She knew they wouldn't abstain until warmer weather and would be smoking in all the non-smoking spots up and down the street. A few people staggered from door to door. Occasionally, one crunched through the snow to the coffee shop a few doors down. She might have already missed him, but it wasn't like she wanted to go home.

She'd reclined her seat and propped her boots on the dash to the side of her steering wheel. She sipped her bottle of Diet Coke. Parker had a paper cup full of coffee that had to be ice cold by now. She kept one eye on the door to Get Lucky's and the other in her rearview mirror at T & A's.

Check the sidewalks? Harass Parker? Harassing Parker would be much more fun. "So, what do ya think about the new A.D.A.?"

Smooth, confident Officer Parker nearly tipped his paper cup full of cold coffee all over his designer holey jeans. "Sir? I mean ma'am. I mean Detective?"

"We're on a stake out together, Parker. Call me Nick or Savage. Drop the detective, and if you call me ma'am again, I'm going to shove your nose into the back of your head."

"I don't think anything about Ms. Vaughn, Detective Savage."

"Bullshit. I'm a cop, remember?" His red face was enough of an answer for her. "Have you told her how you feel? Asked her out?"

"I'm not sure what you're talking about, Detective Savage."

"You know, cute, forty-something redhead? All prim and pretty? Smart?"

"She's in her thirties, Detective Savage."

Nickie shook her head. "Got you. She's thirty-five. I knew that already."

Come on, Jimbo. Show yourself. She needed a

tussle. He would be a satisfying target. She'd lost count of how many times she'd put him away just to have his scumbag lawyer get him off. She was the one who gave him the name Slippery Jimbo, after all.

He staggered out of Get Lucky's escorted by a man a full head taller with a neck as big around as Jimbo's leg. He jerked his arm free of the bouncer's grasp, nearly heading face-first into the exhaust-gray snow along the curb.

CHAPTER 10

Nickie got out of her car and tied the belt from her coat tighter around her waist. "Slippery Jimbo! What a pleasant surprise."

"Oh, fuck me." He shook his head and looked around as if he possibly had a chance at making a run for it.

"Ain't nobody wants to do that with you, Jimbo." She grabbed him by the back of his jacket and hauled him to the brick wall next to the black-painted window of the bar he'd just been ejected from. Over her shoulder, she saw that Parker had followed and realized she hadn't shared with him her wait-in-the-car strategy.

"I've got a woman now, Detective Dude. I told you that." Pathetically, he tried to straighten himself as his arms lifted outward from the way she yanked his coat.

"Oh, that's right. She know you're getting kicked out of the scummiest titty bar in town?"

"You know the scummiest bar in town is T & A's, Detective Dude. Get Lucky's is respectable. I was just coming to see you, man. First thing in the morning, I swear on my mama's grave."

"Your mama lives in public housing." She smacked the side of his head. "And I don't want you coming to see me. You're not my informant."

He didn't come back with a smart-ass retort or a plea to trade money for worthless information. Not a good sign.

"I only saw your Asian dude once, and it wasn't all that long ago," he slurred. "Give me a break, will you? I'm a busy man, and I was coming to see you, I was."

She stood, still holding his coat, and lifted his chin with her other hand. Leaning into him, she put the stench of his cigarette and alcohol-laden breath out of her mind. "Where, when, you little shit?" He took too long to answer, so she pulled him away from the brick wall, then slammed him back against it.

"Don't, dude, don't. I don't feel so well."

She was drawing attention to the three of them and decided to take it inside, just not inside one of the scumbag bars near them. "Come." She dragged him down the street toward the coffeehouse, Parker following close behind.

"It was just once, man. You can't..."

He wouldn't razz her for manhandling him. He knew better.

All eyes turned to them when she opened the door and pushed him in. Since that was only the gal behind the counter and the guy that looked like he was her boyfriend, Nickie decided they were clear.

"Have a seat, Jimbo. While you think good and hard about what you saw and where and why you didn't call me first thing, I'm going to get you some java to help jog your memory before I jog it myself."

"Two creams, one sugar, Detective Dude."

Like hell.

The handcuffs on her bedposts, now this? She

checked her surroundings. Age, height, weight of the people in the coffee shop, anyone who walked past the plate glass windows. The make and model of the parked cars. She always checked her surroundings, but now it was more paranoia than cop work.

She brought back two leaded coffees. Parker slouched in the seat next to Jimbo. She thought Jimbo stayed put because she was buying him coffee, but realized it may have been because the youthful, fast-looking and rather large Parker was intimidating as hell. Sliding the coffees in front of each of them, she sat.

"No coffee for you, Detective Dude?"

"I don't drink coffee."

"You don't drink coffee?"

"Asian man, Jimbo. Focus."

He dropped his head, his expression turning pained.

She folded her hands on the table and leaned closer. "If you don't start talking, asshole, I'm going to clothesline your Adam's apple with the side of my hand."

He winced. "The barbershop. I was getting a trim."

"Sure you were, Jimbo. Phil is still using his shop as a meeting place?" She tsked and shook her head. Phil was on probation for the last time he used his shop for this kind of shit.

"Nothing illegal about getting a haircut, right? Should I talk to him?"

"As if. When did you spot the Asian man, Jimbo? I'm losing my patience."

"Two days ago, I swear. See?"

"You're telling me you saw him Tuesday?"

He considered as he took a drink. "Oh, man. What did you get me? This is tar."

"It's coffee, Jimbo. Drink up. Tuesday? Or no?"

"Yeah, yeah. That's right. I remember 'cause I was getting that trim, ya know? The little lady likes my hair tight."

"Who all was there?"

"I'm not sure—"

Gently, she took his arm, then yanked it back until she heard a snap. The entire upper-half of his body gave in response to the pressure and slid out of the chair toward the floor. "Ow, ow, ow. Phil, his new guy, someone I've never seen before and the Asian dude."

She let her lids drop to half open and held her grasp.

"I swear, Nick. I swear."

She let go and straightened the sleeves of her jacket. "I'm sure you just lost my card." Reaching into the pocket of her coat, she pulled out another. "Here. Take this one, and don't lose it this time or you'll be sorry."

He rubbed his arm and straightened in his chair. She'd nearly forgotten why she came looking for him.

"The Guest House," she barked.

"What about it?" he whined as he rotated his arm.

"What is it?"

"What do you mean, what is it? It's T & A's, Detective Dude."

Nickie left Jimbo to his coffee and sprained elbow. No need to sprint down the street to T & A's, although the adrenaline from his Zheng sighting made her feet ache to burn some nerves. She would give Phil a visit just as soon as she could hunt up his probation officer.

Her car remained intact, even without Parker as lookout. It was one reason she liked it. No one wanted to mess with the old piece. T & A's was how she remembered. The T actually stood for Tommy and the A for Angie, but they'd chosen the initials for a reason, and it showed. She supposed there could be classier tits and asses bars out there, but this wasn't one of them. Braless waitresses in see-through T-shirts who sagged worse than bulls in a barnyard.

The state smoking ban was more of a suggestion around here rather than the law, but she wasn't downtown to bust up smokers or the shit that was going on in the back that must have given this place the nickname The Guest House. She was here to find out who signed a substantial check over to SS8.

She moseyed up to the bar, knowing she wasn't in her best incognito garb. She and Parker certainly didn't look like a couple. It made her think of him in that getup with the A.D.A. She nearly snorted. The bartender glanced over, a cigarette dangling from between his lips as he spoke to an especially ugly woman who may very well have been a man. The plastic bar top was chipped all over. The end nearest Parker peeled at the corners. He sat down on a stool before she could tell him not to. The look on his face said he stuck to it some.

"Diet Coke," Nickie called to the bartender.

He waltzed over and poured half a can of Diet RC with no ice, then pushed it toward her. She scoffed and left it on the counter, turning to scan the crowd. Through the haze, she made out three bikers who stood around the stained pool table. Two couples danced near the jukebox. Or maybe that was dancing. Could be copulating. Some did the same in booths along the back.

"Well, what do we have over there?" she said to Parker. Tommy Juracek. No, that's not right, she thought as she strolled toward him. What was his last name? Ah, yes. Marino. It didn't matter. "I think we've just found the Tommy half of Tommy and Angie's and the son of Mrs. Juracek and likely the one

who forwarded a check from his place nicknamed The
Guest House to SS8. All wrapped up in one kid."
Oops. She just called a guy who was the same age as
Parker a kid. "No offense."

"None taken, Detective Savage. What do we do
now?"

"You hike up your pants and stand back. I'm having
a little chat with the owner."

Tommy sat at a semi-circular booth and wore a
white, buttoned-down shirt with a black jacket. He
had a thousand-pound thug on one side of him and a
blonde with cleavage up to her chin on the other. With
his young face, she thought he looked more like he
just left parochial school instead of a man who had a
bar, a bodyguard and a bimbo. Free country. That is,
unless you forgot to mention you owned a sleazebag
bar, have something to hide and maybe shot your
stepdad three times in the chest.

She rocked her hips as she waltzed toward him. The
expression on his face when he pegged her was
telling. He straightened and nudged his right-side thug
to give Tommy room to get out of the booth.

"Stay put, Tommy." She held up her hand, palm
out, elbow locked in more of gesture that said don't
move rather than please stay put. With her other hand,
she pulled her coat aside, showing said thug her badge
as an added incentive. "You." She gestured to the
bodyguard. "Keep it coming. You, too, Dolly Parton."

Tommy leaned back and started to let his hands
drop to his lap.

Nickie pulled her coat back a little farther and took
her gun off safety. "Hands on the table, Tommy."

"What's this about, Officer?" he said, all thick and
sweet.

So that's how it was going to be, huh? Good. She
preferred it that way. Taking her free hand, she

flipped her hair over her shoulder and tilted her head. "It's Detective Officer to you. Let's have your fine, strong bodyguard take a walk, shall we?" she said, just as thick and sweet. Turning her eyes to the bodyguard, she purred, "Your boss, here, and I have some sorting out to do."

The guy looked to Tommy like he was asking what to do.

She really hated when they did that. "Hey, I'm the one with the gun here." Okay, so maybe the dude did have the gun he was eyeballing under the table, but hers was in plain sight, dammit. She scanned the bodyguard's hands with her peripheral vision as she watched Tommy nod his head in permission for him to step away. Dolly was out and gone in the blink of an eye.

Using her finest hip bump and dumb blonde blink, Nickie slid into the booth and reached her hand under the table. He grabbed her hand and squeezed. Lucky day. She was able to rotate her arm into him, free her hand and grab his wrist in time to teach him a lesson. She used her shoulder as she twisted farther, forcing his arm behind his back. In order to keep it from breaking, his torso rotated until he was facing the back of his seat. His face pressed into the vinyl.

Poor guy. He looked uncomfortable. "Don't even think about it," she barked to the thug, whose eyes were darting between Parker, herself and his boss. "I'll snap his arm like a twig, then break his wrist for fun."

Pressing her shoulder against Tommy, she took one of the cheap paper napkins from the table and used it to reach under the table and pull out his piece. Dipping her head close to his ear, she purred, "This is the state of New York, Tommy. There is no permit that makes this legal."

Large, red blotches starting forming on his neck. This was much better than facing the bag of clothes in her foyer. She craned her head behind her. Parker and Tommy's bodyguard were busy sizing each other up. She slid Tommy's gun into an empty pocket in her coat and released him. He spun like a cat. Some guys learn the hard way. She grabbed his nuts this time and watched him freeze harder than the ice on the road. A few tactics were foolproof.

"Your grandpa sure was hell bent on providing an alibi for you, your mother and baby sis." His eyes were wild, but it could have been because she had hold of his jewels, taken his gun or implied his mother may have needed an alibi; she didn't know or care. "He told me you were home by midnight. I wonder if anyone around here could remember differently with a little green incentive. I'm having a hard time finding anything down yonder, Tommy. So, I'm going to let go. Be a good boy and take a swing at me again, so I can bloody that pretty nose. Okay?" She didn't take her eyes off him or let his thug move from her field of vision, but she outstretched her arms like she was the manager at The Seneca Hotel and Casino showing off the lobby. "And this?" She whistled. "What a place you've made for yourself. Has gramps been in to see? What am I gonna find when I run your illegally concealed gun through ballistics, Tommy boy? Will it match the bullets we took out of stepdad?"

He didn't answer but made the mistake of dipping his gaze to the pocket that held his gun. "No. He doesn't know a thing about it, does he? I'm not here to rat you out, Tommy. I have only one question for you. SS8."

He ground his teeth together before lifting a corner of his mouth. "I don't have anything to tell you."

"You can answer my questions here or downtown. I

prefer the latter."

"Have you ever had a single date in your life, Detective?" He spat out the last word. "Is there any man out there who could tolerate your need to have testicles? Or am I mistaken and you're really a man? Those operations and drugs do wonders these days."

Why was she letting him get to her? "Where were you the night your stepfather was killed?"

"I already answered that question. Several times."

"Not to me, you haven't."

"I bet you need to wear the pants. To be the man. Do you kick out your lovers after you fuck them? Us men don't like to deal with those bitches in the morning, do we?"

It worked, dammit. He distracted her long enough that he was able to clamp his hand around her forearm and twist, making her curl at the waist and her head dip nearly in his lap. He slipped a hand in the pocket of her coat, copped a feel, then took his gun.

She could hear Parker and Tommy's bodyguard grunting on the floor. If he got hurt, she would never forgive herself. Tommy dug his gun beneath her chin. "Bitch, listen to me."

She did her best impersonation of a woman in fear. She whimpered slightly and cowered her head away from him, turning enough to watch his eyes sparkle with power. Men could be so predictable. As she dipped her head, she gathered room for momentum.

"This is my place. You're gonna take your backup and—"

She thrust her head around and butted him in the nose. She saw a few stars and was going to have a healthy bump, but it was worth it. Blood started oozing as she grabbed his gun and kicked her legs out of the booth. Parker had the bodyguard pinned with his arm craned behind his back. Granted the dude was big enough he may not have been able to get up from the floor without help, but Nickie was impressed nonetheless. "Way to go, Parker."

"You have the right—" Parker started.

"No need," Nickie interrupted. "We're good here, right, Tommy?" She forced herself not to rub her arm where he twisted it or her head from the bump that had already started forming. "Oh, and one more thing. Say cheese."

She took a shot of him with her cell. At least she wasn't the one who had to shove paper napkins up her nose. She should have had a better retort, something to leave an impression, but she couldn't get what he said out of her mind. Did she have cold-hearted bitch written across her face? And why did she care what he thought?

She headed out with Parker walking backward close behind. "They aren't coming after us, Parker. He knows I won't tell his grandpa and doesn't know we have a bug on the SS8 phones. And now he knows I know. Time for us to wait." They stepped out into the cold. Her car was untouched.

"You okay?" she asked him. A large drop of blood stuck in his stubble beneath a split lip, and his eye looked like it was swelling with each step they took.

"Yeah, Savage. I'm okay."

"We should get someone to take a look at that."

He jutted a thumb toward her forehead. "Are you going to get someone to look at that?"

"No." But I'm a screwed up bitch who can't face a frigging bag in her foyer.

He smiled. "Then me either."

CHAPTER 11

Nickie stood shivering on Duncan's doorstep. It wasn't from the cold. His key rested in her pocket, but she didn't feel right about using it. She'd driven around town, parked in her spot next to her town house for how long she didn't know. She was sleep deprived and beat up. It may have been her feet that took her here, maybe her heart, maybe what Tommy Marino said. Regardless, she stood on his porch, trembling like a scared child.

He'd parked in his drive. And he drove his Barracuda in the winter. How much else had changed in the time since she'd last seen him?

They'd shared their first kiss on this porch. The weather was similar, but everything else seemed different. Foreign. She heard footsteps inside and ached to run away. It was her knee-jerk, she reminded herself, and forced her feet to stay put.

She hoped with every ounce of her being he didn't shut the door in her face. That he would hear her out. She should have practiced what she wanted to say, should have written it down. Her mind was a cloud of disaster. She was a disaster.

The immense, oak door flew open. Large, dark eyes met hers through the glass storm door. The air escaped his lungs, leaving a cloud in front of him. Then, he dropped his hands to his thighs and dipped his head low. Was he going to get sick? She didn't know what to think, so she waited.

Standing, he ran his hands over his face twice before setting his eyes on her. He opened the door and took her hand. His was cold as he led her into the warmth. Had he just gotten home at this hour? He was breathing hard like he'd been swimming, but he was dry. And she was confused.

There was much she needed to say, to explain, to confess. She truly intended to do each, in that order in fact, but he took the sides of her face and brought his warm lips to hers. The taste of him was like a drug.

Their lips and tongues melted and meshed. His long arms encircled her and drew her against him, making tingles of electricity shoot through every inch of her body and her soul. Tears wet their cheeks as she wrapped her arms around his lanky body and held on. Her mind swirled in a cocoon of sensation and understanding. Her heart burst with more love than any one person should be allowed. In that moment, she forced herself into the reality that she really shouldn't be allowed to be here. Not her.

She slid her reluctant arms from around his back, placed them on his chest and pushed. With the back of one of her hands covering her mouth, she held up the other in a signal to wait. "Hold on," she gasped, the tears coming faster. She wanted to forget her plan, what she needed to tell him. To crawl back in his arms and let his lips take her away from the now. Taking one cleansing breath, she forced herself to do the right thing.

Her eyes looked around as she gathered her

thoughts. His house was a mess. His coat wasn't hung up and had been tossed over his banister. Three pair of shoes lay disorganized on the rug in the foyer. She could see his travel easel and stool, setting out in the middle of his great room and his keys tossed on the coffee table.

Forcing her eyes, she turned them to him. The curve of his jaw, the stubble over his face. She had missed them more than air. Her eyes must be red and swollen from the crying she couldn't seem to stop doing. Just thinking about it made another tear fall over her lid. And he wasn't saying anything, just staring at her with those big, amazing chocolate brown eyes that made her feel small and wrong. No. It wasn't his eyes. Or him. It was her.

"You've been in a fight," he said and lifted his long fingers to the spot on her forehead where she'd head butted Tommy Marino. She nodded and closed her eyes at the feel of his touch.

Keeping her eyes closed, she blurted randomly, "I am Nickie Savage." She opened them weakly.

A corner of his mouth lifted. Was he mocking her?

"I'm messy," she added and began to breathe heavily. "I'm bossy and irrational."

His smile was breathtaking and making her feel all the things that made her run away from him. "I've done things, Duncan. Things you can't imagine."

The smile dropped from his face. Of course, it would.

Her shoulders began to quake. Then, the tips of her fingers. She had to continue or she would never get this out. "I'm not a match for you. I don't even know how to think the word…wife." The last syllable creaked from her throat.

His eyes turned glossy. The room became warm, too warm. Taking a deep breath, she continued. "I'm moody and insecure. I have issues and—"

He took a step forward, and she could smell new car and leather and Duncan. It nearly made her pass out if not for the streams of tears that flowed down her face.

Lifting his hands, he placed them on each of her cheeks and wiped away her tears with his thumbs. She wanted to close her eyes, to pretend this was real and everything was okay.

"I've kept things from you. Important things," she continued.

He pulled back. She knew he would. Should.

His tone wasn't gentle. "I was there when we freed those girls from those rooms. I saw. I know."

It was true. Her brows dropped in deeper confusion. "I hated you for keeping your sightings of Zheng from me, but I've kept my most important secrets from you."

She took his hands from her face and pushed him away once again. Taking off her coat, she laid it over his on the banister. She turned her back to him, then lifted her shirt with her reluctant hands and gathered the material against her chest. He'd seen her back a hundred times, but this was profoundly different. Disgusting.

"My scars." She stood tall, taking advantage of not having to look him in the eye and made herself say it right. "Jun Zheng put these on my back. Every one of them. He liked it. I think it gave him more pleasure than if he'd raped me."

She felt alone and dirty in a way she'd never experienced. Tired and alone and defeated. He stayed behind her, and her eyes moved back and forth along his floor, waiting, wondering, her lungs panting like a scared dog. His long arms came around her, took her shirt and pulled it back over her head. She could hardly blame him. The warmth of his chest covered the scars, and his arms curled around, pulling her into him. She dipped her cheek against his bicep, staring at the fire tattoo on his forearm. Oddly, the flames were comforting.

The waiting was killing her. Slowly, she turned. His face was wet. "I'm here to say I understand if you don't—"

"You're messy." He smiled and kissed the tears on her cheek with his soft lips. "And bossy." He kissed the other side. "You're irrational and insecure. It takes you four bites to eat a single kernel of movie popcorn. You won't get in your rusty car before hanging your feet away from the door to bang the snow and salt from your boots. You throw your clothes over every inch of the floor, but your bathroom is organized like the shelves of a big chain drugstore, and you never have a single dirty dish in your sink."

The tears flowed freely now. What did any of this mean?

"You are compassionate and devoted." He kissed an eyelid, then the other. "I want every part of you to be mine. To be my wife."

It might have been the sound of the four-letter word coming from his magnificent voice. It may have been time away from him. His scent, his voice, his arms. It may have been sixteen years of stuffing her insecurities inside her, in her badge. Whatever it was, her legs gave out from beneath her. He must have sensed she was faltering because his long arms were there, scooping her up.

A ballad of emotion played throughout her body, shaking her until she was sobbing. It was the first time anyone had ever seen her truly cry, and it was like making up for lost time. Her shoulders shook and air sucked into her lungs. This couldn't be real, not in her life. She was supposed to spend her life as a survivor, keeping anything that resembled love as far away from her damaged heart as she could keep it. And here he was, carrying her up the stairs of their home to their bed. The love between them overwhelmed and exhausted her.

He whispered in her ear, "You're safe now." The nearly baritone voice she craved. She was safe. She was home.

It was Duncan's turn to wake with a jolt. Somewhere in his unconsciousness, he realized she was gone. Opening his eyes wide, he placed his hand on the pillow next to him, then the sheets. The slight scent of lavender remained, but the sheets were cool. He scooted to the edge of her side of the bed and looked down at the floor. Her clothes were still in a heap. The shower wasn't on. He hadn't had the chance to tell her she was being followed.

Stuffing the panic, he forced himself to think clearly in his half-conscious state. She no longer had a drawer of extra clothes. Nothing in the closet. And she hadn't carried in a bag when she came to him. Ripping the covers from his lower half, he took off for the stairs in his boxer briefs to check the only other place she could be yet still unharmed.

He took the stairs along the back of the house two at a time, three when he reached the bottom of each set. He heard splashing before he hit the basement level. Relief consumed him as he walked the rest of the way, his lungs sucking air.

She'd put on one of the suits from the changing room. Muscled swimmer's arms and legs pumped through the water before putting on the brakes and standing. Her smile sent palettes of warm colors throughout him. She'd slept curled into him much of the night before, something she'd hardly ever done.

Now, the relief of seeing her in one piece and in…seeing her woke parts of him that weren't beneath fabric that would conceal his condition.

"You're happy to see me." She wasn't looking at his face. When her gaze finally made the trek to his eyes, her expression fell. "You're flushed. What's the matter?"

"Andy and I found something."

"What do you mean, 'found something'?" she asked as she pulled herself from the water.

He took one of the towels folded neatly in his white wicker shelving and walked to her, wrapping it over the goose bumps that were already forming. He could smell the scent of her hair even through the chlorine. His eyes clamped shut. She was here.

"Duncan?" She looked up at him.

"You're beautiful." He kissed her forehead. "And mine." He dropped to her lips and laid his on them, savoring, memorizing.

"And I love you," she added. Her big gray eyes were open and eager. "I want to pretend I don't have a job so that I can stay right here, but I can't be late and you haven't told me what you and Andy found."

Right. He had an eight o'clock appointment scheduled himself. Reality. He allowed himself one more kiss before breaking the news to her. "Someone's been on my property, close to the house."

"That doesn't mean it's Zheng."

She'd read his mind, of course.

"I don't exactly live in a location where someone might need to cut through my yard. That's not all of it."

Her eyes traveled the length of his body. "I can't focus when you're dressed like this, and I really need to get something to eat and get to work. You got anything in your kitchen?"

She wasn't taking this seriously enough, but the way she was looking at him took away his sensibility. She was here. "Our kitchen," he said and let the corner of his mouth lift.

She blinked rapidly three times and lit another smile that evaporated the last ounce of rational thought. He dipped his lips to her ear. "I want to paint you," he growled. "I want to paint you dripping wet."

A pronounced flutter shook her body.

"And, no. I have breakfast pizza, doughnuts and cinnamon crunch bagels. Nothing you would consider food."

"How about this, Duncan," she purred over her shoulder as she headed toward the stairs. "I'll let you paint me in *our* bedroom after I put in a day's work and have lunch with you to discuss what we've found. You pick the time and place."

"We've? You found something, too?"

"It's a hunch."

He followed her, watching her firm backside move beneath his towel as she climbed the stairs.

"But it's better than footprints in the woods," she argued.

CHAPTER 12

Nickie wasn't sure whether they were engaged or not. Her finger stood bare. She didn't need a ring, but wasn't she supposed to have ring? People did that.

She sat in a booth at Mikey's Bar and Grill with lemon ice water and a waitress on hold. The wooden bench seat was older than the hills and the matching tabletop coated with eight-thousand layers of lacquer. At least the patrons here obeyed the no-smoking laws.

How does a woman ask a guy something like this? "Hey, we engaged, or what?"

"Where's my damned ring?" They weren't a conventional couple. Nothing about them individually or as a couple had ever been conventional.

But he wanted her. Literal and metaphorical scars and all.

She wore her belt that came with all the gadgets, making it weigh heavy on her waist. Cuffs, gloves, baton, pepper spray, each with its own heavy leather compartment. And her gun, of course. Feeling especially pleased and cocky that morning, she'd gone to her townhouse and changed into a pair of her tighter, light brown slacks and a snug blouse. What would he have her wear for the painting she promised him? Anything?

He walked through the door, and her belt and the ring left her mind. She was going to be his wife. It was supposed to make her want to run the other direction. To fight it and fight him. Except he was Duncan Reed. He wasn't wearing anything special. In fact, his hair was windblown and not in that good way. She was safe. Home. Forever. For a second, she clamped her eyes shut to keep them from leaking again.

When she opened them, he was standing next to her. She stood as he ringed his fingers around one of hers. Her heels were tall enough that they were nearly nose-to-nose. He leaned in and pressed his lips to her forehead. "I think I forgot to say good morning today."

"Right," she stuttered. "You'll have more chances."

He smiled and ran a hand through the top of his messy hair. The waitress must not have agreed that it was a mess, because as she approached, Nickie seemed to disappear. If the gal swayed her hips any farther on her way to the table, she might break something.

"Welcome to Mikey's," she all but sang before Duncan had a chance to make it to his seat. "What can I get for you, darlin'?"

Darlin'? Nickie didn't get a *darlin'*. She raised a single brow high as she assumed the gal wasn't referring to food.

He knew. He had to see it, but he didn't flinch. Looking at the menu, he ordered. "I'll have a bacon burger with cheddar and fries, please. Nickie, dear? Have you ordered?"

Dear? Snort. It was like the waitress suddenly realized she was there. "Side salad and a turkey wrap.

No mayo." The waitress thanked him and swayed away. She left the menus. "I think you either mesmerized her enough to make her forget them, or her phone number is written in red lipstick on the inside."

He opened the menu. "No phone number. She must be mesmerized."

He leaned in and dropped his gaze to her lips. An electric current pulled her over the table. The scent of him could be her undoing.

"Good morning," he said, even though it was afternoon. "You go first. What did you find?"

"Someone broke into my town house."

As if he stepped into the sun, she could swear his pupils constricted. "What? When?"

"Yours was the first number I wanted to call." She needed him to know this.

"Who? How?"

"Through a window. Must have jimmied the lock. Good job at it, too. I couldn't find a single mark."

"You bought locking bars for your windows."

"You've been watching me?"

"I went by your place last night. Andy and I did some digging."

She hadn't realized how close they'd leaned in as they spoke, but his comment made her pull back against the wooden booth. "You mean you did some illegal hacking with your brother."

"Potato, potahto."

Closing her eyes, she shook her head twice before asking, "And you found something important enough to come looking for me at my place?"

"We searched through pictures linked to the list of people you freed or arrested from Moody's white house. Andy and I found shots of Zheng, more like photo bombs of him in backgrounds."

He'd been researching for her sake, even when he didn't know if they would ever be together again. "I love you." She let her heart guide her tongue.

The comment made him blink. It wasn't like her to say so. Not in a booth at a public bar and grill. He slid his hand halfway across the table. She met him in the middle. His fingers were still chilly from the upstate New York afternoon and should have been soft and smooth from his light work as an artist. But she knew much more about Duncan Reed. His love for working on old cars. The house remodeling and furniture building he did with his uncle. They sat for a moment, speaking without talking.

"You still haven't asked me." His expression seemed to follow her subject change. "An ultimatum, yes. But never the question."

"It hasn't been the right time."

Now, that would really make her crazy. "Slippery Jimbo saw him in town three days ago, and he left handcuffs attached to the four posts on my bed."

He looked like she'd slapped him. His face turned ghostly, and he stood from their booth, walking briskly to the end of the restaurant, then back again. As he sat down, she read the blood thirst in his eyes. She'd seen him lose his temper before. It wasn't pretty.

"I'll kill him." His fingers clenched and released, the veins in his neck pulsed. "I'll choke him with my hands."

She got it. The need. "He thinks I'm still scared of him."

His eyes darted to hers. "He's been following you. I'm not sure how long. At least from the time of last year's Vegas bust."

"The time you spotted him and weren't sure if he

was a civilian or a suspect."

"These are new." He pulled a few four-by-six shots from the inside of his pocket. "The Seneca Hotel and Casino. This is one of the johns arrested from Zheng's operation at Moody's white house. It's dated months before. See? The john was attending a poker tournament and was doing well enough to be tagged in the shot for the newspaper."

Zheng stood, glaring at the man like he'd been waiting for an overdue meeting. "This one was found in Moody's security camera. It was taken the afternoon before the white house bust."

The cold left quickly, and she took off her coat, letting it crumple behind her in the booth. She pushed her chin, cracking her neck one way, then the other. "I'm not a little girl anymore. I'm not scared."

"I'd rather you would be."

Shaking her head, her eyes rolled before she remembered to tell them not to. "I know, I know. I meant, I'm smarter now, Duncan. He uses brutality and fear. Easy tactics on young teens. I'm not a young teen anymore. He doesn't know the first thing to do with an adult trained to fight. And who carries a Smith and Wesson M&P .45."

"I'm going to kill him," he repeated as he folded his shaking hands.

She sighed. There was no sense to argue. No telling him he needed to stay out of trouble, out of jail. "Not if I beat you to it."

He leaned back and seemed to assess her expression. "It looks like we are at an impasse. Until that time comes, I'm afraid I'll need to remain closer to you than you'll like. I'd prefer to start this evening. We should tell our families of our decision. They will be hurt if we don't."

"At this point I doubt you could be closer than I'd

like. However, there is something I need to do before we share our decision with anyone. It will be the last course of action regarding my past that I do alone. That I *need* to do alone. I'm afraid it's going to postpone your plans until tomorrow night. Please."

The look in his eyes turned from comprehension to understanding to reluctant acceptance. She loved this man.

Nickie shifted her beater into park but didn't turn off the engine. Fourteen years had passed since the last time she set foot on this property. Not much had changed. One of the enormous upright evergreens that lined the straight drive was missing. Disease? Storm? It must have happened recently as her parents would have replaced it with one the exact size regardless of the cost.

Inhaling deeply, she assessed her reactions to being here. A weighted cloud not only hung over her but filled the air she breathed. After all she'd accomplished. All the changes she'd made in her life, she stared at the expansive manor feeling as if no time had passed.

Pulling out her phone, she texted Duncan as she'd promised she would. 'the drive was good. peaceful. i'm here.'

A wrought iron gate stood between eight-foot tall brick walls. It didn't open for her, but she knew she wasn't undetected.

Still in her hand, her phone buzzed making her jump. 'thinking of you...my nickie.'

The corners of her mouth lifted, and she pocketed her cell. She opened the car door to a warm breeze. As warm as a breeze gets at the end of February in Maryland. Approaching the buzzer, she pulled out her badge. Since there was really no sense in ringing, she just held it up and spoke. "Detective Nickie Savage here to see Mr. and Mrs. Monticello. I have an appointment." It was a lie, but her parents would be here at this hour and would expect nothing less of her.

Noiselessly, the gate rolled back. She got in her warm car and eased her way down the drive. As if it was alive, the figurative cloud followed her. The job taught her to notice things her teenage eyes never would. Security cameras in the trees. With a place this size, it made sense.

They'd added enormous pillars that flanked the porchless entrance. They were made of the same stones that covered every inch of the vast building. More cameras dotted the roof like jewels in a crown. Her teenage eyes had also never done justice to the enormity of the property. It wasn't a manor. It was a castle.

Ignoring the obvious flow to parking, she followed the circle drive to front and center and parked between the pillars. As she got out of her car, she locked the doors. She never locked her doors. Why did she do that?

Shrugging, she clicked her boots along the stone path to the entrance. It opened before she reached it. A man she didn't recognize bowed slightly and gestured for her to come in. The foyer was just as she remembered. Cathedral ceilings that lifted all the way past the third floor. The balconies for the second and third floor landings had the same wrought iron banisters and spindles as the gate. Since the help didn't offer to take her coat, she slipped out of it as she followed him along the intricate tiled floor. This was new. Different colored tiles formed a falcon with outstretched wings and covered the entire area.

The familiar sensation of a cool, damp basement engulfed her. Over the years, she'd forgotten it. But just like the cloud, it came back as if it had never been absent. It must be from all the stone.

He brought her to one of the rooms her parents had never allowed her to enter. For her, that meant she had kept trying until she'd found a way in. Like everything else, there was nothing of interest in here…other than the thrill of breaking in where she wasn't allowed.

They stood talking as if she or their butler hadn't entered the room. Like they didn't know it was their daughter who was the Detective Nickie Savage making a house call.

Neither the forbidden room nor their reaction altered her cloud. It wasn't heavier, sadder or even more defiant. It was just there. Much like her past. Duncan was right. It wasn't something a person got over. But it was something she could learn to live with. And it was the reason she was here.

As she and the butler waited, her parents finished their conversation. It had something to do with a remodel they had planned for the horse stalls in the back. Nickie had always assumed the only reason they kept the horses was the hope Nickie would someday give in to their demands and learn to ride English. Guess not.

They looked the same, just older. Same large, blonde hair for her mother. Medium brown toupee on her father. They were larger people, both pushing 250. They never exercised. Never cared about what they put in their bodies. She had a sudden urge to eat some celery.

She knew what they were doing. And she knew they knew that she knew what they were doing. None of it mattered. Nickie's only purpose was to fully close this door in her life so she could truly open the one she promised Duncan.

When they were good and ready, they stopped talking and turned expectantly toward their butler. "Detective Nickie Savage to see you, sir. Ma'am." He didn't wait for a response and Nickie knew he wouldn't get one anyway. He did his bow thing and left her standing there.

"Nicole," her mother said as half question/half disdain.

"Ivanna," Nickie responded knowing her informal address toward her mother would put her deeper into the worthless daughter category.

Her mother held out her hand, then flicked her wrist toward a circle of stiff backed upholstered chairs. "Shall we?"

We shall, Nickie thought.

The chairs were arranged in three sets of twos around a tall glass table. They took two next to each other and Nickie sat across from them.

She refrained from taking the deep breath her lungs told her she needed. "I'd like you to tell me about the missing crime scene file from the night I was abducted."

Their expressions were unreadable as they so many times were in her years growing up under this roof. "Missing?" her father asked.

So, that's how this was going to be. She was sure the first thing he would do the minute Nickie walked out their door was to contact the person they had hide the hard copy of the file to see if was still there. Leslie Jacobsen may soon be in trouble.

Which meant this might be her only chance at getting them to talk.

"What are your intentions here, Nicole?" her mother asked emphasizing each word. "Are you have some nostalgic issues regarding your childhood? Some guilt, possibly?" Her voice remained carefully composed.

Don't fall for it Nickie. Keep it together. "It's a question the media would have been interested in." Nickie made sure to use past tense. No reason to threaten so early in the conversation.

Unfortunately, her mother noted the threat and countered with her own. "Despite your stellar upbringing, you were a belligerent child. The media would have made a circus out of the...the things a Maryland Monticello did while she was away. The spoiled runaway story fit. It saved us all the humiliation." What her mother didn't understand was that her threat was empty. Nickie could care less what her mother said about her past to the media, the governor or the President of the United frigging States. She had nothing to hide anymore.

Thinking she'd taken the upper hand, her mother shook her painted nail between Nickie and herself. "We decided together it was best if you finished your upbringing in a home...more suitable to the choices you made. When we learned of your relationship with the Hollywood artist, we'd so hoped our daughter had come to embrace the culture we provided."

"Choices? I chose to be abducted at gunpoint and forced to be repeatedly beaten and sold?"

Her mother curled her nose. Not like a mother who couldn't bear to hear what her daughter had been forced to endure. More like she'd smelled something rotten. Her father maintained his composed Maryland Monticello expression.

Nickie nearly spat. "You've answered my question. I have nothing further." She said it like a cop, and she meant it as a permanent end.

Duncan grabbed another small table as soon as it was unoccupied, pulling it next to the ones he'd already arranged. Nickie stood and reached for the matching chairs. "I can get those," he said.

She smiled. "My arm's not broke." Her sarcasm came as a relief. She'd been oddly serene since she came back from her short trip to Maryland. He tried to convince her they could do this another time, but she insisted. She'd said this was family and important to her. He could assume the reason why.

It was a busy Friday night, but that couldn't be helped. Gil and Teresa created quality background music as they performed in their minute triangle corner stage at The Pub. Their waitress dodged tables and patrons as she juggled a tray full of pitchers of beer and two tall stacks of plastic cups.

Nickie sat down on the front edge of her chair turning her focus to the music. He paused before gathering more chairs and sat next to her. Keeping her eyes on the music, she reached over and took his hand. It both eased his worry and sent a wave of anticipation through him. He replaced the hand she'd taken with the one farther from her and slid his other over her shoulder. "You're beautiful," he whispered close to her ear.

Without moving her eyes from Gil and Teresa, a smile slowly spread across her face.

"Rose texted me," she said. "They're almost here but can only leave baby Andrew with the new sitter for a few hours."

He nodded and pulled her closer. Turning her cheek into his shoulder, she sighed. "You are stuck with me now, Duncan Reed."

"A life sentence I gladly accept." He kissed her forehead and stood to arrange a few more chairs around the outside of the line of tables. The spot he'd chosen was near the stage. Still, when the door opened, a waft of cold air mixed with the smell of cigarette smoke brushed through the area.

"This is embarrassing, just so you know." She was on her feet and placing pitchers of beer on the tables.

"It's better than having my aunt find out from someone else. Or worse than that, Gloria."

She shuddered and nodded her head.

Andy and Rose arrived first, pulling off their scarves and gloves as they made their way to them. "What's with all this?" Andy gestured to the large group of tables.

Neither of them gave a second glance at the sight of him and Nickie back together. They were like that.

Rose. He was thankful she and Nickie had become friends for more than his own, self-fulfilling reasons. It was the first female friend he could remember she had. Now, she would be a sister. Family. Something Nickie needed. Something she deserved.

"Nickie's family is coming, too," he said to Rose. Nickie's cat eyes casually turned to his. He'd referenced Gloria and Gloria's children as family. Would she ever accept the fact that they were exactly that?

"Cool," Rose said and waved over her shoulder to Gil and Teresa. "Too bad they weren't with us the last time we were all here. The boys might not have ended up a bloody mess."

"We didn't start it," Duncan interrupted. He and Andy high-fived.

Nickie smiled. "Bloody almost made me lose my job for failure to report an attempted murder."

"Attempted murder? Nah." Andy shook his head. "Just a few punks taking advantage of three on one."

"Then three on two," Duncan added. "I've got your back, little brother."

Rose held up her hand like a stop sign. "Let's do shots and forget about it."

His aunt and uncle arrived next. They searched for only a moment before spotting him. Brie's green eyes warmed, then found Nickie's and lit. She picked up her pace, making as straight of a line toward her as she could in a crowded bar. "Nickie, dear." She hugged her like Nickie had come back from the dead. "It's good to see your pretty face." Brie pulled away and moved her eyes from Duncan to Nickie, then to Nickie's bare left hand. How did she know everything?

A few more of Nickie's *brothers and sisters* arrived. They, too, didn't seem surprised at the sight of them together. Everyone waited patiently to learn the reason for combining the families at a bar on a Friday night. A group of twenty-somethings played pool. The dartboard stood unused as the place was too packed for pointed flying objects. Duncan ordered a new round of beer for all just as Gloria arrived.

Teresa finished her rendition of "Since U Been Gone," allowed time for applause, then announced a ten-minute break. Gil connected his prerecorded intermission playlist and made his way over. Duncan held out a beer for each of them as the group cheered and gave them room at the table.

It was now or never. He took a moment to recognize that not a single family in this group could be considered nuclear. He and Andy had been raised by their aunt and uncle, Rose by a mother and step-father and his detective by a foster family.

As he stood, the group became quiet, elbowing those who hadn't noticed as if they'd been expecting an announcement. "I'd like to make a toast," he said. "To family." He never saw the need for wordy speeches but was determined to do this right. The sound of plastic thuds clinked as they tapped their glasses together. "Thank you for gathering as one this evening. Nickie and I wanted you to be the first to know we've decided to marry."

They didn't seem surprised. Except that was precisely what Duncan felt. The cheers were more than supportive; they were positively electric. He supposed it mirrored his own emotions. Enthusiastic splatters of beer tipped at each table.

"Finally, you popped the question," his brother said and smacked his shoulder.

"Not exactly," Duncan said more to himself than to answer Andy.

Gil yelled over the noise, "Where's the ring?"

It was as if the room had darkened and a spotlight lit Nickie's left hand. An angry proposal in a restaurant? One as she cried in his arms in his foyer? During lunch at Mikey's Bar and Grill? "It hasn't been the right time."

"What the hell do you mean, 'it hasn't been the right time'?" It was Rose, of course. "You're not engaged without a ring."

He glanced at Nickie. She looked undeniably relieved to hear Rose say so. He hadn't intended to hurt or embarrass her. This was meant to be an evening of celebration.

"Whoa," Nickie said and held up both her hands. "One step at a time, people. How much do you think a girl can take at once?"

"Do you have a date?" Teresa called out.

This time, Nickie grinned at him. Her expression softened. "Soon," she answered for the both of them.

CHAPTER 13

Stuck at a dead end, Nickie pushed her laptop away and set her reading glasses on Duncan's desk. "Police work should be more like television," she whined. "Every case solved with fast action, loads of obvious clues and all in a half hour." Before her eyes crossed from staring at her screen another moment, she closed them and rested her head on the desk in his bedroom. He'd built a fire, the smell of burning wood taking her mind to a picnic in the woods with the horses.

It was a short escape. Even sealed, her eyes betrayed her. She saw the leads that still needed to be followed and reports yet to be completed. It had been way too long since William Juracek was murdered. She had a load of suspects and not a single piece of concrete evidence. The captain wouldn't assign her to anything bigger than a corner store robbery or working as resource for someone else's case. This was high profile for Northridge, and he wanted it solved. She could hardly blame him.

Strong fingers slithered up her shoulders, kneading the knots of tension in them, then traveled up her neck. How had she survived a single day without this?

He laced his fingers through her hair, massaging her scalp and making every muscle in her body turn into a puddle of mush.

Her body's reaction wasn't what she assumed Duncan had been aiming for. She lifted her head and spun her chair 180 degrees. Straddling his legs, she locked the tops of her boots behind him and pulled him to her.

The sharp lines in his jaw flexed and released. "A break from work?" he crooned low and sexy.

She didn't answer with words but slipped her fingers in his waistband. He tucked his magic hands under her backside and lifted as she wrapped her legs the rest of the way around him. Heat found heat.

He set her butt on his desk, and as if pulling them from nowhere, brought one of her necklaces and a pair of earrings from behind his back. He held them out to the side. It was her long, silver necklace. The one with a few dozen interlocking hoops. The matching earrings dangled between his fingertips. "You promised me a painting," he said as he dipped his head and grazed her neck with his teeth.

How could she possibly argue when he did this? Regardless, uncomfortable nerves erupted. Glancing down at the raspberry pink blouse she'd chosen that morning, she spotted the diagonal wrinkles beneath the line where her gun holster had laid from the day. Her pants were too tight, her boots too tall. She liked it that way, but for a Duncan Reed painting? His paintings hung in the homes of politicians, the dripping rich and people so famous even she knew who they were. She, on the other hand, was just…Nickie.

"Now?" she asked. "Wearing this?"

His eyes darkened. A smile, evil and glorious, slowly covered his face.

"Not wearing this." He tugged at the shirt, then brought her jewelry into the small space between them. "Wearing these."

Her phone buzzed on her hip. It was the ring tone for forwarded calls from the police station. "I've got to get this. I'm so sorry." Giving him the most apologetic look she could muster, she pulled it from her pocket and answered. "Savage."

"Savage," the voice on the other end repeated.

She didn't recognize it or understand why the nerves at the back of her neck came alive.

"You changed your name. I like it."

No. He can't have this number. He can't be at the station. Her eyes darted from one side of Duncan to the other, then her legs dropped from around him and hit the floor with a thud.

"You were never a Nicole Monticello. Nickie Savage. It suits you."

She remembered all right. Sixteen years couldn't erase the memory of the voice. She couldn't speak, couldn't move.

"I see you recognize me. Also, I like." He laughed. The same laugh haunted her dreams. The laugh he once used as he put the scars on her back.

Her head turned to a mixture of pissed off, defeated and encouraged. "Where are you, Zheng?"

The veins in Duncan's neck rose, and he began to scramble through his tech equipment.

"Is that your detective work, my savage? Ask me where I'm at so you can come arrest me?"

She closed her eyes. He was right. "How about, what the fuck do you want?"

"Temper." He was right again. "Mmm. How I loved that temper."

With lightning fast fingers, Duncan connected some electronic something to the back of her phone. Zheng wasn't that stupid, but she supposed she would have tried, too, if the tables were turned.

"I don't care what you think about my detective work or honestly what you want. And I'll find out where you are soon enough. Is there anything else?" There. That was better. He was silent long enough on the other end of the phone that she smiled and said figuratively to Duncan, "Do you think we lost him? I think we've lost him. Either that or he can't seem to think of a thing to say to a grown-up. That's right, Zheng. I'm not a little girl anymore. I'm a trained detective, and you're an old man."

"I don't like little girls."

"No shit."

"You know I never touched them that way. But you. You are no longer a child."

Interestingly enough, she felt clearer. The conversation became familiar. "Really? This is how you're going to try and scare me? Is this all you've—" But the line went dead. As useless as it seemed, she glanced to Duncan. He shook his head and pulled away the device he'd placed on the back of her phone.

Nickie popped her head into Eddy's office on her way to check on the guys manning the SS8 phone bug. She wondered how much longer the A.D.A. would give up man-hours for something that was coming up nil.

"Press conference in twenty," she said to him. "Coin toss?"

"No coin toss. It's your turn."

She sighed and placed the palms of her hands together.

"Fine," he said and dug in his pocket. Placing a quarter on his thumb, he looked at her and raised his eyebrows.

"Tails," she called.

He flipped and slapped the quarter in the middle of his desk. Heads. Damn.

"Fine," she said back to him. She hated talking to damned reporters. "I'm gonna check on the guys getting their rocks off listening to the SS8 bugs. I won't be late to the meet and greet and asking of questions we can't answer."

"You'd better be on time. The captain will have your ass if you're not, and I'm throwing you under the bus if you're late."

One more, "Fine," and she spun on her heels, heading for the closet Vaughn had made into what she and Eddy had affectionately named the bug room.

Two IT geeks crammed into the small space wearing enormous head phones. They giggled like schoolgirls, leaning closer to the equipment like they might be able to hear better if they did. One smacked the other's shoulder and snorted. Vaughn hadn't authorized two at a time. Nickie was sure she would come unglued if she knew. Nickie's butt barely fit between machines and tables. She maneuvered through to reach them and hit each on the back of the head. They grabbed their hair and spun around.

Slowly, they pulled their headphones off the rest of the way, then straightened. "Detective," they said in a collaborative greeting.

"What the hell, gentlemen?"

"Sorry, Detective Savage. I was just leaving." The stockier one tried to stand, but there was no room with her in there.

"Sit back down, and tell me what you've got."

"Mostly out of town stuff." The geek, who apparently was the only one actually assigned to be in here, held up his records. "No Joe Johnson. No Seneca Hotel and Casino, Guest House or Tommy

Marino."

She skimmed the entries as she blocked Stocky's escape. "Manhattan, Buffalo, Binghamton. Lisa Jones. Jimmy Thomas. How have they gotten away with this shit for so long using such lame ass covers?"

"We've got a few blatant sex-for-money offers. Some details that weren't coded." They gave each other a look that made her want to lose her lunch.

"We can bust their balls for vice when this is over," she said as she flipped through entries. "I hope you two weren't getting your rocks off. The A.D.A. has cameras in this room." She was joking but suddenly realized how warm it was in here. Hopefully, it was from all the equipment rather than from two IT geeks jerking off.

"I'm kidding gentlemen, but you—" She pointed to Stocky. "—need to get the hell out of here."

"Yes, ma'am."

He stood, but she barely noticed. Her eyes had locked in on a tryst arranged between a Wendy Douglas and someone whose code name was House Guest.

"The Guest House," she mumbled. She picked up her cell and called Eddy. "I've got something," she said.

"Now? The press conference is in ten, and you lost the coin toss."

She did, didn't she? "It will take five. Get your butt in here."

"Press conference. Coin toss."

"Damn it."

Her captain took point. He preferred to do these things close to five o'clock. It was what the public thought was police business closing time. As if. Press conference and run. She'd barely made it in time for the opening statement.

"We are gathered here today—"

Nickie ground her teeth together to keep from laughing.

"—to update you on the Juracek murder investigation. Questions following will be limited due to the sensitivity of an open case. Detectives Savage and Lynx are the lead detectives and will provide any and all information possible at this time."

Dave didn't mention the third-shift beat cop and A.D.A., who stood out of sight behind the curtains. Nickie glanced their way. Parker had ditched the sagging punk cover, and was back to the stiff, humble way she was used to. He stood ramrod straight, facing the podium—except his eyes, which craned in the direction of the assistant district attorney.

Nickie counted fifteen reporters. She recognized the one from Binghamton and another from Rochester. Too bad they weren't as interested when a murder victim was a runaway or one of the homeless that ended up with a knife in his or her side and left in the hills or by the lake.

"Detective Savage will be briefing you this afternoon," the captain said in closing. He stepped out of the way and she stepped forward. "Followed by only a few questions, please," he reminded the silent group on her behalf.

The room was small, but full. She stood behind the wooden podium and glanced out to the people, all dressed in business suits, some with notepads, some with recorders held high like lighters at a concert.

It was a necessary hoop to jump through, and one she'd done dozens of times before. So, why did it bother her so much this time? The eyes that stared back at her seemed to say much the same. They knew this was a dog and pony show. Some would be eager, hoping to make her slip up and say something they could paste on the top of tomorrow's front page.

It was then she detected eyes that were much more personal to her. They were a deep brown, nearly black, and they matched the waves in his hair that framed the sharp lines in his face. Duncan. She would never admit the way he sent a melody of clarity through her. Blinking, she looked down at the podium before anyone realized she was staring and looked over to see why.

"The investigation of the death of Mr. William Juracek of Jackson & Juracek Jewelers continues."

Eddy cleared his throat. It was a jab at her tardiness and made her fight back the urge to elbow him in the ribs.

"First of all, I would like to extend condolences on behalf of the Northridge Police Department to the family and loved ones of the deceased. Know that we are doing everything in our power to find the perpetrator or perpetrators responsible. Mr. Juracek's body was recovered from the alley behind the jewelry business he owned with his father-in-law. Our medical examiner concluded the cause of death was a gunshot wound to the chest. I'm afraid I cannot disclose more than this, as the case is still under investigation."

As the room erupted in questions, she allowed herself one quick glance at Duncan before diving in. His eyes squinted in one of his slight and rare smiles. She meant it, the part about doing everything in her power. He knew that.

"Nick?" It was Captain Nolan.

She shook her head and pointed to the Rochester reporter. "Carol?"

Other hands dropped slightly. "Do you have anyone in custody?"

"I'm afraid I can't answer that question as it might hinder the progress of the investigation," she said with a flat expression, then pointed to the other side of the room. "Matt?"

"Do you have any suspects?"

She forced herself not to roll her eyes. "I can't answer that as it could impede the investigation."

It went on like this for five minutes, maybe ten. Did the killer act alone? How is the family taking the news? How the hell did they think the family was taking the news? She smiled politely until the captain moved her aside.

She knew what his words were, what they would be. They were always the same. But her sense of hearing had disappeared. Along with her others senses other than her sight. It was zoned in on the man in the back who stood between heads. Black eyes, black hair. She would know the eyes anywhere. But here? Jun Zheng. His head jerked sharply to his right before he took off running out the back. She moved her vision to see what spooked him and spotted Duncan sprinting toward the door Zheng had burst open.

Nickie lurched forward, ready to follow as a hand clamped her upper arm. She flipped her glance to find it was Eddy. "What the hell?" she hissed.

"Don't." He said it with surprising force. "You have a dozen sets of eyes on you. All who would like to make their own inferences as to what you're thinking of doing."

He was leaving a mark on her arm, but she ignored it, staring at him with vengeance.

"You'll thank me later," he said but didn't loosen his grip. "No one saw. Let Duncan handle it."

Maybe he was right. As hard as she could, she pinched his hand between the tendons of his thumb and forefinger, forcing his grip open. "Like hell."

Without giving Eddy or her captain a heads up, she took off in a full sprint down the side of the room and out the back door.

CHAPTER 14

Duncan bolted toward the elevator as Zheng stood calmly, grinning between the closing doors. Heat built in Duncan's skull as he reached the elevator and slammed the palm of his hand on the wall once, twice, three times. "Ah," he yelled and checked to see if it was going up or down. Down.

Blood pumping, he spun toward the stairs. The sound of fast boots pounded behind him. Nickie. He burst open the stairwell door and took the first half of the steps three at a time. Grasping the handrails, he catapulted the rest of the way, welcoming the painful shock that traveled up his legs each time he landed. He repeated the process three more times and arrived at ground-level parking. The elevator had been too fucking fast.

He shoved open the door to the concrete half of the parking garage and let it bang against the brick wall. His mind whirled with possibilities as he readied himself to spring. It was a setup; that was obvious. Did that change what needed to be done?

He stood, darting his eyes around the open area and listened. The fast click of shoes echoed on the floor above. They weren't Nickie's boots. Those should have been behind him by now. Sprinting, he took the vehicle exit ramp on foot. Images of Zheng made his legs move faster as he pumped them up the steep concrete.

He heard an engine, the spinning of tires. He listened for the sound of Nickie's boots and, as he reached second floor parking, craned his head to find her. His chest heaved as he sucked air.

He forced himself to top and close his eyes as he used the only one of his senses of use to him now. Nickie's boots. They were faint, but it was her. She'd taken the second floor parking exit with Zheng. Fear gripped him as his legs started running again.

There was no car-to-body impact, only the sound of tires screeching. A black SUV rounded a corner and into his line of vision. And then he saw her. She ran between cars and heaved over concrete barriers before halting to a stop and locking her knees. She raised her Smith and Wesson and stared down the barrel.

Duncan stood his ground in the middle of the throughway, his head pounding, and stared into the black of Zheng's eyes. He saw him sneer as the vehicle picked up speed. *Bam, bam, bam.* Holy shit, she shot her gun. Like bouncing from a springboard, Duncan jumped as the SUV swerved, then squealed into the exit ramp. Duncan dove behind the nearest car, hitting his head on the mirror before slamming to the ground. Metal-on-metal scraped the concrete walls of the exit ramp.

"Duncan!"

Fast footsteps ran in his direction.

"Duncan, where are you? Say something."

A raspy, "Damn," was all he could get out of his throat. The ground was freezing, and his head pounded.

She appeared between cars and slid next to him on her knees. "Are you hurt?" She lifted his arms one at a time, then patted his chest and head.

Other than the large bump throbbing on the side of his face, he didn't think he had more than a few bruises. "I've been through worse."

"I guess you have."

"Nickie?"

She nodded.

"The ground is disgusting," he groaned.

Pressing her hand on his chest, she used him for purchase to rise to her feet, making him groan once more. "Did you see that? He was here. At the police station. Can you believe it?" she asked as she stood tall. "We chased him running scared, Duncan."

He could almost see the euphoria pumping through her veins.

"We took down his operation, and now he's pissed as hell." She fist-bumped the air, then held out a hand.

"No thanks." He'd like to keep his arm. "I've got it. I've also got the make and license number along with what he was wearing from head to toe. He turned north out of parking."

"And he's got three bullets in his hatch." Her brows dropped when her eyes landed on the bump at the side of his head. As she lifted her fingers to it, he jerked back.

"Don't be a baby," she said. "The bump is going out, not in. That's good. Do you feel dizzy? Tired?"

Captain Nolan came running from the second floor door, looking more like a concerned father than a boss. "Nick. What the hell? I heard shots. Eddy's holding back the press." Nolan stopped in front of them. "Duncan. I didn't know you were here."

Nickie looked to Duncan. Her face fell from the high of the chase to torn in a matter of seconds.

Glancing back at her boss, she said, "Dave, it's time we talk."

Avoiding the press, they took the long way around to the captain's office. Nickie felt bad about sticking Eddy with them. Surely, he recognized who she was after. He may not know the extent of her connection to Zheng, but he'd seen the pictures of him—the one he stole from Duncan's printer, the one that stayed taped to the monitor on her office computer.

The captain unlocked his door and stepped into his office. He didn't sit and instead stood in front of his desk, leaned against it and folded his arms.

Before she sat, she glanced back and decided to walk over, close the door and shut the blinds.

When she returned, Duncan was already sitting in one of the captain's guest chairs. He draped an arm over the back of his seat, resting his hand on top of the one she would sit in. Everything was safer when he was with her.

Slowly, she sank into her seat and glanced up at Dave's waiting eyes. He was so tall, so big. Such a contrast to the worried expression on his face.

"I think I need to tell you more about my work with the FBI."

Duncan's hand rested lightly on her shoulder.

Pushing away from his desk, Dave held up his hands protectively. "I already said you don't have to tell me about that."

She knew he meant it as a show of respect.

"Dave."

She never called him by his first name anymore. 'Sir' or 'captain.' Sometimes 'boss.' All the titles he hated. It had been an inside joke between the two of them ever since Tanner went to prison and Dave took his place.

He looked to her now.

"The shots," she explained. "They were on your doorstep. You should know."

His expression was pained.

Looking away, she began. "When I was fourteen, I was abducted from my—"

"I know," he interrupted.

Without turning her head, her eyes darted back to his. "You know?"

His reddened as he nodded. "When you were transferred here, I did a background check. Who was going to be my underling? You know? There were holes, some locked juvie records. I shouldn't have. I checked. It wasn't hard to find you. Nicole Monticello. It's your birth name?"

She nodded. Chronologically, her mind started tracing back to the time she'd been Dave's aide, as his partner. Now, his detective. It started with an offer for a transfer. It had only been a few weeks since she learned it was staged. Shaking her head, she forced herself to be rational. He didn't know about that. Couldn't.

Tilting her head, she looked to Duncan. She wasn't sure why. Advice? Strength. He closed his eyes in a long blink and nodded slightly.

"My files say runaway. It started as an abduction investigation, but the careful lack of evidence regarding the crime scene turned me into a runaway. I was held captive for eighteen months in a child trafficking…" She took a deep breath, sat up and slung a boot over her knee. She'd never had to explain it like this before and wasn't about to let it break her. "A child *sex* trafficking group of girls. I escaped, but when my parents discovered what happened to me, they were disgusted and went back to the runaway story. They hid the files that said otherwise and sent me off to foster care. The decision was pretty much mutual between the three of us."

Dave squatted down in front of her and took both of her hands in his. Oh, boy. Awkward.

"I, uh—" She squirmed but made sure to smile at him. "—changed my name."

"The man."

The smile left her. "Yes," she said.

"He was part of this." It wasn't a question. "If I get my hands on him—"

"Get in line." Duncan may be a man of few words, but the ones he chose generally sent a chill down the spine of anyone within earshot.

Dave stood and walked around to his desk. Expressionless, he booted up his desktop as she continued.

"The FBI wants my knowledge. I've been inside, and they think I'm some sort of source. The activity with them last month. The time I took off—"

"The time you took off for the first time since you started here?" he said as his fingers plucked madly across his keyboard.

"Yes." She swallowed. "We took down an entire operation. Every girl saved. Every perp in custody. You heard about the arrest of the personal assistant to the governor?"

He looked up from the computer, his lips in the form of a small 'o.' "Thurmond Moody?"

"He was key."

Letting her foot fall to the floor, she scooted to the front of the seat. "Moody was key, but he seems to have been second in command. The gunshots in the parking garage were from my gun. I was shooting at the man, or at least the car of the man who was first in command. The man who abducted me as a child."

"I'm getting up the video surveillance now. We'll

have a make and model of his car and description—"

"Dave."

He looked to her with glossy eyes. "Are you calling in the feds?" he asked. He was on overdrive. She'd seen it before.

She sat back and considered. "I don't know. This is backward for us. They call me when they need to. No." She paused, then decided. "No, Zheng came to our town. This is NPD, and it's personal." Moving her gaze to him, she felt a sudden rush of possibilities. "He's got nothing left, Captain. You know what happens when perps have nothing left."

"They make mistakes, yes, but this isn't a game, and I don't like your attitude." His glare bore into her.

"I'm okay, boss. I've got this." Although she knew she shouldn't, she moved her eyes to Duncan. Anyone else would see a flat expression of distance. She knew better. She saw a mixture of worry and pissed off.

"You don't have to do this alone," Dave said. "We're a team, remember?"

"Of course I remember. I guess I'm sort of still on a high from taking down his organization. I'm ready for him." So that no one would notice her quivering hands, she dug them in her pockets and spread a large smile across her face. "He's got nothing left," she repeated. "Payback's a bitch, ain't it?"

CHAPTER 15

Nickie flew so high from the gun chase that Duncan nearly had to haul her home over his shoulder. In order for her to let him drive, he had to agree to drinks at the cop bar with the other officers during the next NPD happy hour. Social interaction with people he actually had to speak with wasn't high on his list.

He'd barely had time to mix a drink at the wet bar in his bedroom before she came out of the bathroom wearing her silk white robe. It was tied loosely, her healthy cleavage speaking to him.

"Nickie," he said cautiously as she sauntered toward him.

A muscled thigh peeked from beneath the material with each step she took.

He held up his hands, palms out. "We need to talk."

Picking up his drink from the wet bar, she took a sip, licked the rim, then reached for the top button on his shirt.

He grabbed the wrist of the hand at his neck and scowled. "This is serious."

"Mmm-hmm," she patronized and took a swig before setting down the glass with her free hand, then reaching for the next button. He took hold of her hands, but she just smiled and led his arms around her back, pressing her cleavage against his chest.

No. He kept hold of her wrists and stepped away. "Zheng."

She sighed and rolled her eyes. "Are you going to make us rehash that whole scene again? Now? I want you." Overtly, she let her gaze move to his pants as she raised her brows. "You want me, too."

"I always want you."

She freed her hands from his grasp and pulled the robe down around her shoulders, hugging it against her chest. "What about that painting?"

"You were reluctant the last time you posed for me."

She shrugged and dropped the robe to her waist, barely holding it to each of her breasts. "We're engaged now."

Her golden skin glimmered in the moonlight under the skylight windows. The soft curves of her cheekbones blushed as she stood in front of him. The light scent of lavender filled his senses. He metaphorically shook his head clear.

"I don't want to paint you when you're like this." He hated knocking her down when she'd opened herself to him. It was necessary.

Her eyes grew large and pained. She pulled up her robe and tied the waist. "Like what?"

"You're drunk from circumstance. I can practically see the adrenaline running through you. You were faced with your childhood nemesis and stood your ground, took a shot at him even. I understand where you're coming from, but we need to talk." He said the last three words separately and with conviction.

She sat at the bar and folded her hands. Her reaction could have been much worse. Had been in the past and it relieved him that they weren't going to debate his wishes.

"You're right," he said flatly and sat next to her.

She took another drink of his whiskey and Coke. "I'm right about a lot of things. Which thing are you talking about?"

Jun Zheng showed up at the fucking press conference. He tried to run Duncan down with his car. Duncan was done with it all and was losing his patience. Making himself think of the reasons for her reaction, he turned her stool to face him. "The part that says Zheng's got nothing left."

She tilted her head to the side as if she might agree with him.

He unbuttoned the next button of his shirt but only because he needed air. The man who put scars on his detective came to her place of employment. In broad daylight. With a few dozen witnesses, many of them reporters. Grabbing his leather-bound notebook from his briefcase, he set it in front of them more forcefully than he intended and opened it.

He wrote the number 1 in the top left corner. Next to it, he scribbled a few words describing the time Zheng was spotted at the press conference after Nickie's teenage escape. Next to the number 2, he listed the time Duncan spotted him in Vegas. The time Slippery Jimbo said Zheng had been asking around about her in Northridge. Zheng was the driver and escaped the day her former police captain and the fire chief abducted and tried to dispose of her. The Seneca Hotel and Casino photo with one of the johns they arrested at the white house bust. There was the shot of Zheng at the white house just a few hours before the bust. As he continued chronologically, he wrote the number 7 before he realized Nickie's hands were quivering next to him.

Shaking his head clear from his focus, he glanced to her face and recognized the look in her eyes. The red, glossy haze made him recall how she earned the nickname savage. "We should take a break," he said.

Her lifeless stare moved to his. "No."

"You haven't eaten."

"Neither have you. Next, are the footprints around your place. I don't think you were wrong about that anymore." Even as a sheen of sweat appeared on her forehead, an evil grin erupted over her face. "He's desperate and sloppy. Just what the doctor ordered."

He took her shivering hand and was glad she didn't pull away and instead squeezed his fingers. Progress. He decided closure might do both of them some good, so he continued. Number 7, the footprints around his house. Number 8, nearly a week ago when Slippery Jimbo said Zheng was spotted at the barbershop. Number 9, when Zheng broke into Nickie's town house and left handcuffs on her four bedposts. This time, he shook. He ground his teeth together and closed his eyes before taking an exaggerated breath.

She ran her hand along the fire tattoo on his left forearm. Slowly, she took the marker from his hand and wrote a number 10. Next to it, she wrote three words. NPD press conference.

He straightened and turned to face her. "I want you to go see Hurst and Goodrich." The mention of the special agents wouldn't sit well, but it had to be done.

"That's not how that works."

It was true. Because of her history, the FBI solicited her for help with missing person cases that involved child trafficking. They had an agreement. Nickie had even finagled a way to involve Duncan when needed. Her soliciting them for help was backward and wasn't part of the deal.

"They would want to know about Zheng," he

argued. "He has to be on their radar."

She shook her head. "I'm not sure about that."

"That can't be true."

"They think Moody was the top man. He was the owner of the white house. He was the one caught with the girls."

He'd never considered the possibility. Sniffing, he sat up and straightened his back.

"I'm going to increase the parameters of the alarm system. You've got the access code and password. It's likely he either has our phones bugged or has access to the content through our carrier. It's something I would do if the positions were reversed."

"Okay, but I'm not sure he's as talented with all that as you are."

She thought that? "Regardless, I'm going to create something small for you to keep in both your shoulder holster and your gun belt. A GPS chip."

"A what? You're going to bug me like a teenager? Are you making me one for you?"

His patience eroded, and he found himself raising his voice. "We don't have time for this. He doesn't want me," he yelled, leaving his bar stool and standing over her.

"Why not use my phone?" she argued like a child, standing with him. Minus the boots, she was significantly shorter than he was, and under the circumstances, it helped.

"Or a prepay where you record the IP address thingy." Her hands flew to her hips, but it didn't have the same effect in the robe versus her detective clothing.

Closing his eyes, he took great effort to calm his bubbling nerves. All it did was play the images of Zheng on the backs of his eyelids like some sort of slide show. "Phones are too obvious," he explained through his teeth. "You won't know it's there. More importantly, he won't know it's there. I'm not asking, Nickie. I'm going to attach a chip to the base of one of the compartments on your holster and on your belt. The one you use for your latex gloves I think."

He felt the warmth of her body but didn't back away. She could push, argue and strut all she wanted. There was no room for compromise here. The scent of mint and lavender made him open his eyes halfway in a determined battle of wits. One he wouldn't lose.

She squinted and pulled her shoulders back in an obvious mode of decision. Looking from one of his eyes to the other, the corners of her lips turned into a grin. Of all the possible reactions? She smiled and dropped her robe to the floor. "It'll cost you."

A flood of release poured from his head. Winning the battle, keeping his detective safely within his grasp. Staring down at her, he reached over her shoulder, twisting her silky hair around his hand, and pulled enough to tilt her mouth to him. Her lips were full and parted, her breath a sweet mixture of liquor and woman.

He dove in as he took hold of the parts of her that had taunted him from beneath the fabric of the robe. The power struggle was long from over as their teeth grazed and tongues fought to take point. Nails dug into his shoulders as a warm, muscled thigh lifted around his hip and the back of her heel pulled their bodies closer. Limbs twined and hands groped. She tore at the rest of his buttons as he yanked at any other piece of clothing that kept him from her. Her soft, warm skin brushed over him turned his need for her into something primal.

Cheating or not, other parts of his body had taken the wheel as he used his size and strength to take her twined limbs and groping hands from him. In one, quick sweep, he cleared the bar, lifted her and plopped her on top.

The feel of the cold bar on her back did little to cool the aching need building in Nickie's core. She lifted to her elbows as she watched the desire in Duncan's deep chocolate eyes. The defined, lanky muscles she'd grown so used to flexed and released as he climbed like a lion over the bar stool and onto the granite top.

The rise and fall in her chest quickened, her body aching to have him over her, around her, in her. He was her drug, one that could satiate and keep her safe all at the same time.

He had some need to be the alpha of alphas that day, and she pushed back just enough to make him writhe in it. Rising up to meet him, he maneuvered between her legs then growled and pressed her shoulders back to the stone.

"Me," he said and ran his hands over her neck, pausing to wrap his fingers around it. He drew a line down her throat and stopped at the indentation in the center of her collarbone.

Never had she been so free.

His hands created trails of fire as he moved them over her, circling, pulling, kneading. Her back arched, and she lifted her arms over her head in release. He growled louder and raised her legs around his neck, traveling lips and tongue over the insides of her calf and thigh. He was hers. Her head craned to the side when he reached her. Sensations flooded from head to toe to her center and back again. He would be hers forever, she thought as she slipped over the first peak.

A tear slipped from her eye as she cried out. It ran down the side of her temple. She shook as he gave, trembled as he gave more. In a moment of reprieve, she lifted to her elbows, his warm, hard body hovering over her. "You broke the glasses." She craned her head toward the floor behind the bar. "You left broken glass—"

But he dug in and over, taking her back to euphoria in seconds. Her chest pounded, her body thrashed. She lost her precious control, her need for boundaries…and for this moment, it was exactly what she needed. She let herself go. No restrictions. No safety barriers. She flew to a place she hadn't been before. Her cries were loud. She could hear them somewhere in her mind. Her hands and legs had become their own entities as they groped, feeling their way over the man that would be her husband.

As her body drifted down the mountain, she took him against her, over her, into her. The air left his lungs as they joined.

"You're mine," he said and pushed. She grabbed hold as they moved into frenzy. Digging her fingers and holding on with hands and legs. His eyes paused on the line of water that ran from her eye, but he didn't wipe it away. "This is ours forever," he choked and pressed his body closer. His honesty sent her over again. Her eyes closed and flashes of light sparkled in the dark, images of the sincere look in his eyes came to her and made her open to him.

The desperation on his face mixed with warmth and need, then turned opaque as he joined her. The stone top of the bar was no longer cold. He collapsed and rested over her, his nose pressing against her neck. "You are going to be my wife," he said as if it were surreal.

And it was. "Freaky, huh?" she said and turned her face into his hair. It smelled like his shampoo and like him. "No looking back."

His hands tucked around her and squeezed in response to her declaration. "What do we have against the bed?" he asked, making her laugh.

She looked around. The bar was taller than she thought. "This was your idea. I wash my hands of it."

Nickie didn't need to look up from her laptop. She could tell it was Eddy in her doorway. This damned case had dragged on long enough. If it weren't for chasing Zheng, she would have gone out to harass Sherie-Wendy-Joe-Johnson-Douglas—as Nickie liked to call her—last night. No. It was Duncan's fault she didn't get to her last night. A slick grin threatened the corners of her mouth, but she realized Eddy was still standing there.

Lifting her eyes, she noticed his legs were spread, knees locked. His expression was far from affectionate.

"What the fuck, Savage?"

"What the fuck and Savage? Ouch, Lynx. I'm sorry I didn't have a chance to thank you for covering for me at the press conference, okay?"

"I don't care about some freaking press conference screw up. You took Parker out on the Juracek case."

It wasn't a question. It was an accusation, and she was guilty as charged. Mostly. "You'd already spent enough overtime with red-eye work. Parker was on graveyard that night, and I had steam to burn."

"That was last fucking Thursday."

"You took Friday off."

"You ever hear of a cell, *partner*," he said the last word through his teeth.

He stepped around her desk and hovered over her. She didn't take too much to bully shit, even if it was possibly deserved. She stood and even with her lower heeled boots, glared at him eye-to-eye. "Make your move, Lynx. I could use a rumble."

He huffed and turned on his heels. "I'm not fighting

a girl. Who the hell do you think I am?"

So, it was okay to get in a girl's face, just not hit her? She decided to keep that question to herself.

"So?" He raised his voice.

Looking at the floor, then up to him, she tried to think of what he might be getting at. Nope. She had nothing.

"So, what the fuck did you find out?" He was flat out yelling now. He paced and waved his arm as he barked, "Parker's got a split lip and his eye is nearly swollen shut. You wanna clue me in on who the two of you cozied up to and what you found out about *our* case?"

Cozied? He was jealous? At least he was out of her face.

She walked over and looked out her single window. Snow came down in buckets. What an insane winter. People were at least driving smarter, she thought, as she watched them on their way to work.

"I went looking for Slippery Jimbo to ask him what the hell The Guest House was. Apparently, it's some official nickname for T & A's." She decided not to tell him about Jimbo spotting Zheng. She could feel the veins start to bulge in her neck thinking about it.

"Nick?"

Shaking her head, she turned at the sound of Eddy's voice as the A.D.A. walked by her office window. Vaughn stopped and looked at Nickie through the slats in the mini-blinds, then to Eddy, then backtracked and came to her doorway. She knocked on the jamb even though the door was opened.

"Good morning, Nickie. Eddy."

What a loser. No one called anyone by his or her first name in a police station.

"I was on my way to an appointment with Captain Nolan."

What's stoppin' ya?

"Any development on the Juracek case? I'm sorry we had to take the guys off the SS8 bug."

It was her SS8 bug that led Nickie to discover Tommy Marino's other life. "The guys heard about a working gal with a name close to the one who William Juracek met with. It sounds like she might be meeting up with Juracek's stepson, too."

"The plot thickens. I suppose I should tell you what you have so far is circumstantial and won't hold up in court."

Nickie felt a twitch in her neck. She had the most solid arrest track record in Tompkins County. She wanted to bark that fact down Miss Miranda Vaughn's throat, but reined in her mouth. "No, you really shouldn't."

Eddy tipped his head to Vaughn. "Good to see you, Miranda. We appreciate your help with the case."

Good to see you? First name basis? What is it about this Vaughn woman that had all her colleagues acting like puppy dogs?

Vaughn tipped her head to him. "You're welcome." She smiled politely. Interesting shit.

"We headed out or what?" Nickie asked him.

"Headed out where?" Eddy said as Vaughn left. "You haven't told me shit."

"I'll tell you on the way."

Eddy followed her down the stairs.

"So, I walk into T & A's, aka The Guest House, and order me a Diet Coke while I took a look around." She wanted to tell him about Parker's frigging amazing undercover getup but thought she better not.

"Did they give you RC?"

"Tried to," she said as they walked through the parking garage to outdoor staff parking. "There was no way I was drinking that crap." Her boots disappeared in the fresh snow. The flakes were as big as dimes and the brightest of white.

"I turn around, and who do I see? Tommy Marino."

"Juracek's stepson?"

"The very one. He is the Tommy in Tommy & Angie's."

"Or the T in tits and asses."

"You got that right. He's got his thug dude on one side and a brainless boob job on the other. I told the gal to scram and for Parker to watch said thug dude."

She'd finished the play-by-play by the time they pulled into Sherie-Wendy-Joe-Johnson-Douglas's condo. "So, Tommy's got this other life I don't think Grandpa or Juracek knew about. It looks like this SS8 was a family habit. Then, Wendy Douglas's name shows up."

"That's not her real name," Eddy added as he sipped his cold coffee from the station.

"I like it. Sherie sounds too obvious, and Sherie-Wendy-Joe-Johnson-Douglas is getting to be a mouthful."

Nickie looked up at the condo. Damn. It was one of the high-class ones where mostly retired rich people lived. Nickie parked her elderly town car near the entrance. It didn't exactly fit in with the rest of the aged metal residents.

They sat and mulled over ideas for fifteen, watching who came and went. The snow had slowed down to a few blowing flurries. There was no doorman, but then again, this wasn't exactly a sprawling metropolitan city.

Nickie almost didn't recognize her minus the red dress and matching pumps. She was with a girl about the age of Gil's twins. Nickie smacked Eddy's arm and got out of her car.

"Sherie," Nickie called out.

The woman turned instinctively. When she spotted
Nickie, she stopped and pulled her daughter into her
side. As Nickie and Eddy made their way to her,
Sherie's eyes moved defiantly between the two of
them.

"The Guest House, Sherie. Tell me what you
know."

Sherie's arms wrapped tighter around her seemingly
oblivious daughter. "I don't know anything."

Another part of her job Nickie hated but was
necessary. She squatted down to eye level with the
little girl. "What's your name, honey? You sure are
pretty."

She was a sweet-looking kid. Sherie had her dressed
in rubber boots. The flurries were gathering on her
matching hat and mittens. "Wendy," the little girl
answered.

Glancing up to Sherie, Nickie lifted a brow.
"Wendy? Are you serious?"

"I told you I only…" She looked down to her
daughter and seemed to be attempting to speak in
code. "I only met with the gentleman one time."

"I'm not talking about the deceased," Nickie said.
"A house guest," she said, using her fingers to make
quotation marks in the air, "was booked to you. You
double dipping with the Juraceks' stepson?"

Sherie shrugged. "It's a coincidence."

"I don't believe in coincidences, and I don't believe
a judge would take too kindly to a mother who holds
your occupation."

Sighing, Sherie looked around and shrugged.
"Tommy is a regular. A freak, okay? The dad
was…different. I thought he was a cop."

"Why?"

"He didn't want to…ya know…" She shrugged
again.

"Yeah, I know. What *did* he want?"

"He wanted to talk. Ask me questions about the business."

"If you don't stop shrugging your shoulders, I am going to book you just for being irritating."

"I think he was checking me out, like he was getting the nerve or deciding if he wanted to…" She looked down at her daughter, who stared at her with wide eyes. "Ya know what I mean. It gave me the creeps."

"Yeah, 'cause I can see how talking to someone could be so much creepier than what you thought you'd be doing." Nickie rubbed her hands over her face. "I'm giving you points for giving me your correct name and address, but taking them away since you didn't tell me about the stepson. Don't leave town."

Eddy kept watching her. It was disconcerting. Did he think she might slip away with Parker out the back door to check out a lead on the Juracek case? Nickie tapped her pencil eraser on her desk. It was like they were getting closer, but they weren't.

She waited until Eddy went to the bathroom. It was pathetic, but she really didn't want to share with him the whole deal with Zheng. Keeping the light on in her office, she ducked into the stairwell.

Eddy never questioned her about why she and Duncan chased a man into the parking garage. She owed him for that, and now she was waiting for him to use the john so she could sneak away. She was scum. Passing the ground floor, she went right to the basement. The jog down the stairs helped wake her and decide how she wanted to handle this.

It was like a dungeon down here, making her thankful for an upstairs office with a window. She usually came down to bother Mr. Henery to hurry up

with the sketch of a suspect. Or maybe to pick the
ME's brain about a case. Today, she was looking for
someone she hadn't met before. A few smaller offices
lined the hallway on the way to evidence and the file
room. Most of the doors were open. Not the one she
wanted.

Mick Grusso was a probation officer. Part time. She
knocked and waited. He opened almost immediately.
He looked like his name. Thick beard, mustache. He
must not be using the services of the offenders in his
charge, because Phil the barber could definitely take a
hack at him.

"Detective Savage."

He knew her? His surprise seemed sincere. That was
a good sign. Scooting around his desk, he stood
behind his chair and waited.

"How's it goin', Grusso? You got a minute?" She
held out a hand and he took it.

They shook before he ducked out of the way,
walked around the back of his desk and waited for her
to sit. She turned sideways, slid through the small
space and took the single guest chair.

"What brings you down here?"

"Phil the barber."

She studied him carefully as he opened a side desk
drawer and pulled out a manila file. His face was
expressionless. Too much so.

"I know he's on three strikes," Grusso said. "He's
got two. Seems to be keeping his nose clean since
then. Is he in some kind of new trouble?"

Nickie didn't answer. "I was going to ask you that."

He flipped through a page or two before answering.
"One count of gun possession without a permit and
one for aiding and abetting."

She knew this already. His place had been the
meeting spot for the old crooked police captain and

fire chief. "Has he been making all his appointments?"

"I don't have record of him missing one."

Does that mean Phil never missed an appointment, or that Mick never recorded him missing one? And is that something you really forget? In fact, do you need to look in a file to know what one of your offenders has on his record? Tilting her head, she smiled sweetly and waited.

"He, uh, hired all new people."

"I have a witness who puts an FBI suspect at his place a few days back." Okay, so she hadn't exactly mentioned Zheng as a suspect to Special Agents Hurst or Goodrich yet, but she planned to and that was close enough. Grusso looked honestly surprised. Points for him. "I plan to visit old Phil. I'd like it if you'd tag along."

"Okay. Sure." He pushed the file to the side, exposing one of those large desk calendars with notes scribbled in each square.

Nickie stood and walked to a hook screwed to the wall near his door. "I'd like to head out now if that's okay with you." She picked up his coat and held it out to him. It was heavy enough she assumed he carried his piece in his pocket.

CHAPTER 16

---◆ ◆ ◆ ◆---

Nickie didn't go upstairs for her coat. She and Grusso went straight to her car and got on the road. She expected him to ask more about the suspect spotted at Phil's, the date he was ID'd and the identity of the informant. Instead, other than the crunch of the snow under her tires, the ride was silent, which suited her fine.

Since the theory that said it couldn't snow when the temps were below zero was dead wrong, the snow had been coming down in buckets for hours. She stopped her car before reaching the curb, giving Grusso room to get out without stepping in the waist-high pile left from the plows.

She parked two stores down. No reason to give Phil time to tidy up before her visit. Accepting her fate, she locked her manual doors and got out coatless.

"Okay, Grusso," she called as she dug her hands in the pockets of her slacks and maneuvered around the crunchy piles of freshly fallen white. "Let's go in and see what Phil has to say for himself."

Indeed, Phil did have new guys standing at chairs, cutting hair or buzzing heads. Phil stood sweeping a small mountain of black hair from beneath a chair, but he noticed them. She supposed that was his job. His eyes went to her, then to Grusso and back to her. He paused for a second, then reached for his dustpan.

Fine. It gave her a chance to browse. She moseyed around the reception thing. Nothing interesting there. No drawers beneath or around the four barber chair stations.

"Detective Savage." It seemed everyone knew her these days, she noted.

"So nice to officially meet you," she said, using her best dumb blonde impersonation. "Mr. Grusso here and I have a few questions for you." She didn't ask about a good place to talk but made her way directly to the only room big enough for three people to sit down and have a visit. It happened to be the same room Phil used for the aiding and abetting part of his two strikes.

She wasn't sure what she was expecting. Was he supposed to remodel the room so no one could meet in there anymore? It looked the same. Cabinets along one side. A table with three chairs. At least it wasn't a big table with a dozen chairs this time.

Tucking one leg beneath the other, she sank down into one of the seats and placed her elbows on the table. As she rested her chin in the palms of her hands she asked, "How's business?"

Phil looked to Grusso, then to her, but he didn't answer.

"She wants to know if you're keeping yourself clean, Phil," Grusso said. "I recommend you answer her questions."

"Business is the same."

"Wrong answer," Nickie interrupted.

"I hired new people. We're cutting hair."

She loved it when guys tried to talk down to her. It

was like her green light to bust balls.

"I'm keeping myself and my place clean," he said sarcastically. "I don't like being harassed."

"And I don't like guys who help out pedophiles. It must just be our little idiosyncrasies." She pulled out a four-by-six picture of Zheng, slung her boots to the floor and slapped it on the table.

Phil let his eyes drop to the picture, then closed them. His shoulders fell and he took a deep breath. "I've never seen this man before in my life," he said, like it was a recording.

She felt pity of all things. "We can protect you."

"No, you can't," he said, looking to her with eyes of steel.

"He's on the run and desperate. Help me find him."

"You're stupid."

"Phil," Grusso interrupted.

She wasn't offended. She was baffled. "So, you think he's not on the run or he's not desperate or you can't help me find him? Throw me a bone here, Phil."

"I said I've never seen him before in my life."

"Why show up here? I would think someone who wasn't desperate wouldn't be coming to a place that already had red flags flying all over it. If some stupid detective thought a dude was on the run and he wasn't, where might he be hiding?"

He looked truly defeated, but in her experience, criminals had loads of practice lying.

"You might try in plain sight."

The Pint was a dive, but it was across the street from the police station, which made it the official happy hour watering hole for the entire NPD. Duncan made a promise to Nickie that he would come with her and made sure to do so pleasantly. A single row of tables sat between a wall of booths and the tattered wooden bar. It had been a classy place when Duncan used fake IDs to sneak in when he was in high school. Now, the floor was sticky and the place carried a musty smell even in this cold, dry weather.

She had been on the Juracek case for over a month. Between it and Zheng looming around, Nickie was on edge. She was as moody as ever and becoming on the jumpy side, suspicious toward most and assuming everyone was guilty until proven innocent.

Standing on the far side of the group of tall tables, she was making nice with the new kid. Dale Parker was tall and blond, young and working on taming his rigid exterior. Lynx leaned toward the new A.D.A., his attempts at flirting overt and shallow. Duncan hoped the woman was smart enough to see it for what it was. The captain used to join the group before he was the captain. No one could get the sketch artist to make an appearance, but Duncan was thankful the ME agreed to join them. Other than Nickie, Leslie Rickard was the only NPD employee he felt truly comfortable speaking with.

Since his agreement with Nickie didn't include drinking light beer from a plastic glass, he carried his whiskey and Coke from the bar and approached the spot next to Leslie. "I think the A.D.A. and I are the only ones in the room unarmed," he said.

"You may be right." The ME tilted her head up once in agreement. "How did Nickie get you to join us?"

"I could ask you the same."

"True." Leslie took a sip of her water with lemon. "She's been stressed."

Duncan had to agree. Nickie also drank water with lemon. His favorite long, linking silver hoops hung from her ears and low around her neck, but she'd worn a baggier pair of khakis and her winter boots that day. It was as out of character as the water with lemon. Instead of one of her regular, brightly colored blouses, she chose one that was a thicker material and navy blue. She was still the most stunning person in the room.

"You went away," Leslie said.

She'd noticed.

"You went away for weeks," she added but didn't pry further. Leslie was intuitive in more ways than analyzing dead bodies.

The group stood around two of the tall tables at the end of the room, talking about bookings gone wrong and working the streets during the winter from hell. With Lynx's attention averted to the new A.D.A., he kept his distance from Nickie. No need for a bar fight, then. How disappointing.

Every few moments, Nickie stopped to glance over at Duncan and smile. Her eyes warmed, and the soft line of her jaw tightened, making him want to drop to one knee and propose right there on the sticky floor. Lynx headed to the bar and the new kid maneuvered to the A.D.A.

Police department drama. Nickie made her way to Duncan and slid a hand around his bicep.

"Mmm," he whispered. "There you are. You smell wonderful."

"I smell like cop work."

He squinted. "There is no such thing. I would know."

She leaned over and reached her lips to his ear. "The smell part of the eidetic memory thing is sort of creepy."

"How are you feeling?" he asked as he brushed a stray lock of hair from her cheek.

She pulled her chin back. "What's that supposed to mean?"

Yes. Suspicious. "You're drinking water." And dressed like a man.

"Oh, that. You should have seen what I had for lunch."

"Did you eat a French fry?"

"More than one. How did you know?"

"You love French fries."

"I called Langley today."

Her contacts at the FBI? "Not something one hears every day. Hurst or Goodrich?"

"Hurst. He said they would come up here to meet with me."

"Northridge here?"

"Exactly. It's creeping me out."

"It's possible they are appreciative of the cases you've helped them solve, and they'd like to return the favor."

She gave him her look that meant he was out of his mind as Lynx came back with a glass of wine in one hand and a mixed drink in the other. Lynx never drank wine. It was another trivial fact Duncan wished he could forget.

"Don't look now," Nickie said low. As if that ever did anything but make someone look. "Lynx doesn't get that Miranda would rather talk to Parker than him."

"They are an odd pair, you must admit. I think she would fall into the cougar category with Parker."

"Stranger things have happened. I stopped by Phil the barber's place today."

The nerves in his body woke.

She must have noted this. "I took Phil's probation officer. He was too chummy with Phil for my liking, but maybe he feels Phil is trying to turn his life around. Yada, yada, yada."

"What happened?"

"Zheng has been back to the barbershop. I'm sure of it."

"Sure of it? You never say *sure* unless you have proof."

"Phil was scared when I showed him Zheng's picture. They can't be meeting about anything. We took down their operation. There is no regrouping. There's nothing to regroup. Unless he's trying to start over again, but then why is he hanging around here? No girls have been reported missing. If Zheng is looking for ways to get to me, he's gonna have to work a little harder."

"That's not funny."

Her gaze softened when it met his. "You're right. I'm being careful. I promise. Hey, Rickard," she called over her shoulder. "I'm careful, aren't I?"

"I am afraid you are the queen of not careful, Nickie." Leslie's returning smile was one of a friend. "It's getting late. It looks like I'm going to have to call Lynx a cab."

Nickie's head rested against Duncan's seat as he drove. It was the second time in a week she agreed to leave her car at the station. Why did this worry him?

"How are you feeling?" he asked.

"You've already asked me that tonight," she answered and patted his thigh without moving her head or opening her eyes.

He'd driven his Audi and cracked the windows, letting the crisp clean air of the rural highway fill their senses, or his at least. The turn into his drive was barely visible. He down shifted and climbed the hill.

"I've noticed you judging others," he explained. "Not maliciously and likely well deserving, but it's not like you."

"Example?"

"You assumed Lynx is after the new A.D.A. as well as the new guy, Parker."

"Well, duh."

"I agree. It's just not like you to say so. And you assumed Phil is allowing Zheng back in his shop."

"I have an eyewitness."

"You have Slippery Jimbo."

He pulled into his garage, shifted into first and set the emergency brake.

"Ugh. I hate when you're right."

"And I enjoy it enough for both of us."

She gave him one of her annoyed looks that somehow turned him on.

She never waited for him to open her door but did meet him at the one to the house. He ran the back of his gloved hand down her cheek. "Why does it please me that you have no overnight bag for your overnight stay? Or that your overnight stay is assumed?"

Her smile was breathtaking. Perfect. Striking. He bent down and kissed her once, twice, then dipped in farther. Her long arms wrapped around him. "You are covered in far too many layers," he said, pulling away.

"You started it."

He opened the door and reset the alarm to the new setting for when they were inside. "We were debating the legitimacy of Slippery Jimbo's testimony."

She laughed. It was musical. "No debate. I give."

They took off their coats and hung them in the closet, then pulled off their boots and left them on the rug before turning for the two flights of stairs to the master bedroom. "You're right about the judging thing. I suppose I'm at odds with what parts of my life are real."

"Example?"

She smiled at his attempt to throw her question back at her. Then, she paused mid-climb. "I spent fourteen years thinking my teenage stay with Gloria was legal, only to discover it was staged. What if she had gotten hurt? I'd never forgive myself." Her feet started moving again.

"And my transfer to Northridge? Staged. Captain Tanner?" She was raising her voice now and pushed open the French doors leading into the master bedroom, both at once. "I trusted him. Looked up to him. How did I not see he was a pedophile sicko like the ones I…" Her face turned to him, her expression pained and embarrassed.

He took her soft face in his hands and rubbed his thumbs along her cheeks. "I am a part of your life that is real and that is true. So are Rose, Andy, Gloria, Gil."

She blinked her long lashes at him, her eyes warming. "I'm so in love with you."

"Let me paint you."

"Now?"

"Mmm."

"It's embarrassing."

"Now it's embarrassing?" He ran a thumb along her lips. And to think at one time he thought they were disproportioned. "Come," he said and took her hand. He led her to the walnut settee he had made to replace the one he lost…*they* lost in the fire.

Positioning one of the velvet pillows, he laid her back and positioned her arms, one resting by her side and the other draped over her head. He'd imagined how he wanted her to pose for him since the day the first painting turned to ashes. He had hoped for less clothing, he would admit.

Taking an empty canvass, he prepared his best

brushes and paints. He heard rustling on the settee and turned to find her pulling off her ugly slacks. He tried not to stop and stare, truly he did. He'd painted nude subjects dozens of times. And he'd seen her legs hundreds of times. Her endless, golden brown legs. He slid onto his wooden, swivel stool.

Her smile was sweet and slight as she stood in her wooly socks and ugly shirt. It turned sly as she ruffled her hair and brought the waves around her shoulders. She stepped on one of the socks and pulled out her foot, balancing on one leg as she dangled her bright pink painted toes to him. She repeated with the other, then ran her hands from the outstretched foot, around her ankle, up her toned calf, and along the muscles on her thighs.

His lips wanted to mention that she didn't seem embarrassed anymore, but his voice wasn't working. Something dropped from his hands. He looked and noticed his brush on the floor, but left it there and flipped his gaze back to his detective.

She turned in a slow circle as her fingers worked the buttons on her shirt. The shirt that was too damned long in the back. The tail covered the majority of her round, smooth backside. The muscles in her legs flexed and released as she stepped slowly. Stopping front and center, she locked her knees, legs spread in a stance much like she was preparing to draw her gun.

She continued with the buttons over her navel. The bra and panties she wore were far from ugly or khaki. They were the ones in matching blue jean material each with ivory-colored lace lining. His pants were becoming unbearably uncomfortable.

The long string of linked silver hoops dangled between the healthy cleavage that always seemed to call to him. She slipped the ugly shirt from her flawless shoulders, exposing the soft lines along her collarbone and the hollow at the base of her neck, where he liked to nuzzle his lips and his nose. When she dropped the shirt to the floor, it took every ounce of willpower he had to keep his ass on the stool. He'd already clicked a dozen poses in his eidetic memory that he wanted to start painting, but this. His Nickie standing in front of him. Healthy female curves and smooth golden skin.

Her face was flushed giving away the desires that matched his own. Leaving the brush on the floor, he stood but she held out an arm, palm facing him. He closed his eyes in defeat and sat back down. She turned her back to him and reached behind, grasping the clasp that held her prisoner. He barely noticed her scars as his eyes were glued to her backside that was no longer covered with an ugly shirt. The click of the clasp as it released was small but took the air from his lungs nonetheless. She held the bits of fabric to her body as she turned, two strong hands covering what he wanted to paint, needed to have in his hands and in his mouth.

His breath quickened. "You're killing me."

Her smile was pure evil and all his. She dropped her hands, letting the blue jean laced material drop to the pile of clothing that circled her feet. Her hair. Her honey-wheat waves covered all the wrong places. He craned his neck to get a glimpse as she laced her thumbs through the sides of the matching panties.

To hell with her stop sign hand signal, he had to touch her and started to stand. "No," she said earnestly, her breath as ragged as his. "Paint." And with that, she dropped her last piece of clothing on the floor.

Paint? Was she serious? She must have been, because she lay back on his settee wearing nothing but the lines of silver hoops. They dangled from her ears and down her neck, resting along the breast that wouldn't let them drop to the seat of the settee.

She was right. Her face was full of color, her body warm and taut. It would be the perfect start to his painting.

Painfully, he picked his brush up from the floor and began smoothing strokes over his canvas. The sight of her chest rising and falling beneath the silver links was as alluring as she was. Was this truly forever? He dipped his brush again and again. Time was moot as he worked. She fell asleep with the slightest of smiles on her lips. Her breathing slowed, and he painted.

Hours passed as he worked, gaining momentum with time. The temperature from his automated furnace dropped, but he was warm, almost perspiring as his detective took form on his canvas. The process was a drug he couldn't get enough of. His hands threatened to cramp, but he continued. Sometime during his hours of work, he'd removed his shirt, his shoes, but he had little recollection of doing so.

She slept like a rock, moving only slightly. It was simple to work around. He knew every inch of her.

His gaze did a double take at her skin when she developed slight goose bumps in the chill. How long had she been cold? He abandoned his painting and approached her. He didn't remember to use caution in case she woke with fists clenched and swinging, but slid his arms around her shoulders and beneath her knees, lifting carefully as not to disturb her. She crooned and turned her face into his shoulder, her nose tucking into the fresh, pink scar from his gunshot wound. More than anything, he wanted the ring that rested in his pocket on her finger. Silently, he made the declaration that he wouldn't finish the painting until it was.

He slipped her naked body between his sheets and

tucked them around her. She moaned and turned away from him, exposing the scars on her back. His brows dropped as he studied them. They weren't pink as was the new scar on his shoulder. They'd turned nearly the same color as her golden brown skin, only a shade lighter. The pain that swelled inside of him was sudden and profound.

Zheng would pay.

CHAPTER 17

◢ ◆ ◆ ◢

Nickie's lungs threatened to burst from her rib cage. She threw her head back in triumph before climbing off Duncan and plopping on the bed next to him. She moaned. "That was much better than a workout in the pool."

"Mmm," Duncan hummed but lay still like the dead. The rapid pace of his lungs was the only evidence that he was still with the living.

She flipped the covers from them, making him growl and pull them back before rolling over. Unashamed, she made her way to the settee and the pile of clothes she left the night before. She reached for her shirt as she turned to the painting. She was speechless. Paintings took him days. Weeks. This one seemed nearly finished.

Her hand covered her mouth. Is this how he saw her? The person in the painting was soft and…nice. She glanced down at her naked body, then back to the painting. The last time he painted her less-than-dressed, she'd worn a shirt and her underwear. She stifled a snort at the thought of the striptease she'd performed. What had she been thinking? Slipping into the shirt, she stood gazing at his work.

And, at that moment, it didn't matter to her whether he ever officially proposed or if he ever gave her the ring he didn't know she knew was in his pocket. He wanted her. Forever. And this was how he saw her.

As she headed for the bathroom—their bathroom— she realized he must have been up nearly the entire night to get so far on the portrait. The sheets over his body rose and fell slowly. He was already sleeping after what they'd just done? She smiled, revived and ready to take on her day.

She stepped into the shower and turned the water to blazing. This case was becoming a permanent resident in her head and had gone on far too long. Either Tommy Marino found out his stepdad took interest in his special Sherie Douglas hooker, or else Mrs. Juracek discovered her husband's visits with the ruby red Sherie and killed him in a crime of rage. Did Mrs. Juracek want to get her hands on the inheritance before it went to her son? Did she know about his double life? Or did Sherie somehow think she could benefit from a dead William Juracek? Could Tommy have made empty promises of riches and inheritance? Tommy hadn't been officially made the heir of the deceased's half of the business yet. Maybe Tommy didn't know that. Maybe Sherie didn't know. She realized she'd just washed her hair a third time and decided she better move on to the conditioner.

Every joint in her body was unhinged. Every muscle loose and taut at the same time. The hot water beat on her body, the combination making her alive and energized. She reminded herself to keep an open mind to the possibilities that might be outside of her circle of suspects.

As she sat to spend her routine forty-five minutes on hair and makeup, she realized Duncan wasn't getting up anytime soon and her car was at the station. See? He should listen to her when she told him they needed to drive separately. She cringed as she texted Eddy for a ride. She would catch hell, but he was the one had to leave his car at The Pint last night, and she would shove the hell right back at him.

She tiptoed to the dresser that now held nearly all of her belongings, then to the half of the closet that was hers. Even when she brought the rest of her clothes to this house, they would barely take up half the space of Duncan's.

The rise and fall of the sheets never changed as she slipped out the door.

"I feel like we should have a spot in the garage," Eddy said as he pulled to the curb in front of the Juracek home. Nickie let him drive after he had to call a taxi to The Pint, then came all the way out to the house to pick her up. It wasn't exactly on the way. It didn't mean she had to like it.

"I'm tired of coming out here, too. Maybe she'll confess," Nickie said sarcastically as she shut the car door behind her.

The walk wasn't shoveled, and she'd worn her favorite damn boots. No one answered the bell for a solid five minutes. They almost left when Mrs. Juracek came to the door in a housecoat. Her eyes were swollen. It was the only way Nickie had ever seen them.

"Good morning, Sylvia. May we come in?"

She nodded and strode toward the same small living room off the foyer where they questioned her the last time. As they followed, Nickie noticed the place was beginning to look more like her town house than the tidy Juracek home. Nickie and Eddy took their spots on the loveseat. How could there be more snow than the last time? No yard lights today. The green of the bushes was completely covered, making them look like mounds instead of snow-covered plants.

"Do you mind?" Nickie asked, placing her ancient recorder on the coffee table in front of the loveseat.

"I give permission for you to record me," she said blandly. "Oh, and this is Sylvia Juracek speaking."

Nickie turned it off. "Can I ask you something off record, Sylvia?"

The expression on her face was the first glimpse at interest Nickie recognized since they arrived. "What is it?"

"How are you holding up? Um, your house, your sidewalk…We can arrange for someone you can talk to."

Sylvia waved her hand in front of her face like she was shooing a fly. "Cleaning ladies quit. I'll find new ones. What can I do for you, Detectives?"

Nickie turned her recorder on again and asked, "Do you know about a place called The Guest House?"

"I'm afraid I don't. Where are my manners? Can I get you anything to drink?" Sylvia pulled the housecoat closer around her.

"No, thank you. What about T & A's?"

Mrs. Juracek dropped her eyes. The tears were instant.

"He's a good boy. He's just going through that college stage boys do when they get themselves into things they shouldn't."

A twenty-five-year-old bar owner was a boy?

"He'll come around." The tears that dipped from her eyes said she didn't completely believe that.

For the record, Nickie prodded. "So, you are aware that your son, Tommy, is the owner or partial owner of Tommy and Angie's?"

Sylvia nodded.

"For the record, please."

"Yes, I know." Her voice was rising.

"Thank you, Sylvia. This is a difficult time for you."

"What's difficult is that you haven't found who did this to my husband. The murderer is still out there. I have a daughter."

Nickie sighed, then repeated the question she'd asked once before. "Do you know of a business named SS8?"

Mrs. Juracek's eyes turned to blood rage. Interesting new reaction.

Her hands shook as she pointed a finger to Nickie and said low through her teeth, "If I ever find a single SS8 *employee*." Spit sprayed from her mouth as she said the last word. "They're dead."

Eddy stepped on Nickie's foot. She trusted him and scooted back in her seat a few inches.

He took Sylvia's hand and patted the top of it. "It's a terrible place, we know, Sylvia. We want to catch the person responsible for the death of your husband. The murder might be part of that despicable SS8 place."

'Despicable SS8 place?' Nickie had to work to keep a straight face.

Sylvia nodded. "Tommy got mixed up there. He's going to stop as soon as he has some time to grow up."

"Of course he is, Sylvia." Eddy was nearly singing her a lullaby. "What about your husband?"

Mrs. Juracek blinked. "What do you mean by that?" She yanked her hand from Eddy's. "What do you mean by that?" she repeated hysterically.

"Your husband went to see one of the *employees* of SS8 a few weeks ago."

"You're wrong. You're lying. William was faithful. Oh no." She started rocking forward and back. "Oh no."

He kept at her. It was painful to watch, and Nickie wondered if this is what Eddy felt when she was the one badgering a person of interest.

"But you slept in different rooms. He was killed in the middle of the night dressed in a suit."

"He snores. I can't slee—" She buried her face in her hands and bent over, nearly touching her face to her knees. "I don't know why he was out. Oh no."

"We're going to call your father, Sylvia," Nickie said and sifted through some business cards, leaving one on the table. "Let's get him out here to help you with some things. And here is a number you can call. These people are good listeners. They can help you."

"Get out," Mrs. Juracek whispered. "Get out. Get out, get out!" she said louder and louder.

"We'll see ourselves out," Eddy said calmly.

They trudged through the snow on the way down the path to his car.

"A little hard on her, don't you think, Lynx?"

"You mean the woman who said if she ever found a single SS8 employee, she'd kill them?"

"She didn't do it."

"Come on, Nick. You saw her reaction."

"She may have her head in the sand about her son, but she did not know her husband had been cheating on her."

"Do you ever go with your gut?"

"Sure, but I'm careful my gut doesn't cloud my vision to the rest of what's going on. She knew about Tommy's secret bar owner life. I wonder if Mr. Juracek knew."

* * *

"Boss?" Nickie knocked on Dave's door.

The door was open. Eddy would have just walked in, but that seemed rude. Dave nodded in recognition. "Come in, Nick. What's up?"

"Remember the special agents I spoke with you about?"

"Which couple of special agents? The first ones or the second ones?"

She sank in his cushioned guest chair and slung a boot on her knee. "The second ones."

"Hurst and Goodrich."

"Yep. They're sort of on their way."

"Here?"

"Yeah. Sorry I didn't give you a heads up earlier. I just found out yesterday."

"They want you on a case? You don't have to tell me specifics. I just need to know if I'm losing a detective and for how long."

"No, I called *them*."

"You called—" His expression softened. She could practically see Zheng register in his mind. "Oh."

"Yeah."

"They're coming here?"

"I know. It's creepy. Wasn't my idea for them to come here, of course. Anyway, I wanted you to know."

He nodded. "I noticed your car's been here overnight a few times this past week."

What the hell? "Is that a problem?"

"Of course not. I'm trying to pry into your personal life without prying into your personal life, but is it broken down?"

Ah. "I rode with Duncan a few times." Awkward conversation both answered and averted.

He jerked his head toward the commons area, then fooled with some papers on his desk. She turned her head to investigate and spotted Hurst and Goodrich hanging around the door to her office. They were dressed casually, much like the last time they were hanging out near her office. What did she expect? she wondered as she headed toward them without saying good-bye to Dave.

Hurst was the bigger one. Tight, black hair. Clean shaven. Goodrich was lankier. Brown hair with a unibrow making his scowl look all the worse.

They didn't offer a wave, a greeting or even a nod, but waited for her to speak. She held out a hand and shook with Goodrich first, then Hurst. "Thank you for coming on such short notice. Please come in. Can I take your coats?"

She'd cleared off the chairs so they had a place to sit. Her office might be embarrassing, but it was still her office. Small and messy. They could very well get splinters from her chairs. It might be a bad thing for an FBI special agent to get a splinter in his ass, but she couldn't do anything about it now.

They hung up their coats on their own next to hers on the freestanding, wobbly coat rack that stood next to her door. Then, they each took a seat in her only two spots for guests.

"I appreciate your expediency. I have some information to share with you." And some questions.

They looked at each other from the corners of their eyes. Oh, right. She'd forgotten special agent types did that.

No sense beating around the bush. She peeled the picture of Jun Zheng she kept taped to her desk monitor and placed it in front of them. They looked at it, each other, then to her. Their expressions weren't nearly as easy to read as Mrs. Juracek's.

"Thurmond Moody was highly involved in the sex trafficking ring we took down in January. The evening's illegal trysts may have been staged at the white house located on his property, but as you know, the girls were delivered all over the country for use at different events. What I'm trying to tell you is he was not the top of that food chain. I believe this man is." She moved her gaze back and forth between the two of them, studying their reactions carefully. She saw what she was looking for. Recognition.

They didn't look at each other. Why did she think that was a bad sign? "We need a minute," Hurst said.

"Are you serious?"

"'Fraid so."

CHAPTER 18

Nickie should be grateful. They came *here*. On a day's notice. But they recognized Zheng and instinct took over. Instead of leaving her office so they could have their moment, she leaned back and folded her arms over her chest.

They didn't react but instead stood and walked out the door. She rubbed both hands over her face, then laced them through her hair. They knew something. They knew something about the case that involved her personally, and they were considering what or how much they would share with her.

She should have gone to see Tanner. Would go to see Tanner. At least she could bully and threaten information out of him. If it didn't take all damned day to fly to the federal pen in Terre Haute, she'd go right then and leave Hurst and Goodrich to their *moment*.

She was still sitting back with her hands folded when they returned. Using her knuckles, she turned her jaw until it cracked.

"We know this is personal to you," Hurst said.

"How. How do you know?"

"Special Agents Strong and Lewis sold out. They're being held at an undisclosed location. We don't know where they are."

Sold out? What? "Define 'sold out.'" This wasn't going where it needed to go.

"They were assigned to this case. Your case." He held up a hand before she could protest. "Somewhere along the line—maybe before it was assigned to them—they sold out to the other side. Both of them. They were working for the bad guys, Nickie." Without looking at it, he tapped her picture of Zheng that still lay on her desk.

She had questions. Questions and wanted answers about Strong and Lewis. But her focus needed to be Zheng. "It makes sense," she explained. "Zheng had connections—corrupt connections. The former Northridge captain of police, the assistant to the governor of New York. He prefers to use middle men. But he's lost his trafficking ring—his source of income—and with it any leverage he may have had to extort whoever Strong and Lewis answered to." She set her elbows on her desk and rubbed her face in her hands. "Strong and Lewis," she repeated. "Were you even going to tell me?"

Goodrich remained expressionless. Hurst sighed. His expression reminded her of Dave.

As if thinking out loud, she said, "They fought me, ignored my advice, my warnings. My pleadings."

"Yeah, they knew," Hurst said dropping his formal articulation. "It ain't right. The only reason they backed you up with SWAT at Moody's white house was because you tapped the security cameras and recorded more still shots than they could ignore and stay out of prison. And the audio? You stuck them in a damned fine corner." His smile was all cop.

Under different circumstances, she might appreciate

the grin on his face.

"We didn't know his name," Hurst confessed.

Zheng. A fresh stab of betrayal shot through her gut.

Leaving his face expressionless, Goodrich retorted this time. "We didn't know his name. Only that he was part of this. He's shown up on our radar too many times to be a coincidence."

"I think he is the top man. Or was before we took everything away from him. He seems to have a score to settle with me." She explained about the break-in at her townhouse, about the press conference he crashed. The sighting at Phil's barbershop.

Almost as if Hurst ignored what she just said, he interrupted. "Strong and Lewis kept files on you." She knew this already. What good cop, detective, special agent or frigging rookie wouldn't know to look into the people you're using? Except, his face told her there was more.

"They kept files, organizing the details regarding your childhood. From the time you were abducted to present. The night of your escape. Your transfer to New York foster care. Your time at the academy. All of it."

Goodrich sighed.

So, they knew. She nodded. She'd suspected this, of course. It was why they contacted in her in the first place. For her *expertise*. It was still disconcerting to hear them speak of it. "Where are the files? Did you bring them?"

The look on Goodrich's face said he wasn't happy where the conversation was leading.

"I want those files."

Without checking his partner for their creepy special agent silent pow wow, Hurst agreed. He closed his eyes and nodded. "We'll ship those overnight insured as soon as we get back."

Her foster home was staged when she was in high school. Her position as Northridge detective fixed. Her former police captain had been involved with the trafficking operation she had been hunting. "How do I know you haven't *sold out*?" She said the last two words with vengeance.

"We understand your reluctance to put your trust in anyone of legal authority," Goodrich said still expressionless. There were no red flags where these two were concerned, but she hadn't sensed any red flags with Strong or Lewis either and she was an excellent judge of male character.

"Why all the care and share now?"

"There wasn't a tactical reason to tell you," Goodrich said. "You know how this goes."

"Stop talking like the two of you are one person. You." She pointed to Hurst. "I want to know why *you* decided there is a *tactical* reason to tell me all of a sudden that the last sixteen years of my life have been a lie. That I've been staged like a string puppet."

"It's what we...I wanted to talk to Goodrich about. You have intel on this man." Hurst pointed to her photo of Zheng. "But mostly, this shit ain't right, Detective. You've done a lot for the department. You deserve to know. We'll send you those files first thing when we get back. And we'll show your picture to people we trust." He lifted her picture of Zheng from her desk and asked, "May I?"

She nodded before countering. "How about for now you show his picture around to people you trust. I'm curious about Phil the bartender. I'd appreciate it if you'd look him up. He's easy to find." Although she had zero trust in them. "Jun Zheng," she continued. "Yes, I know him. I'm sure your *files* tell you just how personally I know him. He's on the run and has nothing left. He doesn't know what to do with a grown woman trained in defense who carries a Smith and Wesson M&P .45. I'd like to get him in custody before he hurts someone, or worse yet tries to rebuild."

The longer Nickie tried to sort through her meeting with the feds, the more she needed to get away. A swim. It would do her some good. Duncan's house was twenty minutes away. The gym was closer. Yanking her coat from her rack, she slung it over her shoulders as she headed for the stairs.

Be smart, Savage. You're better than this. A workout in the middle of the afternoon wasn't exactly routine. She spun on her heels and headed for Eddy's office. As she popped her head in, she barked, "I'm taking an hour if anyone asks."

"What's the matter?"

Did she have it written on her forehead? "Nothing's the matter. I'm bringing Duncan in on the Juracek case," she added as a side note. She almost felt bad throwing that one at him, but then, no.

She beat down the stairs on the balls of her feet, then let her heels knock the concrete as she strutted toward her car. The blast of cold air burned her lungs and opened her head. Her town car was a block of ice and took a solid ten minutes to free. The contrast between the sweat forming around her collar and the numbness in her extremities was ridiculous. The pain in her fingers and toes was welcomed.

Sitting in her warmed car, she shook her head. Strong and Lewis were in on it. She smacked her steering wheel with the palm of her frozen hand. Shifting the gear into drive, she pulled out of her spot.

Gravel spun beneath her tires as she turned out of staff parking. She smacked the wheel two more times and let her head scream.

Some asshole pulled in behind her and got close enough to her tail that she couldn't see his headlights. Brake check? Nah, she might scratch the rust on her beloved tank. His was a shiny new Lexus SUV gold edition. She would take the high ground, pick a spot in the lane so he couldn't pass and slow down to ten miles an hour.

Tinted windshield. She could pull him over and ticket him just for that, but she had a workout to get to. And at ten miles an hour, he was already making her late.

She took the corner into the working class subdivision. It was her short cut to the gym. Hurst and Goodrich came all the way up here to *discuss privately* whether to tell her about Strong and Lewis. About *her* file. She hit her steering wheel one more time for good measure.

The muscles in her face fell, and her eyes trained on her rearview mirror. The SUV turned with her into the subdivision. There was nothing in this neighborhood that could possibly interest the owner of a new Lexus. She didn't even know if he was a he. She couldn't see a damned thing through the tinted windshield and the sun reflecting from the fresh snowfall.

She made a random corner. A sunbeam shot through the Lexus as it followed her around it. It was enough for her to see an outline of a person, a man. Short, spiky, dark hair. Jun Zheng.

He waited for her to leave work? Tailed her from a police department?

Bring it.

She tapped her brakes and heard his make a quick screech. The next corner led her back to the main road. She had a plan. Anywhere near the station wasn't going to work. He would be too cautious. But she had him. His cockiness was going to be the end of him. Her heart raced. She pushed back in her seat and gripped the steering wheel.

Purposely, she smiled and trained her eyes on her rearview mirror, hoping he would see the glee on her face. As soon as they neared the outskirts of town, he crept closer. The gold-plated headlights disappeared once again.

Her head jerked forward and whiplashed enough that she hit her forehead against the steering wheel. He rear-ended her doing forty- five? Anticipation raced through her veins. So, it was going to be that way, was it? She was expected to be the scared little girl she once was? Afraid of a little metal on metal? And to think she refrained from her first brake check so she wouldn't hurt his fancy car.

Her foot pressed on the accelerator. She hoped the stink from her ancient engine went right through his air circulation. He sped to catch up, of course. She was nearly bouncing in her seat. The town car was almost on two wheels as she took the last turn onto the highway that led toward Duncan's house. Not that she was going there. She just needed the open road.

This beloved girl was so old that it had no air bag and no ABS. Which also meant metal, thick and unbreakable. Just what the doctor ordered. Tightening her seat belt with one hand, she grabbed hold of the wheel with the other, then locked up her brakes.

The thrust of his car threw her entire face into the steering wheel this time. Deafening sounds of screeching metal and the long burn of tires filled most of her head. The fact that she was rolling filled the rest. Somehow, she knew she landed upside down. Sharp pains shot through her ribs, shoulders and arms. Stars blinded her vision. The smell of burnt rubber and gasoline filled her nostrils just as everything went black.

* * *

It had been an hour since Duncan texted her. Not that they had the kind of relationship that demanded expediency in responses, but under the circumstances, she needed to get the hell back to him. He hadn't had a chance to get the GPS chip secured in her holster and gun belt yet. Damn it. Why hadn't he done that?

Instead, he booted up his laptop and decided on cell phone triangulation. His fingers flew across his keyboard. He hacked into AT&T, then into her phone number. A smile spread across his face as he recognized that she was only a mile down the highway on the way from town.

He'd slept in late that morning and woke with the same drive to work on her painting as he'd had the night before. It nearly killed him to make it into town for his single lunch appointment. The rest he was able to do from home—between working on his painting.

He checked the triangulation again. It hadn't moved. She must have pulled over to use her cell. No. Cops never did that. Text yes, phone no. And no one takes that long to text.

He sprinted for the stairs. It was nothing. It was nothing. He didn't come close to convincing himself. He skipped the last six stairs and his coat, darting for the garage and punching the door opener. His Audi was still warm from his lunch meeting. He took it and burned rubber as he completed a quick three-point turn.

It was then he saw it. The smoke. Tears instantly burned his eyes as his commander yelled to him from the cockpit. "How many are gone, Private?" Heat swirled around him as the fire grew. "All of them, sir," he heard himself say and turned at the end of his drive.

No. He couldn't go there. Not now. Two cars. He

saw two cars. Not a helicopter. Not the desert. His Nickie. He clutched a chunk of the hair on top of his head as he skidded next to her car in the ditch. It was upside down. A white Lexus wrapped around a tree and was engulfed in flames.

Without coming to a complete stop, he opened his door, and stepping off the clutch, killed the engine. The deep snow was like wading through quicksand. He could see her. She dangled upside down from her seat belt. No, he begged, but there was no movement.

"Nickie!" he screamed as his hands shook and tugged on the door. It wasn't from the cold. Yanking and heaving, his eyes burned from tears when it didn't budge. He trudged through the snow around the car to the other side. "Nickie," he yelled over and over. She hung lifeless, her arms dangling. A line of blood went from her nose to her eye socket.

"Nickie, please." He hauled on the passenger door. "Not now. You can't. You promised." His arms became like lead as he pulled and pulled, then pounded on the glass. Stepping back, he ran and sank his elbow into the back passenger window. It didn't shatter but broke into long fingers of pointed glass. He knocked a few pieces away, then reached in and lifted the lock on the front passenger door.

His fingers were frozen stiff and barely helped in opening the upside down car door. Crawling along the inside of the roof, he took her face in his hands. She was cold. "No, baby. No. Not cold. Come on." Taking her shoulders, he shook. "Nickie. You can't." He reached for the seat belt release and pushed. His damned fingers wouldn't work. He blew on them and pushed until it felt like his fingers might shatter into pieces.

She fell with a thud to the roof. "Ow!" she moaned.

"Oh hell. Oh bloody hell." He scurried to right her

until he had her on her back with her head in his lap. "My Nickie. I thought you were…My Nickie."

"You're brushing my head like you're petting a dog." Her eyes were closed, but she was smiling. "Wait." She opened her eyes. "Zheng. He hit me. Or I hit him." She shifted and struggled, then fell back, winced and held her head.

"There isn't anyone alive in that car."

Together, they craned their heads and watched as the flames around the Lexus exploded into an oval of orange that lifted like an enormous balloon toward the sky.

Distant sirens became barely audible. She was bloody and bruised and had a goose egg the size of a goose egg forming on the middle of her forehead, but she was laughing.

"I see nothing funny about any of this. I thought you were dead."

She laughed harder, coughing and sucking air.

"Did you just snort?" he asked. "That's it. That. Is. It. Marry me, Nickie Savage."

She turned her swollen, tattered face to him. It flickered in the light of the erupting flames. He dug in his pocket and pulled out the velvet bag. Opening it, he took the solitaire, circular diamond ring and held it out to her. "I can't really get on one knee—"

She tackled him, both of them groaning with pain, and showered his face with kisses. Her cold lips ended on his, her icy fingers holding the sides of his face. She pulled back. "The ring. Give."

He held it out of her reach. "No. I do this part, and you haven't said, 'yes.'"

"Yes. Yes, I'll marry you, Duncan. I love you. Now give me the damned ring."

He could feel his smile spread wide. She blinked three times before he lowered the ring to her hand and slipped it on her finger. She held it out like Nickie Savage never would, admiring it as the sirens came closer.

Tucking herself into him like they were home in bed, she whispered as if someone might hear her. "Duncan, you're wearing your house shoes."

CHAPTER 19

Every inch of Nickie's body hurt. Sirens flashed around them like a disco ball from the eight black and whites, three ambulances, one tow truck, three fire trucks, and a handful of unmarkeds. That was what happened when a cop was down. She got that. But she was engaged to Duncan Reed—officially—and she really wanted to go home and celebrate.

There was no sign that Jun Zheng or any other person had ever been in the Lexus—what was left of it. And even sitting in the back of the heated ambulance, she was frozen to the bone.

"If you touch me with that one more time," she barked at the EMT holding the wet swab. "I'm going to kick your ass and see that you work at a desk for the next three months."

Duncan smiled from the other side of the ambulance. It still took her breath away. Regardless, she was able to glare at him in return. A woman had an image to maintain.

Dave and Eddy scoured the area, something she should be doing if not for the fact that she wasn't sure if she'd ever walk again.

"The detective needs her bag from the trunk of her car," Duncan said to the EMT.

The dude started to object. It wasn't his job, but one look at Duncan and he nodded his head and left.

"I don't really need the bag from my car, Duncan."

"You have a bag in your car?"

How could she feel such peace at a time like this?

"Was it worth it?" he asked.

"Was what worth it?"

"You were going how fast on the highway? No car did that much damage by rear-ending a moving vehicle. You slammed on your brakes, didn't you?"

She couldn't help it. She smiled from ear to ear. "Locked 'em up."

His face fell. The expression that replaced it was much like the one he wore at Rossetti's when he gave her that awful proposal. "I've accepted what comes with being married to a cop. I won't accept you putting yourself purposely in danger." His chest rose and fell, and the veins along the sides of his neck turned purple.

"Okay."

"What the hell do you mean, okay?"

She lifted her brows. Even they hurt. "I mean I get your point. You're right. Don't rub it in."

"That's it? That was our first engagement fight?"

It was painful, but she maneuvered over to sit next to him. She patted his knee. "Don't worry. I'm sure there will be worse ones."

"I thought you were..." He lifted his hand and brushed his thumb over her goose egg. "We need to get out of here."

Dave walked to the back of the ambulance. "We found a blood trail. The K-9 unit from Rochester is on the way." He held up a plastic bag. Inside, she could make out a branch with dark red stains brushed along the leaves. Her mind went to the day she escaped Moody's white house as a young teen. She, too, had to run alone through the trees in the cold. There weren't as many trees as there were here, and it wasn't as cold as this crazy winter, but the whole scenario was damned justifying.

She wanted that bag. She knew Zheng would be long gone and she wanted the bag, wanted to have Hurst and Goodrich run the DNA through CODIS.

"You slammed on your brakes, didn't you, Nick?" Dave asked.

Duncan rudely interrupted before she had a chance to answer. "Locked 'em up." He even had the nerve to imitate her voice.

Dave nodded. "That an engagement ring on your finger?"

"Yes." She hadn't felt so guilty since the first grade.

"Anything else major you haven't told me?"

"Nope. That about covers it."

Dave smiled and nodded. "Congratulations. Both of you." He turned to Duncan. "She's a good woman. You should take her home. We can finish up in the morning."

He was coming. He was coming and Nicole was ready.

They'd put her in the red room. Each was named for the color of the walls. How stupid. They made her wear a white, lacy bra with matching underwear. She didn't even have enough boobs to fill a bra. They didn't put any makeup on her. They wanted her to look like a virgin. She hadn't been one of those for a long time.

This one liked her, she remembered. He called her Savage like everyone else. She would be a savage, then.

He came in, busting out in laughter over something the man who stood at the door had said to him. Lifting his hand to the guard, he shut the door and turned his beady eyes to her. She hurried to the edge of the bed and curled her legs so she was like a ball. It was only sort of an act.

He laughed so hard, he wheezed as if he had asthma, then emptied his pockets like her father did when he came home from work.

"I hoped you'd be that way, honey." He talked to her like she was a little girl. They'd taken that away a long time ago, too.

She shook with fear, more because of her plan than because of him.

He tossed his jacket over a chair and pulled at his tie.

"They," she croaked. "They record us, you know."

His hands stopped. He didn't move his head, but moved his eyes from one side of the room to the other.

"There," she said, pointing to the lion head on the wall.

He continued with his tie, tossed it on the bed, then untucked his shirt.

He didn't believe her. No. He had to believe her. Please believe her. He was going to ruin everything.

He took off his shirt. His blubber hung over his pants so bad she couldn't tell if he wore a belt. Taking his jacket from the chair, he tossed it over the lion head before he came to her. "There we go, honey. Now, it's just you and me."

She put her mind somewhere else. Somewhere safe. Her lip trembled as the weight of him on the bed rolled her toward him.

"Now, where did we leave off last time?"

Braced, she let him yank her horizontal and reached with her arm as his clammy body pressed against her. She could smell smoke and alcohol as his hands prodded inside the bra and underwear.

She found it. She found his tie and she was going to do it. She took it and started thrashing like a fish. He'd expected it. That's why he liked her. Always be smarter than the bad guys, she reminded herself, as she wrapped the tie around his neck.

Startled, he stopped. It gave her enough time to scramble around to the back of him, twist the tie around his neck and pull until her arms shook. Lifting, he turned from side to side, reaching for her. But he was too fat, and she was too strong. She was like a savage and held on. Even when the muscles in her arms ached, she hung on. Even when he quit moving and fell forward, facedown.

Her arms shook, partly from the ache of what she just did and partly because she really did it. Her eyes jerked from his lifeless body to the door, to the covered lion head, to the window. Like she planned in her head a hundred times, she ran to the silk robe they made her wear. In the pocket, there were old slices of bread and some Cheetos.

She didn't even think to put on the robe; she just ran. Ran to the window, opened it and jumped to the ground, dropping the food. She picked up as much as she could before she sprinted to the trees, to anywhere away from the white house. The dogs were coming. It was okay, she reminded herself. She knew what to do.

She stopped and stuck one knee to the ground, holding out the food. The dogs wagged their tails when they spotted her. She'd worked for months gaining their trust, and she rewarded them with the bread and Cheetos before she headed for the tree closest to the fence.

Her feet were cold, but Duncan wrapped a blanket around them, warming them instantly.

The feel of his gentle hands woke her. She blinked and looked around. She wasn't outside, and she wasn't a young girl. She was home.

"You were dreaming."

"I remember."

The sadness in his eyes told her he knew what she'd been dreaming about. "You covered my feet."

"They were sticking out. You tossed and turned the blankets into a heap. I thought your toes might get cold."

She didn't wake up swinging. She'd dreamt the dream and didn't wake swinging her fists. She was going to make it. She would be all right. "How do you feel about getting a dog?"

Duncan smelled the cocktail of Nickie's shampoo and lavender-scented body lotion. It was a drug.

"The ends of your hair curl when they're wet." Still barefoot, she lifted on her toes and set her warm lips on his. She'd covered the large bump on her forehead with makeup. It wasn't going to fool anyone.

He linked fingers with her left hand and brought them into the small space between them. "I like this," he said and kissed the ring on her third finger.

Her free hand slithered around his back and she spoke in a low, sexy tone. "I heard couples are supposed to kiss for at least six seconds before they leave for work in the morning and again when they get home."

Dropping his lips to hers, he took in the soft warmth. His hands laced through the back of her hair, then he sank deeper. The curves of her female shape pressed against him, sending him from zero to sixty in seconds. When she pulled back, they were both breathing heavily. She pressed the back of her hand to her mouth.

"So the idea," he said between breaths, "is that leaving a man with a hard on makes a marriage stronger?"

"Seems like." She adjusted her blouse and shook her head. "I was planning to ask you something. A favor."

He lifted his brows. "Does it have anything to do with a four-legged animal?"

"Oh, well that too. But the Juracek case has got me in tangles. I was hoping you might take a look at it with fresh eyes."

"What does Miranda have to say about it?"

"What does the A.D.A. have to do with anything?" she said as she slid her bruised arm gingerly through her holster. She paused and craned to look in the compartment that held her plastic gloves. "Hey, did you put your GPS thingy in here, yet?"

"Possibly. And Miranda is the A.D.A."

She sighed before checking the safety on her Smith and Wesson. "She keeps trying to warn me that I don't have solid evidence yet."

"She doesn't know your record."

"She could look." Gently, she sat down on the settee. "And she's right. I have a body. I have about a dozen motives and suspects, but I don't even have a murder weapon."

"We could play hooky, get you naked, have...energetic sex in the pool, then let me work on your painting." He sighed, realizing she hadn't yet truly started healing from the car accident and that he wasn't speaking with the head on his shoulders. "Or I could take a look at your files. I have an eight o'clock. The rest is busy work I can juggle around."

"You'll stop in around ten, then?" She paused and

spun on her heels. "Unless you've already hacked into my files and checked it out."

"We're going to be married. I wouldn't do that without your knowledge. Although, I could take a look from the computer at my office."

She rolled her eyes as she placed her bag over her shoulder. "I hear nothing, see nothing. I appreciate the extra set of eyes."

She gave him a much shorter peck before heading for the stairs. Her feet stopped before she reached the door. He wondered when she would realize.

"About my car…."

"Take the Audi. There is, surprisingly, no snow in the forecast. It will be the most comfortable."

She shook her head as she turned the knob on the French doors. "Comfortable? The guys will never let me live this down."

CHAPTER 20

———◆ ◆ ◆ ◆———

Duncan owned the entire top floor of the tallest office building in downtown Northridge. Since that was only four stories, it wasn't as impressive as it sounded. His was the first car in the parking lot and entered through the back door.

Old man Jimmy's janitorial cart clicked over each ceramic square as Duncan headed for the elevator. "Good morning, Mr. Reed," Jimmy croaked in his decades-of-smoking voice. "Fine morning we're having now, isn't it?"

"That it is, Jimmy, and please call me Duncan."

"Will do, Mr. Reed." He nodded as he made his way down the hall.

Duncan grinned as he rode the elevator to the top. His part-time secretary would be here in forty-five. His appointment shortly after. It gave him enough time to dip into the Northridge Police Department database and take a look at Nickie's files on Juracek. He could hear his brother scolding him for hacking into a government site from work. He had permission, but that might not exactly count.

After setting his Keurig, he sat down to work. He

didn't know how to leave the intricate maze of trails and lack of entrails that Andy did, but his work wasn't incompetent.

The file stated time of death, stomach contents and a list of surviving loved ones. He leaned back, considering the fact that Juracek's family had been without a body for funeral proceedings all this time.

Reports from the questioning of each family member and person of interest were included. He soon understood what Nickie meant when she said the case had her in tangles. Everyone had a motive and seemingly the psychological state of mind as well as a weak alibi.

It was the photographs that most interested him. The body bag clearly said premeditated. It wasn't a clean hit. The three shots were sloppy; only one of them was a kill shot. And the circular wounds. He zoomed in on each, then compared them to the ones Leslie Rickard took of the wounds as the body lay on her stainless steel table.

They were perfect circles, or partials of. One had additional abrasions inside the circle. He zoomed closer yet and realized it was another circle.

As long as he was in, he would check if they extracted DNA from Zheng's blood samples yet and if they ran them through CODIS. It read, *In Process*.

He planned to ask her to let him study the scenes of Juracek's murder, both the actual murder and where the body had been recovered.

It seemed as if only a few moments had passed, but he heard the purposeful footsteps of his secretary, then checked the clock. Seven forty-five. Damn. He doubled back the way he'd gone in and shut down, just as Andy had taught him.

It was a terrible time for Nickie to ask Duncan in on

this. She knew he had to fly out as soon as he could. Luckily, when you own your own plane, you don't have set departure times. She felt like she needed to give him a disclaimer before entering the jewelry store. "I have to warn you," she said as he pulled to the side of the alley behind Jackson & Juracek Jewelers, "the missus isn't the most stable brick in the building."

The place was just opening for the day. Since the showroom wasn't where they'd be looking, she thought they didn't need to do this after hours. She wasn't sure yet if it was a good thing that Mrs. Juracek was the one doing the opening. Every time Nickie saw her, she was a mess and she said she hadn't worked the store in over a dozen years.

Nickie had gotten the okay from her captain to use Duncan as a resident specialist. Oddly, that process was becoming easier and easier. She supposed when you had a good track record, the boss trusted your judgment.

It was a warmer morning, but still below freezing. A dozen snowfalls had changed the landscape around where Juracek's body had been found. Duncan traded his leather driving gloves for his thicker ones, then cut the engine of his SUV. He got out and wandered to the dumpster. She followed and decided less was more and didn't ad-lib. The cool air soothed the still-purple bump on her head.

Squatting, he checked beneath the dumpster. Even without the yellow tape or chalk lines, he knew right where the body had been disposed of. So, he *had* read her files. He walked around the dumpster, down the alley and up. He looked toward the roof. It was nearly exactly what she had done six weeks ago.

"Is this is the door?" he asked, gesturing to one of the unmarked, steel doors that led to the alley. She nodded. He tried the knob, then rapped on the door.

"I told Mrs. Juracek we'd call when we were ready to come in. I don't think she'll open a door that doesn't have a peephole." She pulled out her cell and searched for the number.

"Jackson & Juracek Jewelers. How can I help you?" Mrs. Juracek's voice was clear, confident and sultry.

"Good morning, Sylvia. This is Detective Savage. My advisor and I are the ones knocking on your back door."

Her voice dropped several decibels. "I didn't hear any knocking. I'll be right there."

"Every time I've seen her, she's had a bad case of the red eye. I'm not sure if it's from the antidepressants or from crying or both. She's got motive. She's the only inheritor of the business at the death of her husband. There was loads of talk about passing it on to the stepson."

She looked to him and tilted her head. "You already know all of this."

He lifted a corner of his mouth as the door opened. Not to be picky, but it had been a solid five minutes since Nickie had called her.

"Oh, there you are. Come in."

Mrs. Juracek wore loads of makeup and a tight-fitting navy blue suit. She slumped as she walked.

She and Duncan followed her to the scene of the crime. The tape had been removed from the door leading to the J & JJ business office. The desk still stood with a hole in the corner. The bullet had been removed and sat in evidence.

Duncan entered the room, and did his thing where he stopped and looked around. It was like he was rolling a video feed of the area. Nickie assumed that was exactly what he was doing.

The missus fidgeted, checking the hallway often.

"Mr. Juracek was standing here." Nickie stood and faced the way the reenactment dictated he'd been placed and facing. "The bullet that entered and exited landed in this wooden desk...here." She walked over and pointed out the splintered hole.

With one foot out the door, Mrs. Juracek spoke in a squeak, "I should assist our newest staff with the front end."

"What do you keep in the safe?" Duncan asked her before she had a chance to escape.

Mrs. Juracek turned and focused on the built-in floor safe at the corner of the office. It looked like one of those mini-sewers where you could only put shit in and nothing out unless you had the combination, synchronized keys and possibly knew the secret dance.

"Not that one." He walked around the desk and gestured his hand toward the low paneled wall.

"Wait." Nickie almost yelled. She handed him a pair of gloves.

He put them on and ran his fingers around the outside of a single panel. It was at about his hip level and was one of a dozen matching panels that circled the room in a horizontal line.

"This is wainscoting."

Nickie figured he was talking to her and not Mrs. Juracek. He gestured with his plastic gloves to the bottom half of the wall. "See how the trim creating this panel is separated from the backing? The backing is a separate piece." His fingers continued around the perimeter of the frame thing, pulling and seemingly checking for weak spots.

Casually, Nickie glanced to judge Mrs. Juracek's reaction. She was back to looking either drugged or numb or both.

Pop. The panel opened like a mini-fridge, revealing

a metal door that had been hiding behind it. "Oh, dear," Mrs. Juracek exclaimed.

Oh, dear? Nickie was losing her patience with the widow.

She forced her voice to remain cooperative. "May we have the key, please, Sylvia?"

"I don't think I have a key."

"You don't *think* you have a key to a safe in your store?"

"I am telling you exactly that."

Mrs. Juracek seemed surprised enough. *Seemed* wasn't going to hold up in court. "Can you call your father, ma'am, and ask him about it?"

Her expression was thoughtful. "Hang on a minute." She left. Her heels clicked behind her.

"I can't believe you saw that." Nickie turned to Duncan. "I also can't believe I just said that."

"I've worked on furniture with my uncle long enough. It's not natural for the trim on a panel to be separated like this."

Mrs. Juracek came back with a large metal ring of keys. This could be a long morning. She skipped a few, then started with the smaller ones.

Looking around Mrs. Juracek's back, Nickie turned her eyes to Duncan, then shrugged. He was still analyzing, she could tell.

Click. The hinges squeaked as Mrs. Juracek pulled the small door, then gasped and clutched her chest. It was a shallow space, no bigger than a small P.O. Box. Nickie supposed many jewelers might have one. It made sense. A place to keep the better rocks, extra cash. But this one held just one thing. A nice, shiny gun. It looked like a Colt from this distance.

The safe came up clean. No prints. A safe in a business with no prints on the outside? Inside? Or on the gun? That alone told her it was the murder weapon. Forensics said the same was true for the gun and bullets. The make of the gun matched the one that killed Juracek, but Nickie still had to wait for a positive ID. The boys were going to get to play with shooting the Colt, then compare the shell casings with the ones taken out of the vic.

Nickie had decided it was time to turn up the heat and call in the old man for questioning. She pulled her Diet Coke from the door of the station's machine. It was hard enough to believe Mrs. Juracek had no idea about the safe, but Jackson? He owned the place long before the deceased came along. Twisting the top of her soda about a quarter turn, she closed her eyes and took in the sound of the sizzle. It was always good for a needed mental boost.

She headed back to her office, although she wanted to stop by reception and see if Fed Ex had delivered her files. But, the results on Zheng's DNA search were in. She couldn't tackle both that and her mysterious FBI file plus keep herself from taking out her frustrations on the nearest colleague or perp. Knowing your issues was half the battle. She smiled, taking a long swig as she made her way to her office.

The part-time paper-pusher who used the desk outside of Nickie's office was the perfect kind of colleague for taking out frustrations. On the corner of the desk sat a tabloid. It had been pushed off the edge far enough that Nickie would have to be blind to miss it. Duncan was on the cover in the bottom-right corner. He was lip-locked with that Coral Francesca woman. The actress's hand was plastered to his ass. It was at the fundraiser thing he went to two trips ago in L.A. If little miss nosy wanted Nickie to have a reaction, she should have picked a paparazzi shot that didn't so obviously depict Duncan in a situation he didn't want to be in.

She sat down to dig through the DNA results as her phone buzzed. Her heart did a small jump when she saw the text was from Duncan. 'landed safely. see you tomorrow evening.'

She planned to stay at her town house that night. It would give her time to pack.

The results on Zheng were several pages long. That was a good sign and a bad one. His DNA was a match. It was good for her investigation. And it was just plain sad.

He was a match to evidence found on three dead girls. Each case was over ten years old. She printed each. Nothing in ten years? He must have become more careful as he got older or else he had others doing his dirty work for him for the past ten years.

No. Her fingers gripped the sides of her desk. He would want to do it himself.

Darkness covered her as she adjusted her glasses and looked at the pictures. They were so young. Had she looked like that? How could a man possibly get off on a child? The freaks were always sorry when they were caught. None ever came forward on their own. Every single perp seemed to use the abused-as-a-child excuse. Nickie didn't buy it. She was abused as a child and didn't have a need to hurt children.

Two of the girls had his hair on them, one his skin beneath her fingernails. Good for you, Nickie thought of the girl who took a piece of him with her on her way down. Each showed signs of a struggle. Defensive wounds on their forearms, several blows to their heads. It wasn't always that way, she remembered. Some died from a single gunshot wound. Those were usually the ones who were getting too old or started showing physical effects from the drugs that were pumped into them. And those were probably the ones difficult to pin on him. No DNA. The ones that went down hard were the ones used as examples to scare the hell out of everyone else.

Her intercom light flashed, making her jump.

"Savage," she answered.

"We've got Mr. Jackson in interrogation one for you."

"I'll be right there."

She leaned back in her chair and stretched the bruises that were yellowing but sore as hell and seemed to cover every inch of her body. Good cop or bad cop? She decided to play it by ear.

They left him alone in the room as Eddy watched on the other side of the one-way glass. He wore an old school, tailored, three-piece suit, and he had unbuttoned the jacket.

"Good afternoon, Mr. Jackson." She came in and stood across from him at the stainless steel table. "Thank you for coming. Can I offer you some coffee?"

"No, thank you, Detective. I need to get back to work. What is this about?"

Nickie sat down gently in the chair at the other side of the table and folded her hands in her lap. "Mrs. Juracek hasn't had a chance to get ahold of you?"

"No." He looked like he might pop out of his chair. "Did you find the person who did this to William?"

"I'm afraid not, but we found a gun."

His eyes darted to hers. "You have the murder weapon?"

No need to argue over semantics. "The safe in your office."

"You mean the office at the store?"

She nodded.

"That's impossible. A gun couldn't fit into the slot.

It's made for bills and sometimes padded envelopes holding exquisite jewels. It can't be opened unless two people are present—"

"The other safe."

He looked around like he was searching for something. "You mean the one in the wall?"

"Sylvia didn't mention that we discovered it?"

"No, why would she?" His eyes grew large. "That's where you found the murder weapon?"

She set her folded hands on the table and sat forward in her chair. "We need your help. Tell me why you didn't mention the safe or the gun when we questioned you before?"

"That old thing?"

Yep. That old thing.

"The safe is useless. Even you could pull the door off with your hands."

She let the chauvinist comment pass. "The gun."

"Why would there be...? Who would put...?" His eyes turned back to her. "You don't think I...?"

"This is all routine. You understand. We'd like to get a DNA sample from you. It's a simple cheek swab. And fingerprints, if you would. It can all be done before you leave."

"I. Will. Not." He thrust his pointed finger toward her as he said each word, then stood and staggered before he caught his balance. "This is why you called me down here? Are you desperate? Accusing innocent people because you can't solve this case?" He limped to the door. "Am I a prisoner? Or can I leave?"

"You are free to go."

Mrs. Juracek was next.

CHAPTER 21

Nickie forced herself to ride coach. The seat was dirt cheap. Points for her. It was okay that she couldn't straighten her legs. The trip was under two hours. It didn't matter that her armrest was busted and flipped open every time she touched it.

But the dude next to her who kept crossing the invisible line separating their air space with his elbow was about to get his ass kicked. This was all Duncan's fault. She didn't know about first class or what it was like to ride in a private plane until he came along. Drive an Audi? Ride first class? She absolutely would not let him make her soft.

Where was that stewardess with the basket of complimentary snacks?

She lifted a hand to the one who walked by, her crisp navy blue suit brushing Nickie's shoulder in the cramped space. "Excuse me, miss." Discreetly, Nickie flashed her badge. Maybe she could turn slightly soft. "I have an appointment I need to get to. I'll need to get off first when we land."

The gal was actually contemplating turning her down?

"We don't have notifica—"

"Would you like me to speak with your supervisor?" Nickie interrupted.

"We generally let first class out—"

"Fine. After first class." All Duncan's fault.

She really wanted to do the Mrs. Juracek interrogation herself. Eddy was a fine detective. He would do a good job, but Nickie liked to do things herself. It was part of her doesn't-play-well-with-others. It had always worked for her.

Today was important. She had questions no one else could answer. It didn't mean he *would* answer. Her former captain spent his days in one of the most maximum-security federal prisons in the country. Housed interestingly in the college town of Terre Haute, Indiana.

It was an easy trip. Over and back, she convinced herself. No carryon bags. No overnight. Just her briefcase filled with her tablet and the files she may or may not need to shove in Tanner's face.

She'd personally gotten him an individual cell. It wasn't exactly solitary confinement. More like a keep-the-inmates-from-using-the-pedophile-as-a-shower-toy individual cell. They had an understanding, she and Tanner. She kept him safe, and he told her what she wanted to know.

Usually.

She wished she could check on Eddy, but there was no way she was going to pay money for Wi-Fi. Who couldn't go for two hours without using their phone? She might possibly have been convincing herself rather than complaining.

She'd called the prison ahead of time. The penitentiary would have Tanner ready when she arrived. They'd been more than helpful during her past visits. She despised meeting with Tanner. It was a necessary evil.

The image of him handcuffed and shackled to a chair that was dead-bolted to the floor helped.

Duncan had spent three days and nights at home working on the impromptu painting of his detective. It put him behind schedule. Cause and effect. Behavior and consequences. It may have been worth it but did little to ease his schedule. To add insult to injury, the painting of her sat unfinished on his easel in Northridge.

She received the DNA results from Zheng. Her files from the FBI were en route. He should be with her. He had no closure from the unfinished painting, and he should be with his detective.

Sitting in his hotel suite, he put the finishing touches on his final painting of Sophia Colour. She was a picturesque woman. Perfect nose, high cheekbones. Her hair extensions blended seamlessly, draping her hair in thick, silky, black waves.

She was an easy subject to paint. She had personality and expression. The painting he worked on was for her agent's office. It wasn't four-foot-by-eight like the ones he'd completed for so many in L.A. She stood facing away from the camera in a bright turquoise, floor-length gown with an open back. She was one of the few actresses in Hollywood he truly enjoyed spending time with.

She wasn't his detective.

His detective was checking out a rental car in Indianapolis right about then. He checked the time on his phone, adjusted over time zones and corrected his thoughts. She was probably arriving at the prison. She was going to face the man who held her captive in the back of a truck. Tanner had probably been heading to Seneca Lake in order to attach weights to her ankles and sink her to the bottom at the time he was captured.

It wasn't that she couldn't take care of herself. She'd scoffed at the idea of taking his plane, mumbling something about what the officers at work would say about it. It was that she shouldn't have to do this alone.

He checked his phone again for a text letting him know she landed safely. The idea of riding coach made him shiver. If they were going to be a married couple, they would need to come to an agreement regarding sending a message when the other didn't crash into a fiery ball and instead landed safely after a flight on a commercial plane. He'd checked the flight status and saw that it reached Indy. That wasn't the point.

The view out his window was of smog and rush hour traffic. Not exactly pristine working conditions. He finished with his smallest strokes—size 000 brushes—to create the final, most intricate of details. His goal was for viewers to second-guess whether his work was a portrait or a photograph. After the final touches, he had just enough drying time to deliver the piece to Sophia's agent the following day.

His phone buzzed, indicating a text. He nearly dropped it as he checked the screen. Except it wasn't Nickie. It was his aunt?

'check the cover of the daily rich and famous'

The cover? Ah. A shot from the fundraiser. Good, he thought with the caution of a person experienced with tabloids. Sophia deserved the exposure, even if it was from a shady magazine such as *The Daily Rich and Famous*. Brie enjoyed the times his picture showed up on the arm of one of his clients. She seemed more than pleased that his clients were no longer love interests. Those times seemed long ago, he thought, as he booted his tablet.

He poured a fresh cup of coffee as the Internet connected. His detective was far from rich or famous. His memory brushed a quick hint of her lavender scent through his mind. He smiled and decided he was going to give her hell for not letting him know she'd landed safely.

Plugging *The Daily Rich and Famous* into the search engine, he came up with the one of Johnny and Bebe Lyons. Apparently, they publically announced an open marriage and were looking for couples with similar beliefs. Duncan knew the couple well enough to know nothing could be further from the truth.

His coffee tipped and ran across the desk in a steady stream to the floor. He couldn't bring himself to reach for a napkin with his eyes stuck on the screen. He remembered the *photographer* who took the picture. He just didn't remember it this way. No. No, no, no.

He stood and clutched his cell. Dialing Nickie's number, he grabbed a handful of hair as he stared at the picture of him and Coral Francesca embraced in a kiss with her hand on his backside. The caption read, 'Oscar award-winning Coral Francesca reminisces with artist ex Duncan Reed.'

"Nickie. Answer," he yelled as he darted his eyes around the room. Hanging up, he thumbed through his contacts until he found his pilot's number.

As he held the phone between his ear and shoulder, he packed his things.

"Andrew, this is Duncan. How fast can we get airborne?"

"Today, sir?"

"Yes. Tell me you can make it work."

"The little lady will be glad to have me home early, sir. I'll make the arrangements and contact you when I have an estimate on our departure clearance."

His pilot was a good man. Duncan would
compensate him accordingly for the last-minute
change.

His next call was to Sophia's agent. "Good day,
Duncan." He must have read his caller ID. "You
sound rushed. You're going to have the painting here,
yes? I have people coming."

"Yes, yes, it will be ready, but it needs drying time,
and I have to get home. I've booked my hotel room
for another night. You'll have to come and pick it up
here."

"Pick it up? I'm busy. Why can't you bring it by on
your way?"

"Alex, I have an emergency. It needs to dry. I'm
leaving."

The prison guard escort was waiting for Nickie after
the first check-in and search. "You'll need to leave
your personal belongings here, Detective. You
understand."

She did understand and unfortunately was getting
accustomed to the routine. "Are you the one taking
me back?"

"Yes, I am."

She emptied her pockets and left her briefcase,
taking only her manila file folder with her. "Do you
need to look through this?" she asked, holding out the
file.

The guard shook his head. No file search? This was
new. She must be getting a good rep around here.

"I need to give you a heads up, Detective. Some of
the guards don't like that Tanner has his own cell."

Then again, maybe not. "I get that. He's still a key
witness and a source to an ongoing investigation." She
wouldn't mention that she only learned the
investigation was ongoing a few days ago. "I hope

you understand."

"Ain't no skin off my back."

They put Tanner in one of the rooms they'd met in before. He looked thinner each time she saw him. But his color was still good and his face and arms were clear of the defensive wounds and abrasions from the time he had been placed with a roommate and ate with the rest of the prisoners.

He sat in a metal chair at a metal desk. His hands were free of cuffs, which told her he'd been keeping his nose clean.

"No greeting, Captain?" She turned her chair backward and slung her leg over the top. "I'm hurt."

He didn't look like this break in his routine was a welcomed distraction.

"How's life, Tanner? Are you getting rehabilitated and all that?"

"I'm in for life, no chance for parole. I don't need to rehabilitate."

"You have a point. What about the cell, then? Are you all cozy? I see you haven't had anyone kick your ass lately. Or worse." She smiled. It couldn't be helped.

He obviously wasn't interested in their usual bantering. And here she'd flown all the way out. Riding coach.

"You told me Zheng was beyond you. I want to know how far beyond you."

"I don't like to be manipulated."

"Says the man who manipulated children for nearly thirty years. How far?"

"I heard you took in Moody." He shook his head like he was impressed.

"Moody and each and every one of the girls," she corrected.

He leaned forward like a kid who couldn't wait to tell a secret. The guard stepped forward at his proximity but Tanner didn't back off. He looked back and forth from one of her eyes to the other. His smile sent a chill down her spine. "There's always more where they came from." He lifted his brows up and down once.

There was more to what he just said. She could taste it in the damp air. Of course, there were more girls. Did he mean more girls to abduct? Or was he referring to the mind boggling number of children that were sold into sex trafficking every day? It was with great force that she made her lips ask the question she somehow, somewhere thought she already knew the answer to.

It came out in a whisper…a choked whisper. "Where?"

He leaned away from her and slung his arm on the back of his chair. He hadn't looked so smug since his days at the station. Reflexively, her heart started beating like it was trying to get out of her chest. She knew this answer, but she couldn't let it come to fruition in her mind.

Shrugging, he stuck a finger in his mouth and picked at his teeth. "Arkansas, Washington State. Everywhere, Nick."

Zheng wasn't there the night they took down the operation at Moody's white house. Of course. In an obvious gesture her shoulders fell. She didn't care that it brought pleasure to Tanner. It was difficult to make her dry lips move. "Are you telling me Zheng has more groups of girls?" she croaked. The look on her face was probably that of a little girl. A little girl who had been beaten until all of her will was gone.

"You're kinda slow, Nick." His laugh was deep and guttural. "You just getting that now?"

The next question was like a painful fever sore in the back of her mouth. One she had to touch with her tongue. "How many?"

He rubbed his nose with the side of his thumb. "Hard telling."

This time, she growled. "Estimate."

"Ten? A dozen maybe?"

The muscles in her face fell, and her mouth opened into a little 'o.'

He smiled. "Give it up, little girl. Go back to your little town. Find your little jewelry store perp. Go home to your boyfriend. Nice rock, by the way."

The room became cold, damn cold. She refused to wrap her arms around her for warmth. Or to hide her left hand. In fact, she forced herself to lift it, ring facing out and held up two fingers. "Arkansas and Washington state. Where else?"

He shrugged.

"That answer's not going to keep you in isolation."

"I dunno. They move around a lot. I just had to keep tabs on you."

Her hands shook and heat built at the back of her neck. "That's right. You were just the low-level john working off his addiction, you sick motherfucker. I'll find Juracek's killer, all right. And I'll put him away just like I did you." Her chest rose and fell like she'd finished a race.

"Temper, Nick. You're losing your edge. Desperate makes mistakes. Did I teach you nothing?"

CHAPTER 22

The town house was chilly. Since Nickie left her house shoes at Duncan's, she kept on her coat and boots as she turned up the thermostat and did a quick search. No sign that the window locking bars had been tampered with. If Zheng truly ran ten to twelve groups of girls, he had bigger issues to address than a small town detective.

Taking a cleansing breath, she tried to make sense of it all. She surveyed her place. Not much here. Not because she'd moved nearly everything to Duncan's house. The only things there were most of her clothes and bathroom stuff. Well, and her dry beans, spices, canned vegetables, and protein bars. She simply didn't have a lot of things.

Cops don't make much money, she rationalized as she checked each room. No, that wasn't it. She wasn't a homemaker. None of it seemed to matter.

Taking down Zheng's group of girls had been euphoric. It all seemed distant and less significant now. Surprisingly, the files the FBI sent her may serve as a needed distraction. She would take the time to sit down and comb through them. Tomorrow. Or maybe the next day.

The last room she checked was the kitchen. "All clear," she whispered.

Chicken noodle soup and saltines for dinner. As it heated on the stove, she checked her phone and decided the place had warmed enough to shed the coat. Duncan had texted her earlier in the day, asking where she was sleeping that night. Did he still view her as a flight risk? When she gave him her answer, she expected a responding text arguing that his house was their house. Instead, she got nada. Get a grip, Savage.

The soup began to steam, and she took down a cereal bowl. A few crushed crackers in the bottom and she had the perfect dinner for mulling over the loads of crap that were screwing with her head.

The knock on her door made her jump nearly out of her seat. Since when did she jump at knocks on a door? She'd just left Eddy. Duncan was in L.A. Tiptoeing to the foyer, she slipped her gun from the holster as it hung from her coat rack, then took it off safety. Glancing through the peephole, she gaped for a solid ten seconds, wondering if she was in an alternate universe.

It was Duncan. He just left for L.A. yesterday. The L.A. that was on the other side of the country. He texted her when he landed. Yanking open the door, she said, "What are you—?"

"I can explain."

"That's good, because either you have the ability to apparate or you stayed in L.A. for about ten hours."

"You don't know." He said it like a statement. Either way, she wasn't following his meaning.

"Apparently, there are a lot of things I don't know, but which thing do you mean exactly?" Shit. The soup. She turned for the kitchen. "My soup is going to boil over. Why did you cut your trip so short?"

An arm came from behind her and beat her to the knob. She turned to find his hands gripping the sides of the stove, his face an inch from hers. His scent filled her, making her eyes drift closed. She forgot about dinner, Tanner and the file in her briefcase.

"I need you to hear me out."

Her eyes opened. She found his dilated and all too sincere.

Pushing away from her, he started pacing. "It's not what it looks like." His hands ran over his face, through his hair, then rested on the top of his head. He looked like Andy when he did that.

"You're sort of freaking me out," she said and folded her arms over her chest.

"No." He shook his head.

"Excuse me. Earth to Duncan. Are you losing it on me here in my kitchen?"

She was sure he didn't hear her.

"That's wrong. It's backward. I was." He looked back at her with his brows dug deeply over his eyes. "It was at the fundraiser, the one in L.A. the last time I went."

Ah. The muscles in her face relaxed as she realized where he was going with this. A much nicer woman would stop him.

"The paparazzo were there. Of course. There is a picture. I was there for Sophia. No, that sounds all wrong."

She couldn't take it anymore. He didn't even sound like himself. "If Coral touches your ass when we're married, I'm going to break every finger in her Oscar award-winning hands."

He stopped pacing. That was a good thing anyway.

"You know?" he asked.

"I saw the picture in *The Daily Rich and Famous*, if that's what you're getting at."

"But I was kissing Coral Francesca. Her hands were on my ass."

Not that this was all about Nickie, but it sure was a pleasant distraction. "Must I repeat my threat? And do you think I'm going to go all jealous nutso every time some paparazzi grabs a shot of a bimbo throwing herself at you?"

"But—"

"You had your hand on her wrist. I expect she didn't like it too much when you peeled her fingers from your tight, muscular, gorgeous ass." She reached both hands around him and took hold just to make sure it was still tight and muscular.

Dropping his forehead to hers, he squeezed his eyes shut. The muscles beneath her fingers seemed to relax as he expelled a long, deep breath. "I can't ever lose you." He moved his forehead from side to side against hers. "I thought—"

"You could have called." Men hated to be interrupted. Sometimes, it made it all the more necessary. "We're going to have to have a serious talk about this issue of yours." She moved her hands to the sides of his face. His eyes had turned nearly oynx like they did when he worked himself up about something.

Talk could wait. Zheng could wait. So could dinner and the FBI files. She smirked as she threw his catch phrase at him. "I haven't seen you naked in three days."

His sexy lips turned into a grin. The small lines that so rarely radiated from the corners of his eyes made him look smart and sexy.

He kissed her temple. "I'm in love with you." Painfully slow, he lowered his lips to hers. The kiss was long and careful. Did he sense something had changed? Her head spun and her heart thumped.

"Shall we eat?" he asked as he drizzled his lips along her cheek and jaw.

She didn't tell it to, but her head shook quickly back and forth before falling back, inviting him to her neck. Long, strong arms scooped her up.

"I'm going to make love to you in a bed." He said it like an objective as he carried her toward her bedroom. "Under the sheets."

Although his body was warm against hers, she still shivered at his declaration.

As they reached the side of the bed, he kissed her once more before releasing her to the floor. He went to turn down the sheets, and she wrapped her arms around him. He turned into her as she pulled his shirt from his pants. He grabbed her wrists. "Bed. Covers."

She bit her lip and lifted a knee, reaching for the side of the mattress, but he scooped her up again and gradually laid her down. They took lazy turns exploring and caressing with lips and hands. She selfishly used him as she sank into a warm cocoon of escape.

There was no internal debate in Duncan's mind or body. He released each button and zipper purposely with the greatest of attention, then followed the lines of newly exposed flesh with his lips. Her body responded to his pace with equal serenity as if they were dancing a slow waltz—very different from their usual tango frenzy. They rotated and turned as they took their time relearning each other's bodies with touch and tongue.

Her skin quivered beneath his patient touch. His fingers dipped, barely brushing over her, and she instantly responded, crying out promises of forever. Even through her aftershocks, she rotated again, drawing lazy lines over him with her teeth and body.

He sent her over again and then again, until she tossed the sheets and blankets to the floor, sucking air and clutching a fist to the center of her chest.

As he grinned and reached for her again, it was her turn to grab his wrists. "What," she said, panting, "do you think I am?" As if she'd just run a marathon, her breath labored and she climbed over him, hovering cruelly. In contrast to her heaving chest, her lips curled into an evil grin.

Instinctively, he took hold of her hips and lowered her around him. The shock to his system left him clutching her sides. His vision blurred. When his focus returned, his Nickie was there, watching with steel gray eyes that were drunk with need. She held her arms out, and he answered her request by taking hold and linking their fingers together. They used their arms for purchase as they began to sink and move in a pace that grew symbiotically.

Her mesmerizing body moved over him. The lines of her face, the intoxicating droop of her eyes. Every part of her clutched him tighter as she neared her final peak.

"Nickie," he groaned and spilled over the edge. Everything around him disappeared. He pulled her deeper and her thighs contracted around him. His Nickie. He couldn't stop. She didn't stop. They moved together right up to the last ounce of pleasure, clutching fingers and bodies slick with sweat.

She fell on top of him like the dead. Her arms lay awkwardly to the sides, her chest heaving in long, deep breaths. "Welcome." She heaved a few more breaths of air. "Home."

The only light was the one coming from the ice maker on Nickie's refrigerator. Duncan hadn't eaten since yesterday's lunch, and his stomach rebelled.

Greek yogurt, Naked Juice, a drawer full of green things and hard-boiled eggs. She should be as thin as Sophia for what she ate. Thankfully, she wasn't.

Eggs. The raw kind. He pulled out the carton, some of her low fat cheese, some green and red peppers that still had some stiffness to them, mushrooms, skim milk, and butter. He would make himself an enormous omelet. Add some toast and possibly some of the juice and he might have a decent meal.

There was something she wasn't telling him. Something bigger than an overly confident actress who couldn't keep her hands to herself.

He flipped on the light above the stove and starting beating the eggs. Three should do it. The sudden burst of light didn't make him jump, but it did make him want to hit the bulb with the whisk hard enough to break it into several pieces.

"You're naked in my kitchen."

He kept beating and turned to her. "My robe is at home." Unfortunately, hers was on her body.

She tossed him his boxer briefs.

"Put these on, at least. I can't focus on eating—" She wandered over and surveyed her counter. "—an omelet with you naked."

As he pulled on his boxers, she bumped him with her hip and picked up his whisk. "Mind if I add a few eggs?"

"Please do," he said as he pulled her cutting board from the cabinet below and started chopping peppers. The smells of food and his woman began to wake him enough to forgive the light. "I flew from L.A., because I assumed you would think—"

"You didn't trust me."

"This was supposed to be a discussion about you trusting *me*, not the other way around, but you're right. I should have called. I was frightened I might lose you." The fear may be relieved, but the concern over the worry lines on her forehead was not. "I'm not used to feeling helpless. I didn't want to discuss it over the phone and certainly not through texting."

"It's going to happen again, you know."

"Another thing I should be telling you, not the other way around."

"You're going to need to get over it."

He shook his head. "Here's my proposal. You agree to text me when you arrive in out-of-town locations, especially ones that require an airplane, and I'll agree to communicate with you regarding any insecurity going on in my head instead of flying across the country."

She poured the egg mixture into two pans, and he sprinkled the ingredients. Then, she turned to him and held out a hand. He took it, and they shook. Without letting go of her fingers, he traced her knuckles with his thumb. "Now for what's bothering you."

Her lungs expanded fully before she exhaled.

Releasing her hand, he moved his to the dark circles beneath her eyes, tracing them with his fingers. The aroma of omelets filled the kitchen. She turned from him and set the table. He poured the juice.

"You're hungry," she said without looking him the eye. "You should eat."

The worry grew, making it impossible to think of food. "Is it the FBI?"

"The FBI seems like days ago."

"It was days ago."

"Only two. And a half." She placed salt and pepper on the table.

"Stop." He took her wrists this time, locking them together between his hands. Her eyes clamped shut, but she didn't fight him. Taking her hands, he shifted to hold them by just her fingers. He curled the ones on her left hand, kissing his ring. "I'm here for you. For the rest of our lives."

He led her to one of her kitchen chairs, then turned the heat to low. They sat in silence and he swore the circles darkened before his eyes.

"It's been a big few days," she started. "I'm still taking it in." A small smile erupted at the corners of her mouth, but it didn't reach her eyes. "Two thousand yards in your pool didn't even help."

"You swam in our pool? Alone?" In the house where Zheng had been most likely been keeping an eye? "With Zheng after you?"

She shrugged. "I'm not so sure he's really concerned about me after all."

He leaned back and gave her time.

"I should have realized…I mean why else would he be absent the night we took down the white house?" Her tortured gray eyes turned to him. He hoped she saw warmth in his. "Tanner told me there are more groups of girls. A lot more."

Oh. It took his mind some time to grasp. He could only imagine—or at least empathize with—her reservations in sharing this. It changed everything.

"Strong and Lewis sold out to the other side. They're in an undisclosed location. Hurst and Goodrich told me they found a file on me. It was more than the one you and Andy found. Supposedly, it included the details from the time of my escape to now. Fifteen years."

Strong and Lewis sold out to the other side. It made sense and wasn't something he would be forgetting any time soon even without his eidetic memory.

"I was a fool for thinking he would have just the single group of girls. Not after doing this for sixteen years."

He couldn't grasp this. Not even with all the extra

space an eidetic memory allowed. "How do you continue to trust people?" He shook his head wanting nothing more than to take away her pain.

She didn't look puzzled. She knew exactly what he referred to, and instead, stood and folded the omelets, then popped some bread in the toaster.

"A good man reminded me once of who I can trust." She smiled warmly and leaned down to kiss him once on the lips. "You, Dave, Gloria. Andy, Rose, Gil. That's a lot of people I have in my life. I'm not so bad off. I just need some time to get used to this bigger picture." Her brows sunk low and her chin turned to the side like she'd been slapped. "An appreciative woman would say Gloria saved me. Not that she didn't. But I do it for the girls. You saw them. They are so young. And now it looks like they are still out there. There will always be girls out there who need me. The rest is water over the bridge." She looked to the ceiling. "Or is that under the bridge?"

"Where is this file?"

"You have a one track mind."

"Yes, and it is you." He stood next to her at the stove and placed his hand on her cheek. Moisture in her eyes began to pool.

"It's in my briefcase."

"Here?"

She nodded.

"Have you looked through it?"

She shook her head.

"Do you have a reason there is a file that was kept by crooked FBI special agents that is sitting untouched in your briefcase?"

"I plead the fifth."

CHAPTER 23

"I see. Shall we look through the file together?" Carefully, Duncan linked his tense fingers with hers. He couldn't think of a single time before now that Nickie's had been cold and clammy.

"Onward." Nickie smiled weakly. "It's my new motto."

They took their time. Buttered the toast, placed the steamy egg masterpieces on the plates and situated themselves at her small table in the middle of the night, her in her robe and him his boxers.

The file was huge yet organized, all papers ordered chronologically.

She scooted her chair closer to his. The file rested between the plates that sat at the edge of their private circle.

The first several pages listed each of the foster homes she either was kicked out of or ran away from. She should not have to relive this. The arrangement to have her drugged, taken from her final placement in Maryland to an unsuspecting Gloria.

She yawned and stretched, then craned her neck. "They have my high school grades? That's just creepy as hell."

It was more than creepy. It was more than illegal. Someone was going to pay.

"You okay?" she asked.

She should not have to be asking that. He forced a smile and nodded.

Her college records, the police academy. Her first job as a cop in Liberty. The omelets were long gone by the time they reached her transfer to Northridge. They'd moved and sat together on the couch with the papers spread over her coffee table. The light in here was softer and, as the windows faced the east, was beginning to show signs of sunrise.

Tanner had been assigned to keep an eye on her.

"He told me he drew the short straw."

"I should have killed him when I had the chance."

"And make me miss out on all of our cozy prison visits? Psht."

She was joking. She was joking like she often did at times like this. He needed desperately to crush something, and she was making jokes.

"Look, there is information in here about when I took on your aunt's case. Zheng chose to put me in a small town, not expecting I would get in the middle of everything between her and Tanner. Not smart."

He stood and paced.

"You wanna take a break?"

Yes. "No."

Her head dipped closer to the coffee table before she snatched a page and pulled it to her face.

He didn't ask, but sat next to her and leaned toward the paper. "I don't see anything. Tell me."

He felt the heavy sigh from her shoulders and watched as her lids closed. Her chin dropped to her chest as she handed the paper to him.

It was like most of the other pages. It listed bits of pertinent correspondence copied and pasted from her emails and text messages. He didn't see it, damn it. She stood and laced her fingers over her head and through her hair.

"Who?" she asked the air.

The date stamp. There was a correspondence from someone on the inside updating Strong and Lewis on Nickie. It was dated after Tanner went to prison.

"Someone at the station." He said it to himself.

She chanted as she paced. "Don't let it be Dave. I can't deal if it's Dave."

"It's not." He stood and grabbed her forearms, making her stop and look at him. "You just said you know you can trust him. It's not," he said louder. "He's been friends with my uncle since high school. Rose is his step-daughter. His wife works at homeless shelters. He loves you."

Tears gathered in her eyes. "I can take anyone. Henery, Rickard, Vaughn. No Vaughn is too new. I could even deal with Eddy, but not Dave." She clasped her hands to his chest and laid her cheek to his shoulder. He wrapped his arms around her as far as they would go and held on.

The sun was up fully now. "It is a new day. We will get through this. I am here for you."

Her chest expanded fully against him, then expelled slowly. Jostling her shoulders, she stepped back. Her eyes were angry. So many had betrayed her, still betrayed her.

"I can take anyone," she repeated, then stabbed him in the chest with her finger three times as she said, "Just. Not. Dave."

"Holy shit." She put her hands on the sides of her head like she was trying to keep it from exploding. "Duncan."

What now? He waited.

"The marks on Juracek's chest. The circle things. There were three of them," she yelled as if triumphant.

"You have me so damned confused."

She rattled her hands as if she was shaking something from them.

"Go through that crazy superhero mind of yours."

He would try to take that as a compliment.

"Gerald Jackson walks with a limp. Do you remember seeing a cane at the store?"

"You think Jackson killed Juracek?" The marks on Juracek's chest could most definitely be from the bottom of a cane thrust into a chest.

"Cane? Store?" she repeated.

He nodded. "The umbrella stand near the back door."

Nickie had driven—Duncan in his SUV and her in his Audi—all the way to his house to use his pool. The Audi may be embarrassing, but until she could convince the insurance company to keep her on her policy, she used a black and white by day and the Audi by night. The two house thing was stupid enough, let alone the two car thing, she had to admit.

She got to work ridiculously early, before everyone except overnight reception. It wasn't like she was going to get anything else done with this new revelation she'd had. The graveyard guys were still out. She sat tapping pencils in her office, waiting for Dave to show up, waiting for Eddy so she could tell him what she discovered, waiting for the okay to call Jackson back in here, hopefully in handcuffs. She was also trying to ignore the fact that someone who worked within these walls was stabbing her in the back every chance he got.

The workout had done little to burn off the buzz running through her body. Even minus a night's sleep, the last thing she needed was caffeine. She made her way to the soda machine regardless. She knew what Dave was going to say. It was circumstantial. Most canes had similar rubber foot patterns. But it was Jackson. She could get him to confess. She'd had almost two months to learn the ins and outs of this family, and she was sure she could get him to confess.

The Diet Coke was sold out. The horror. She recognized the thump of Dave's shoes. At six-foot-four, they were unmistakable. Without the soda, she hurried toward him. He paused at his door and lifted a brow to her.

"Early morning, Nick?"

"Yep."

"You need something?"

"Yep again."

His hair was damp and his tie still hung undone around his neck. "Who did it?"

"The Juracek case?" He always could read her when it came to their work. "What makes you think I know who did it?"

"You're bouncing."

She was not bouncing. Exactly. "What if I'm wrong?"

He gave her the look like that would be silly. Points for him. "Juracek had three gunshots and three red, circular marks."

He nodded as he turned on lamps and booted up his computer.

"I believe the circular marks were made from the end of a cane. Gerald Jackson walks with a pronounced limp."

Dave dropped in his chair and stared at her. "I'm not going to say this case has dragged on and you're grasping. You don't grasp. And you don't point fingers unless you're sure. But a limp? Talk to Vaughn before you make a move."

She threw her head back and let it lay along the top of the back of Dave's guest chair. "Not Vaughn. Anything but Vaughn."

"Jackson has no previous criminal record. Play nice."

This was worse than no Diet Coke.

"But he knew about the safe. Knew about the gun. It's been confirmed that bullets shot from the gun match the ones we pulled out of Juracek. It's the murder weapon. And he thrust his finger at me three times during interrogation. Three times."

"He thrust his finger? What about motive?"

Okay, it was starting to sound stupid even to her. "I have a hunch."

"What did you say?"

"I know, I know. Just give me a chance." She explained her theory on Jackson's motive. It made even more sense to her hearing it out loud.

"Vaughn first."

"Captain Nolan asked me to come see you?" Vaughn said it like it was half-question/half-irritation.

"Don't shoot the middleman, Vaughn. I don't like it any better than you do."

Vaughn stood in her burgundy suit and matching pumps in front of Nickie's desk. "I don't like being summoned." She said the last word with spite.

"I don't like answering to lawyers." Nickie refused to stand or offer her a seat.

"Listen, Savage. I'm not just a lawyer. I'm the assistant district attorney. In fact, in these parts, I'm *the* assistant district attorney. You need me. *Don't* piss me off."

Well, shit. After all that, Nickie was forced to respect her. Her day was going to hell.

"Sit down, would you?" Nickie offered. "I want to bend the rules a bit and need to know if it will hold up." It didn't even kill her to say the words.

Nickie went on to explain her list of evidence, as circumstantial as it was, to Miranda.

"I can crack him. I know I can. I just need the okay to bring him in and permission to possibly mislead, trick and lie to him while on police property." She went on to elaborate as Miranda nodded.

The A.D.A. took a deep breath. "The lobby is public. Go for it." She rose from Nickie's guest chair.

"Vaughn," Nickie called before she left. "Between us girls, you're a female in a building full of mostly men. That makes you fresh meat, and I don't mean for bitchy detectives."

Miranda sighed and sat back down. "You mean Eddy."

Ah. So, she wasn't completely stupid.

"I mean Lynx and Parker."

"Parker?"

"Yep. As a favor, I'm going to tell you that if you decide to dabble, it's a free country. Lynx is fine if you're looking for a roll. Parker is the real deal. Hurt him and I'll kill you in your sleep."

"It sounds like you're speaking from experience."

"Not with Parker, no. But Lynx? In fact, I say go with Lynx. It'll get him off my back."

"You're engaged, aren't you?"

"Yeah." It made her smile, damn it. Right there in front of the new girl. "Doesn't mean the fiancé and Lynx don't throw jabs at each other now and then, sometimes the kind that include fists."

"Good to know, although I don't mix work with…extracurriculars."

Not stupid at all. "Oh, and one last thing, Vaughn. Stop calling people by their first names. You're in a police station. It's embarrassing."

Nickie had Duncan cleared to be the one to stand by the entrance with a tray of mini-water bottles. It was the funniest damned sight she'd ever seen. Duncan Reed, who had graced the cover of a number of magazines. Granted they were tabloids, but still. There he stood, handing out bottles of water like he was on probation doing community service. She would owe him sex with outfits for this.

Parker took point at the security check. He was instructed to add bottled liquid to the list of things not allowed past the security checkpoint. Guns, knives and bottled water. It didn't have to make sense. Parker just had to enforce it with a straight face.

It would have been much more fun to be a fly on the wall in the lobby, but she needed to be ready upstairs. She thought of the discussion she and Duncan had about communication. He was right. If they were going to be a married couple, they needed to work on it. He needed to trust her, and she could admit she should remember to give him a heads up as to which part of the country she was in.

In Jackson's case, more was at stake than a plane ride across the country or a pissed off man who didn't hear from his girlfriend. It was murder. Overly confident, self-motivated murder.

She spotted Eddy as he escorted Jackson up. Eddy glanced her way and winked. Jackson turned toward interrogation one, and Eddy placed his hand on his elbow, steering him toward two. Jackson jerked his arm away and limped toward the right room.

Ten to twelve groups of girls were subjected to Zheng's torture. More people than Nickie could count had betrayed her. A woman lost her husband, a child her father. The world was a hard, hard place. The result wasn't going to allow for much peace, but she would do her best to at least find justice.

She needed Jackson off balance and let him wait to sweeten his frustration and suspicion. For a solid hour, she did what she never thought she would need to do. She used her personal tablet via satellite to do background checks on each and every person at the station who had been there since Tanner was captain. Everyone except Dave. He was family. She had to draw the line somewhere.

George Henery was an OCD poster child and an excellent sketch artist. Leslie Rickard may have been aloof and too smart to be human, but she was solid. Or she seemed to be. Eddy was her partner, although she would never say that out loud. He cared about her and put his neck on the line for her more times than she could count. Bird was their bomb guy. Li was the profiler they brought in from the city when they needed to. It was all confusing. The desk bitch who liked to stir things up between Nickie and Duncan was too obvious.

When it had been enough time, she pushed away the confusion to do what she did best. Standing and stretching, she grabbed the file she prepared and made her way to interrogation two.

She opened the door and poked her head in using her softest voice. "Is there anything I can get you, Mr. Jackson? I remember you offered me cranberry juice. I made sure to stock some in the fridge in case you'd like some."

"Do you know how long I've been waiting here?" he yelled. "I don't want any damned juice."

Which was a good thing since she didn't have any damned juice.

"I want to know why I'm being held in here," he barked.

Nodding, she opened the door, carrying a walking cane that she then hung by the handle on the side of the table. "I know it seems like it's been a long time. I apologize. It gets busy here."

She placed the file on the table and sat carefully in the chair across from him. His eyes went to the cane, to the file and back again a few times. It wasn't his cane. Probably wasn't even the same color, but as Miranda so annoyingly reminded her, almost all canes had the same circle-inside-a-circle pattern at the bottom of the rubber gripping end.

"I'm afraid I have some news about your grandson."

His eyes opened wide. "Tommy? Is he okay?"

"Oh yes, sir. He's at work right now."

"He isn't scheduled to work today."

"Not the jewelry store, Mr. Jackson. I don't know how to tell you this, but Tommy has sort of a second life." She opened the file and took out a picture of the front of T & A's. Beneath the neon T & A's was the name Tommy and Angie's.

In great theatrics, Jackson moved his head from one side to the other. "Miss Savage, do you think there might be more than one Tommy in Northridge?"

Cracking her neck, she chanted in her head, 'I will not correct the title he used to address me. I will not correct the title he used to address me.'

Instead, she pulled out the next photo. It was the picture she took of Tommy with her cell phone when he sat in the bar booth with blood gushing from his nose from where she'd head butted him.

Jackson's face fell. "What happened to him?"

Oops. No need to confess she was the one who did

that. "I'm not sure, sir. T & A's is his bar. We're sure of this. I'm so sorry to have to be the one to tell you, and I'm afraid there's more."

"Tommy's a good boy."

She nodded. "I really think he is," she lied. "But I need to show you something." She took out the copy of the check made out to The Guest House. "This is the nickname of the bar Tommy owns."

"He does not own—"

"Well, it's the nickname people use for the bar called Tommy and Angie's." She turned over the check. On the back, it was signed, 'Pay to the order of SS8.'

Jackson's mouth fell open. He didn't try to hide it. She took the moment to take the cane and lay it across the table.

She let Tommy's SS8 habit and the cane sink in as she dumped more on him. Without opening the file completely, she slid one of the ME's shots of Juracek's chest. Three bullets and three circular wounds. She recalled the last time she had him in interrogation when he thrust his wrinkly finger at her three times.

"I know this is difficult to see. He was such a good man, but I need you to look here at these circular wounds. If you look closely." She bent over, putting her nose nearly to the photo. "You'll see there is a distinct circle inside of a circle." Tilting her head, she pulled back. "I suppose it might be a crescent inside of a crescent. Regardless, it is the markings of the end of a cane."

He was sure now; she could see it in his face. He knew she knew he was the accused. If she hadn't hit him with Tommy's nasty habit, he may have bolted on her. There would be nothing she could have done to stop him.

His wrinkled hands began to shake. "There must be thousands of canes with that pattern. Millions." Ugh. That was almost exactly what Vaughn had said.

Lifting her phone, she pretended to notice the time or get a text. It didn't really matter which. "Oh, I'm terribly sorry. Could you excuse me a moment, please?"

CHAPTER 24

She went to the door and cracked it open. Parker was there and handed Nickie a mini-water bottle zipped in a plastic bag. 'Where's Duncan,' she mouthed. Parker nodded toward the room on the other side of the one-way glass from interrogation two.

Duncan was watching. Now, she was just embarrassed. Biting her lip, she took the bag and made her way back to Jackson.

It really didn't matter if his fingerprints were on the bottle or not. They didn't find a single usable print anywhere on the body, the body bag, the safe, the gun, or unused bullets to compare them to. She just needed him to think they did.

He looked honestly pained. She could almost feel sorry for the guy if he hadn't premeditatedly put a handful of bullets into the chest of his daughter's husband.

"I wanted to let you know, it was a misunderstanding. Anyone would have thought so."

He remained statue still, his attention frozen on the water bottle.

"You see, your son-in-law wasn't visiting the girls

at SS8. It was Tommy. William met with one of the girls who Tommy *liked*. Her name is Wendy. She has a little girl. About the age of your granddaughter." The lies were coming out as smooth as silk now. "Wendy told us your son-in-law met with her to ask her questions about Tommy."

"No."

She took his trembling hand in both of hers. He didn't pull away. "I'm so sorry, sir. William was trying to save your grandson."

Sadly, this was the part that was the complete truth.

"He wanted Tommy to get his life together. Just like you do. To inherit Jackson & Juracek Jewelers, just like you wanted."

Jackson pulled his hand back and held both to his chest like a girl. "I didn't know." He sucked in air. "I thought William was…"

"It was a misunderstanding, I know. We all know. It could have happened to anyone. Get it out now."

He sucked in air. "I thought William was using prostitutes behind my Sylvia's back. I thought he was lying. Who knew what kind of deadly disease he could have brought home? You understand, don't you, Detective?"

She pulled out a tablet of paper and a pen from the file. "I do. Write it exactly the way it happened. Make sure to include the misunderstanding. I'm confident it will make a difference to the A.D.A." When hell freezes over.

Nickie sat at the largest, most stunning oak table she'd ever seen. Duncan and his uncle were bent over laughing at the story of when Andy and Rose were catching crawfish in Black Creek as children. Apparently, Andy was scared as hell of the pinchers, and Rose was picking them out, one after another, and tossing them into a bucket for dinner.

They spoke of the three other children Nathan and Brie had after adopting Duncan and Andy. One was graduating in a few months. The twin boys would end their second years in college.

William Juracek would never see his daughter graduate from anywhere. Nickie could still hear echoes of the sobs from Sylvia's and Renee's lips and see the honest regret in Tommy's eyes.

The Reed golden retriever sat next to Nickie with its snout on her leg. She scratched him between his eyes and watched as his lids threatened to drift closed. He was a gorgeous creature, but she had a soft spot for Rottweilers. She'd spent valuable time with the breed. They may have saved her life. Granted, her time with the breed was through a basement window as she fed them scraps of food, but it was important.

"The ring is stunning," Brie said to her. "May I see it?"

Nickie didn't know if she was supposed to take it off or hold it up like a debutant. Luckily, Brie took her hand and pulled it closer for a better look. "So strong and simple. It suits you. And the rock. Sheesh, Duncan. It's you."

They laughed, and life was good. She had much to do, but life was good. She was going to be okay. Her phone buzzed. She checked the number. It was a voice mail from Gloria. She smiled. Yes, life was good. "I'll be just a minute," she said, excusing herself and making her way to the front room.

As she swiped her phone open and chose her voice mail, she looked over at the painting of Niagara Falls Duncan had drawn when he was seven, or was it eight years old? He truly was a superhero.

"Nicole."

Tears instantly filled her eyes and panic in her heart.

Zheng. Zheng had Gloria's phone. She ducked from the view of the kitchen and squatted down on the hardwood floor. Biting the backs of her fingers, she listened until she tasted blood. "I have your Gloria. I expect you to come alone. Come to the southeast corner of the hospital. Now. You have fifteen minutes. Leave your phone where you are. I'll be able to triangulate its location."

Without telling them to do so, her feet moved softly. She slipped into the coat closet and took Duncan's keys from his pocket, then crept out the front door and pulled it closed gently. She took off in a full out sprint for the Audi, listening as she ran in the cold.

"On second thought, keep your phone and bring someone with you. I'd love to have an excuse to play with this delightful, caramel woman. Wouldn't we like to play, Gloria?" Nickie recognized the whimpers of the only true mother she'd ever known.

She tossed the phone in the trees, bolted to Duncan's Audi and put it in neutral. Rolling down the hill to the end of the street, she started the engine as she reached the Black Creek Bridge, then squealed the tires toward the hospital.

They all stood in the foyer, Red whimpering at the front door.

His uncle grabbed Duncan's shoulders. His fingers sank in until it hurt.

"Get it together," Nathan said. "Think."

"I can't think. I need to get home," he said as he searched his empty coat pockets. "I can find her cell from there."

The door was closed. She'd left without a word. After her phone call.

"You can find a cell phone?" Nathan asked as if he wasn't sure if Duncan was playing with a full deck of cards.

"Let Red out," Brie said. "He can find her trail."

Of course. Duncan opened the door. "Go on, boy. Find Nickie for me."

Red's feet sped down the drive to where Duncan had parked his car. His nose moved along the space void of snow and in the shape of the car. He seemed to find what he was looking for and sniffed in a straight line up the drive.

"No, boy. She's not this way. Red!" The dog ignored Duncan and kept sniffing low to the ground as he made his way up the side of the drive.

Duncan needed to get home to his equipment. His mind spun from taking Nathan's car to how fast he could locate the signal from her phone once he got home.

She wouldn't do this. Something wasn't right. His Nickie was in danger. He started for Nathan's car when Red took a detour into the trees. Was she in the trees? Duncan lifted his head and watched.

Red dug his nose in the snow and came up with something in his mouth. Wagging his tail and whining, he walked over to Brie, sat and spit out Nickie's phone.

Nathan's expression was pained as he looked to Duncan. Slowly, Duncan reached for the cell and brushed it clean. It was still working. He opened it to check her last text. The text was the one from him he'd sent the night before they met for dinner.

He changed to recent calls and found one from Gloria just fifteen minutes prior. Relief was short but intense. It was Gloria. She needed something. Okay. This would be okay. Was she sick? Someone in the family in an accident? Why didn't Nickie come tell him?

Waving his hands, Duncan breathed a sigh of relief.

"It's okay, everyone. I overreacted. We've been under a great deal of pressure recently. It was just Nickie's foster mom. I'll call and make sure everything's okay."

He pulled out his cell and punched in Gil's number. His hands were shaking. He must be cold. As casually as he could, he started back for the house as it rang, but then realized no one else was moving. Nathan, Brie, Andy. Rose with Andrew Jr. Even the dog stayed put, everyone having some silent conversation between the six of them.

Brows dropping, Duncan continued. Let them stand out in the cold for nothing if they wanted. The phone shook in his hands as it rang. This was nothing. "Gil, it's Duncan."

"A little early for a Sunday, Duncan. Is everything okay?"

"Fine, fine. Everything is fine. Nickie got a call from Gloria this morning. Just a few minutes ago, actually. She didn't mention what it was about and left suddenly. I was calling to see if you knew anything about it."

There was a pause. It wasn't long but gave Duncan too much time to think. He realized his feet had stopped, too.

"She didn't show up for morning Mass and doesn't answer her cell. I'm in the car on my way over to check on her now."

Duncan squatted down like a catcher at the plate, except this catcher dropped his head between his knees. He needed his equipment. Now. Standing, he let the blood rush to his head and make him dizzy as he took off toward the garage.

"Duncan!" He couldn't ever remember Nathan raising his voice to him before.

"Nickie's in trouble. I need your car. I need to go.

Now!"

"Let me get my coat. I'm coming with you."

"This is big." Duncan didn't have time for this. "It could be dangerous. I've got to go."

"You're going to wait," Nathan said, using the same tone minus the volume.

This was no time to be scolded like a high school boy. Duncan rubbed his hands over his face as he watched Andy jog to the house after him. "Where the hell does he think he's going?" Duncan asked Rose.

"I think they should take Red, too," she said. "He might be of help."

Nickie's hands shook so hard she could barely turn the steering wheel into the lane that led to the hospital. She had six minutes left and pulled over. Scanning the area, she couldn't find anything out of the ordinary. Duncan's GPS chip. She pulled her gun belt out from beneath her seat and secured it around her waist as she drove.

"Come on, Duncan," she begged. "I need you."

She inched to the southeast corner of the hospital with three minutes to spare. This didn't feel right. There was nothing here but the corner of a building. Snow-covered grass went for several yards between the brick corner and the parking lot. The back entrance was halfway down the length of the building. Time was running out. She needed more time.

Throwing her gearshift into park, she left the car running and got out. A man turned the corner wearing a waist-length jacket with the hood up. It wasn't him; she could tell. She walked his way regardless.

"Jimbo?" His face looked like meatloaf, fresh cuts and bright red swollen lips, cheeks and eye.

"Nickie." Tears were dripping over his cuts and off his chin. "I swear I didn't...They made..." He reached for her hands. His were covered in swollen red bruises. She took one of them and pulled his sleeve, exposing defensive wounds up and down the side of his hand and forearm.

"Take this," he said, pulling his arm away. He took a piece of paper from his pocket and handed it to her. "I don't know what it means. He's not alone."

He's not alone? Who else? How?

"He's crazy, Nickie. Crazy. I've never seen anything like it. He said he was going after my woman if I didn't meet you here. Go now. He told me to tell you, you have ten minutes."

"Ten? From when?"

"Go!"

She took the paper, reading it as she ran to her car. "Go to the warehouse by our crash." Their crash? That was by Duncan's house. There was no warehouse by Duncan's house. She backed up and floored it through the lot. As she drove, she pulled out her tablet and found a Google Earth app. What the hell was she doing?

As she powered up, movement down the road caught her eye. A line of what looked like every squad car and emergency vehicle in town barreled toward the hospital. She wasn't in her usual town car. It was smashed. Or in one of the black and whites she drove during the day. That meant no access to a radio. Why hadn't someone called her cell? Instinctively, her foot left the accelerator and hovered over the brake as she reached for her phone. It was in the snow at the Reed home.

Gloria. She pressed the gas as she craned her head from the Audi's rearview mirror to the side mirror and back again. Nothing looked off at the hospital, but this had to be Zheng's doing.

She drove as she watched her tablet load, then typed

in Duncan's address into Google Earth. There was
nothing but trees. A truck driver laid on his horn as
she swerved into his lane while manipulating the
screen on her tablet. She searched around Duncan's
house and found Andy and Rose's place. The fence
around their backyard. Their barn. Could he mean
their barn? No.

On the other side of the highway, back in the trees,
she found something. It was a row of metal buildings.
The access was from highway ten, not this road.
Tossing the tablet on her passenger seat, she slammed
on her brakes and spun into a U-turn.

Please be alive. Please, Gloria. Hang in there. I'm
coming. Why didn't she think of this? Of course he
would fucking go after the people she loved. Duncan
knew to be cautious. His damned GPS. She even
scoffed at him for it, she thought as she spun onto a
gravel road with tall weeds sticking out of the snow.
The tiny chip may be the only way she would get out
of this alive.

She stopped in front of the largest building. It stood
at the end of three smaller ones, all with single,
oversized garage doors. She remembered this was the
abandoned spot one of the town's contractors once
used to store his equipment.

Movement caught her eye. A door opened.

Gloria.

Zheng stood behind her, one arm around her
shoulders and the other holding a gun pressed into her
temple. Her eyes were wide with fear, her mouth
stuffed with a cloth and duct taped shut.

Nickie's heart pounded as she got out of her car.
She did everything she could to be smart, to be calm.
"Me for her, Zheng," she said as smoothly as possible.
Her eyes scanned the area. There were two large
garage doors to the left of a short, concrete staircase

that led to a door; a regular door between the garage doors, another at the opposite end of the building's single window near the door Zheng stood in. No sign of the other people Jimbo mentioned.

He smiled. Over the years, lines had formed around his eyes and the corners of his mouth, but it was him. That same fucking demented smile. Backing up, he dragged Gloria into the dark.

Nickie ducked low and ran to the side of the building. She pulled her M&P .45 ACP from her gun belt and took it off safety. The glock in her boot pressed against her shin as she took the short stack of stairs to the open doorway.

She realized she was walking into a trap. She also realized she couldn't live another day if she didn't try to free Gloria. All she had to do was stall until Duncan found her. If he found her.

Gun drawn, she spun into the passageway and made her way back. This must have been the office wing of the building, while the other side stored the excavation equipment. The sweat forming at the base of her neck chilled in the cold air. Her breath led the way in front of her, giving away her location.

With few windows, it was dark. She hardly made it around a folding chair that sat in the hallway before his voice told her to stop. Without moving her head, she turned her eyes to the direction of it. He stepped out of the room just behind her with Gloria limp and defeated in his arms.

Nickie held up both hands and the gun. "Let her go, Zheng. This is you and me now."

"It would be nice to have some quality time between the two of us, yes. Think of the times we have to reminisce about. The years we need to make up for." He jostled Gloria, making her whimper. "Slowly, set the gun at your feet."

The exit door was open behind him; the room he'd just left was dimly lit like a window was in there. Still no sign of others. She obeyed, then pushed her .45 toward him with her foot, saving him the need to tell her to.

As he kicked it farther into the room, he said, "Now the one bulging from your boot. You really should learn to wear looser pants, Nicole. You might give someone the impression you enjoy exchanging sex for money."

Tears ran down Gloria's face.

"It's going to be okay," Nickie said to her as she removed the glock from her boot and pushed it along the floor.

"No, it's really not. You see, you don't care what I do to you, Nicole. You helped me learn that from your reactions to my presence in your townhouse and when I took part in your press conference." He reached for the glock with his foot as he tightened his grip on Gloria. Gloria squeezed her eyes shut and her shoulders shook. Pushing with the side of his shoe, he brought her glock close to where he stood. "You really should see a shrink about your self-worth issues. You have no fear of pain. No fear of what a person like myself might be capable of."

He brushed his gun from the crown of Gloria's black hair, digging it down her cheek and over her shoulder. "The ones you love, on the other hand…"

"Okay." Nickie couldn't stand it any longer. "You're right. I need a shrink. You've got me scared. You're right," she repeated as her eyes burned. "Let her go." She inched her way to him.

Using the toe of his boot, he pulled a chair from the room and sat Gloria in it. He pulled something from his pocket and took her arms behind her. Nickie heard the unmistakable sound of a zip tie.

"Have a seat, my Nicole." He gestured with his head toward the folding chair already in the hall.

CHAPTER 25

Andy had insisted on taking his Jeep. Duncan bounced in the passenger seat on the way to his house with Nathan and Red in the back. His leg bounced with nerves. His leg never did that. He was about to put more of his loved ones in jeopardy. Instead of his platoon, this time it would be his family.

"Pull up to the front," he said. Opening the door before the Jeep stopped completely, Duncan took off over the brittle, dry asphalt to his granite steps. Taking them two at a time, he realized Nickie had his keys.

He ran the length of the porch, then jumped. Punching in the code to the garage door, he looked around as it raised enough for him duck beneath. His uncle, brother and Red were close on his heels. He dipped beneath the moving door and through the one to his service entry. Adrenaline soared through him enough to make him nearly forget to disengage the alarm.

Sprinting the two flights of stairs, he sucked air as he barged through the French doors to where he kept the equipment used to hack into a phone's GPS. Except, he wouldn't be searching for a phone's GPS.

The sounds of the pounding feet that followed him were of little consequence. Red's barking was barely heard.

He hooked the equipment needed to locate Nickie's two GPS chips up to his desk computer. If she didn't at least have them in his Audi, he had no other plan of how to find her.

Holster first. He connected the system, then used the lengthy code matched with the chip. As he waited, his leg shook and he realized his uncle was on the phone.

"Who are you calling?" It came out harsher than he'd intended.

"Dave."

"Captain Nolan? Of course. Wait." Duncan couldn't think of a reason not to. It simply wasn't sitting well with him. "Good. You're right. Good." His entire body began to rock with the leg.

Andy and the dog stood next to Nathan, both statue still.

A soft *ting* sounded and Duncan turned to find the location of Nickie's holster. Zooming in, he realized it was in his house. Of course it was. She left it on one of the hooks near the coat closet in the foyer. He pounded the sides of his fist on his desk. Forcing his body to calm, he ground his teeth at his stupidity and switched over to the code for the chip in her gun belt.

As he kept his eyes glued to the screen, he leaned back in his chair and ran a hand along the top of his head. He held on to a clump to keep his head from exploding, to keep the sounds, images and smells from his stint in the Middle East from imploding his brain, keeping him from his Nickie.

This blip was monumentally more discouraging. The closer it came to his house, the more air that seeped from his lungs, threatening never to return. Upstate New York, near Seneca Lake, to Northridge, to just outside of the north west side of town, right where his house stood.

His face fell into the palms of his hands. She'd left it here, too. Of course she did. Why would she carry a holster or a gun belt to a visit with his aunt and uncle for scones on a Sunday morning?

Somewhere he sensed a large body standing behind him. It was his commander. Together, they surveyed the line of limp bodies they had dragged from the helicopter. Forcing his glance downward, he surveyed the blood that covered his hands. Only some of it belonged to him.

"Duncan, we have work to do." He nodded. Body bags to fill. Paperwork to complete. But first, they needed to protect their fallen chopper from insurgents. Except, he had no will to protect anything.

"Duncan," the voice said louder. "Look at the damned screen." Strong hands shook his shoulders, and he opened his eyes.

Squinting, he blinked and dipped his face closer to the monitor. Her gun belt wasn't here. It wasn't in his house. Elation caused him to wipe the sweat that had formed along his forehead and blink again. "What? That's less than a mile away." It wasn't in his house, he repeated somewhere in his head.

"Those are the buildings Greenberg Contractors used to own." It was Andy's voice.

Duncan pulled himself back fully to the present and spun to find Nathan and Andy. "Dave. What did Dave say?"

Nathan and Andy glanced at each other. Oh no, how long had Duncan been in the flashback?

"We couldn't get through to him. We tried the station and Detective Lynx. No one is answering."

Duncan ran for the doors. He went down one flight of stairs before he turned for one of his spare rooms.

Opening a wooden wall cabinet, he chose a handful of vials, some smaller containers of C4 and a pocketknife. His Beretta lay under the seat of his SUV, but he needed more. He moved to the next cabinet. Next to the bigger blocks of C4 were his guns.

"What the hell, Duncan?" Andy asked from behind him, Red running in circles. "You've got a freaking arsenal in here."

Ignoring his brother, Duncan stuffed a smaller glock in the back of his belt along with a few replacement magazines in the pocket of his pants. Nathan reached next to him and took a semiautomatic.

"I can't let you do that. It's not registered to you."

"Try and stop me," Nathan said.

Zip ties dug into Nickie's wrists and locked her knees and feet together. Her gun belt hung from the knob of the door to the room Gloria was in. Zheng stuck her M&P .45 in the front of his pants. The glock lay on the floor by the door to the room. The outside door had been left open letting cold air blow onto the side of Nickie's face. Zheng hadn't gagged her as he had Gloria. That wasn't a good sign. He paced as he listened to someone on the other end of his cell, then smiled wide and clicked off.

"Gentlemen," he yelled and stopped in front of Nickie.

Tanner hadn't lied. She'd tried to shake off the thought. Zheng had people here and others to communicate with on his cell. He wasn't desperate. She hadn't put him on the run when she rescued the group of captive girls.

He stopped in front of her chair and leaned down to her. "You're the only one who ever got away." He crooned in her ear. "Alive, that is."

Slowly, she pulled her face away from the scent of him. Cologne and soap. "You always were special," he said.

Quick as a weasel, she jutted her head toward him, ready for the stars to spin in her head from the blow. He skipped back and roared with laughter. "That's not going to work on me, my savage. I know you far too well."

Three men dressed in matching dark mock-turtlenecks came from down the hall. Zheng kept his eyes on Nickie but pointed his finger into the room where he'd placed Gloria. "Take her and secure the rest of the entrances," he said to the men as he barked in Nickie's face. "Don't take her too far. I might need her if Detective Savage is less than cooperative."

"No!" Nickie screamed. She shook and shook her secured body enough to move the chair three full feet. Glaring in dread, two of them stuck a hand under Gloria's shoulders and dragged her, chair and all, backward down the hall. Gloria's eyes were saucers, red with fear, growing smaller as Nickie watched her taken away.

The third man carried a blowtorch and started sealing the exit door Nickie had entered through.

She blinked away the tears as she strained against the zip ties that began cutting her wrists.

"Look at your face, my Nicole. Panic. Fear. That's an expression I've never been privy to before. How positively wonderful. Come," he said as if she could move. "Let's talk."

He spun her around in her chair enough to make her neck whip and crack. Then, he dragged her chair into the room vacated by Gloria. Clamping her eyes shut, she tuned out Zheng and listened attentively at the sound of the men's footsteps and Gloria's chair as it scraped along the concrete. Another turn, then one more.

Andy soared down Duncan's drive. It was too fast. He was never going to make the turn. "Andy! Slow the hell down."

Duncan grasped the roll bar and braced, but Andy didn't attempt to turn.

"Short cut, brother," Andy yelled and blew over the highway, bouncing between the trees across the ditch. He shifted into four-wheel drive, then headed into the woods.

Through the noise of crunching snow and aching metal bouncing through the woods, Duncan's phone rang.

"Eddy? What a relief," Duncan yelled in the phone. "Nickie's in trouble. We need backup. No one's answering their phones."

Duncan dipped his head from the wind and covered his other ear. "What? Is anyone hurt? How much damage? Are you sure?"

He rattled off rapid-fire questions as a picture of what was going on came into his head. A diversion.

"Motherfucker," Duncan said as he hung up the phone. "Bombs are planted all over the hospital. They are going off in fifteen minutes increments. Eddy is coming to us regardless. I think he's all we get."

Andy busted through the edge of the trees to a clearing and nearly ran into a smaller warehouse at the end of a row of four. His Audi. Duncan had one focus. Nickie.

Andy slowed down, passed the Audi and crept to the back of the largest building. Tire tracks littered the gravel. Only one set belonged to the Audi.

Nathan told Red to stay as the three of them each took a door. Duncan came in low and against the metal side of the building as he made his way up a few concrete stairs. His heart sped, and his senses were on overdrive as he took his bare hand and wrapped it around the handle to the door, then shook. It was locked as he expected. Glancing to Nathan and Andy, they both shook their heads, signaling theirs were locked, too.

Duncan dug in a pocket and pulled out the first vial of C4. He chipped a piece of the sticky compound and stuck it into the lock. Taking his lighter, he lit the material and ducked, covering his face. A small *poof* and he was in. Giving a thumbs up to Nathan and Andy, he put on his gloves and gently pulled on the door.

It didn't move.

He pulled harder. Nothing. Not a millimeter of movement. Nathan and Andy had reached him by then. "I think he's welded it fucking shut. Let's try the next one."

And they did. And the next and the next. With each door they tried, Duncan's hope diminished.

"It's no use," Andy said. "I have an idea. We're going to need more explosives."

"Nicole Monticello of *the* Maryland Monticellos." Zheng walked in a circle around Nickie. "I cannot tell you how much trouble that name has given me." She recognized the smell of him as if sixteen years ago was sixteen days. "Our clientele like them fresh and clean." This was too familiar. Her eyes followed him, and she dipped her lids to half-closed. Her body changed to autopilot.

He reached like he was going to brush the backs of his fingers down the side of her face. She jerked her mouth to his fingers and tried to bite.

He pulled his hand back but stared at her like she was some drugged freak as he continued. "But I would have never picked you if I had been in charge all those long years ago. Much too high profile. Then, you changed your name. I was like a proud father the day I was told this."

She didn't have time for this. "I didn't do it because of you," she said and waited until his psychotic pacing took him around the back of her chair. In her fit, she'd shaken it to nearly under the window. She heard no gunshots and no cries from Gloria. The feet of Gloria's chair had stopped scraping about three rooms from here.

"Not for me? Ah," he said. "As a tribute, then?" From behind, his voice came close and low. "For the cries from the girls as I punished them for your betrayal? Can you still hear them?"

Her shoulders fell. Yes. Yes, she could hear them. She knew, always knew what would happen if she ran. And she ran anyway.

He laughed the laugh that haunted her dreams and mixed with the cries of young girls.

"I was forced to allow you to carry on due to…your status. I had to keep an eye on you. Babysitters and all that. But the stunt you pulled at Moody's white house, Nicole, was the end of you. Your liability has become a risk larger than the killing of a Maryland Monticello. Than the killing of a cop."

He ran his hand along the top of her hair, making bile rise in her throat. "I need to know how you did it, my Nicole." His hand brushed over her shoulder. "How did you find out about Moody's? The timing? The placement of the guards? The security system was state of the art. Who did you include in your circle of information?"

His hand trailed to her neck, circled and grasped. His other hand slithered low around her waist. "I was sincere, my Nicole. I've never had interest in young girls. You know that." He slid his hand to her breast. "Not that way. But this." He squeezed and her feet and legs reflexively exploded. The chair tumbled backward on top of him. Her head fell on his. She heard the unmistakable sound of skull hitting concrete. The blurred vision from the impact was well worth it. He scooted himself from beneath her, but not before she had the chance to give him another head butt. It probably hurt her more than it did him. Still worth it.

He didn't bother righting her chair, but came around and closed-fist punched her three times in the face as she lay toppled. The sight of blood dripping from his nose thrilled her. Through the pain and taste of blood, she smiled, hoping her teeth were covered in it.

"Yeah," he said as he reached behind his head. When he pulled his hand around, blood covered his fingertips. The sight was pure elation.

"You never did care about pain. I'm going to go get the spic."

"Okay," she said. "I'll tell you. You'd have to be an idiot not to figure out your pimping schedule. Just follow the big games where guys need to grab their cocks after a big win, or have someone else do it for them after they lose."

"The security system?"

She shrugged and readied herself for the next blow.

CHAPTER 26

Duncan grasped the steering wheel as he bounced in Andy's Jeep with Nathan in the passenger seat and Red in the back. Andy drove an oversized end-loader with a line of C4 bricks stuck along the outside of the bucket. The smaller trees that were in Andy's way became fallen logs as he rolled over them. Too much time had passed. She could be anywhere or in any kind of condition. Or no condition.

He had to get to her. On Nathan's lap rested Duncan's tablet. Duncan had programmed it to do two things: detect Nickie's GPS chip and ignite the C4 bricks. Random blips flashed on the monitor as the device gave off pieces of information locating Nickie's gun belt within the largest warehouse.

It was a gamble, but he decided her belt would no longer be on her. Zheng would have taken it. It was still a gamble. He had no choice. He had to get through. Every damned door had been welded shut. How the fuck did Zheng plan to leave? Probably a similar way to how Andy planned to get in.

Did Zheng think the diversion at the hospital wouldn't last? That the police would be out here in force? Was it all precautionary? It didn't matter, Duncan thought, as Andy made his way through the clearing. He stopped the machine, then turned to get the signal from Duncan.

Duncan studied the blip on the monitor although he didn't need to. It hadn't moved. Looking up, he noticed the spot would be about ten yards behind an entrance door at the top of the short stack of stairs. He'd tried to blow the lock on that door himself. This time, he planned to blow the door and wall that surrounded it. He pointed to the spot for Andy to drive into and slipped out of the Jeep.

Shoving the machine in gear, Andy drove it straight for the spot between the closest garage door and the human door at the top of the stairs. Nathan hovered his fingers over the enter button on his tablet, waiting for the Duncan's signal. Just before Andy made impact, Duncan spotted the face of an unfamiliar man peering through the window.

As Andy's end-loader made contact, Duncan waved his hand to Nathan who remotely ignited the explosives, blowing a hole the size of a small country in the wall. Debris rained from the sky: metal, hunks of concrete and glass. They took cover, waiting for it to clear before they ran in the direction of the hole.

Red beat them to the building, climbing up crumbled walls with his nose to the ground. A man wearing a black mock-turtleneck lay sprawled partially under the debris with blood dripping from his nose and ears. Red growled and dipped his head. They all turned.

Zheng.

He came from a room toward the end, then staggered around the corner. Red sprinted after him, followed by Nathan and Andy. Duncan's fingers longed to choke him until he looked like the man in the black turtleneck, but he needed to find Nickie. He headed for the room Zheng had exited. It was the second time in a few short weeks he'd found her lifeless. She was covered in dust and laid on her side, tied to a chair by her feet and hands. He slid to the ground on his knees and grabbed her bruised face.

She blinked, showing him a glimpse of her steel gray.

"Nickie. Where does it hurt?" He ran his hands along her face, cleaning the dust.

"My wrists."

"Oh shit." Of course. He dug in his pockets and grabbed his knife. As he sliced the freaking zip ties, her feet and hands sprang forward and she rolled on her back and rubbed them.

Her wrists were bleeding, and still she got up on her hands and knees and crawled toward the door.

"What are you doing?" he yelled. "Zheng is hurt. He's not going far. Red is after him."

"Gloria," she croaked, picking up a glock from the rubble and pushing up from her hands.

"Gloria? What are you talking about?"

"There are at least three more, plus Zheng. They have Gloria."

He helped her to her feet and hobbled toward the hallway. "One of the three is buried under concrete." Their feet crunched over broken glass.

"What did you do?" she asked, looking at the gaping hole.

"I wanted my detective."

She sighed heavily and poured her weight on the arm that held her up. "I'm the one who got away."

They found Gloria in a room, eyes wide and sobbing through a rag stuffed in her mouth. The look in her eyes at the sight of Nickie was the serene relief of a mother reunited with her daughter.

"Go," Nickie said. "I'm going to get her out of here."

He wouldn't leave her. "I just got you back. I'm at least getting you to the Audi first."

"I've got this. Don't you let him get away. Go!" she yelled, and he ran. He ran until he caught up to the barking. Red stood baring his teeth with the hair on his back raised. Another man who looked much like the dead one near the hole in the wall stood staring at Red with contempt. Andy had one of Duncan's rifles pointed at his head.

"They went that way." Andy nodded toward the garage area. "I've got this one."

A single siren screamed toward the group of buildings as Duncan followed the hallway Andy suggested. Throwing his body into it, he pushed opened a steel door. Four SUVs were parked in a line inside. He heard three sets of footsteps. His memory helped him recognize that one belonged to Nathan.

"Get down, Nathan," Duncan warned. The sound of his voice gave away his location, but it was necessary. With soft feet, he hurried along the wall of garage doors. Piles of rusty equipment lined the back on the other side of the SUVs. He ducked low, then rolled covering himself in dust, much like he did during his time in the desert.

He spotted Nathan's black shoes and a pair of boots covered in the kind of dirt that meant they'd been near an explosion. Zheng. Drawing his gun, Duncan rose to a squatting position and moved silently to the other side of the only thing that stood between them—one of the SUVs. He heard the unmistakable sound of an unlatching car door.

His mind was suddenly clear. No clutter from years of sights and sounds. No need to throw his mind back to the Middle East.

Catapulting, he leapt into the air and over the hood of the vehicle. He let off round after round, nearly emptying the magazine of his Beretta into the opened door Zheng used as a shield. Zheng may have ducked the bullets but not the car door as Duncan kicked it shut on his way to landing on the concrete. An unbridled need to get his hands on Zheng kept his mind clear.

Zheng kicked his legs in the air and landed on his feet. He bounced on the balls of his feet and straightened his fingers like a black belt ready to spar.

Duncan wasn't trained in martial arts. He'd been trained to fight quick and dirty. Fast and precise, Zheng jumped and spun, but Duncan was faster. He dodged the foot that came out of nowhere toward his face. That was the trouble with these cocky karate assholes. They didn't know the first thing to do in street fight. Duncan took advantage of Zheng's exposed nuts and landed his fist square in the center of them.

Zheng howled and dropped to the floor like a newborn giraffe. Duncan bent over him, his fist aching to bloody his face. Zheng writhed on the ground. "No," Duncan yelled. "Get up. Get up and fight."

Duncan nudged him with his shoe probably harder than he needed to. Clutching the side of the vehicle he just tried to enter, Zheng lifted to one knee.

"Get up, motherfucker. Get up."

Still clutching his junk, Zheng dipped his head between his arms, then spun and landed a solid hook to the side of Duncan's head.

Pain erupted somewhere in his vision, his hearing, his head. None of it mattered. Duncan charged, making Zheng's spinning, turning ballet shit useless, and flew a quick jab, stunning him before following up with a punch that came from Duncan's chest, through his arm and out his knuckles. Again and again, Duncan pummeled him, ignoring the pain searing in his knuckles.

The click from a gun taken off safety made Duncan turn his attention away. One of Zheng's men stood with a gun pointed at Duncan's head. Carefully, Duncan lifted from Zheng and held up his hands. He spotted his uncle as Nathan slinked from behind the man. Duncan desperately hoped Zheng wouldn't see him, too.

The car door clicked again. With hands still in the air, Duncan kept his head facing forward but moved his gaze to Zheng just as...Nathan pulled the trigger? The man went down but not before sending off two rounds, making Duncan and Nathan duck for cover. Momentarily stunned, Duncan took in the idea that Nathan shot a man. Relief flooded Duncan as the man rolled on the concrete between cars, clutching his leg. Nathan hadn't killed a man.

The garage door began to rise as the SUV's starter ignited.

The single siren grew closer as the sound of more approached from farther away. Any injuries were buried in endorphins. Duncan was well prepared to jump the hood of the vehicle when he noticed black boots that stood on the other side of the rising door. Black boots, planted in the gravel, feet spread, knees locked.

Nickie.

Zheng would run her over without a second thought. As the door lifted to halfway, Zheng jerked the front end of the SUV through the opening. Then, Duncan saw it. She had her arms raised and her glock aimed at Zheng's head. Her expression was highly conflicted. The muscles in her jaw flexed as she jerked her aim up a fraction.

Pop, pop. Her arms stayed in place. Blood splattered the driver-side window and Zheng's car scraped the side of the garage door opening before coming to a stop. Even with the vehicle halted at her feet, she didn't move. Not her legs or the gun she grasped in both hands.

Duncan walked to her with his arms up. "Nickie?"

Her eyes darted to his, wide and crazed.

"It's okay. It's me. It's over. Where's Gloria?"

An unmarked Camry with lights flashing from the grill came barreling down the weeded drive. Lynx.

"She's in the Audi," Nickie said and shoved the glock in the back of her slacks before walking toward Zheng. She stood and stared at him with lifeless eyes, half-opened eyes.

Duncan staggered around to the passenger side and opened the door. "You got him in the head and the shoulder. He's breathing. You didn't kill him." That fact confused him. "You shot him, point blank range, and you didn't kill him."

Her sigh was pronounced. "No. I didn't kill him. We need him to the find the other girls."

Eddy skidded a few yards from the SUV and flew out of his unmarked. "Mother fuck, Nick. You're okay. You had us all scared shitless." His eyes grew bigger as they zoned on her battered face. "Or *are* you okay?"

"We've got a stiff inside and two secured. One is injured in the car, here. There may be others unaccounted for." The line of emergency vehicles grew closer. "Can you cover the perp in the car? I don't think he's going anywhere." She started to head inside the building. "I have no radio or phone. Tell the guys to call in an ambulance for the one in the car and get the ones held inside."

"Wait. Nick. Those aren't our black and whites coming." Eddy put his fingers to the bruises on the side of her face.

"What are you talking about? Who the hell is it?"

"The hospital was targeted. The captain called in everyone to take care of it. Those guys are either from Ithaca or Geneva. Who is in the car?" he asked.

"Jun Zheng. The hospital was his doing." She said it as a fact, not a hunch. "I'll fill you in later. Try not to shoot him again. I need him for information." She took off into the garage.

Lynx rotated his gaze to Duncan before approaching the vehicle. Duncan took off behind Nickie.

CHAPTER 27

The steam from Nickie's breath led her way as she headed down the first hallway. "You shouldn't come with me." He had family to check on. So did she.

"Like hell," she heard him say from behind her in the dark.

"I didn't kill him," she whispered in a sort of disbelief. "I wanted to. We need him, and we need to bring in the other two alive." The dust hadn't completely settled. Not in here or out there.

"Nickie, wait," Duncan said, but she'd already spun to the growling in the side room and had her glock pointed at Andy.

"Put that thing down. We're family," Andy said and smiled. "I heard the sirens. Tell them to hurry it up. I'm tired of babysitting this scumbag."

She followed the hallway all the way out the door Duncan had blown away. "Holy shit, Duncan. What did you use?" Holding up a hand, she corrected herself. "Don't tell me."

The Audi was still there. Gloria. She didn't see anyone in it. Nickie stumbled, hurrying over the crumbled stairs and around the stiff Duncan had told her about.

Gloria lay on the floor in the backseat. Slowly, Nickie opened the back driver's side door. Relief flooded Nickie as Gloria craned her head and looked over her shoulder at her with her warm and smiling dark eyes.

"It's over," Nickie whispered. "It's okay. Do you hear the sirens?"

Gloria came out, and Nickie wrapped her arms around her.

"Let me look at you, child," Gloria said as she pulled back and took Nickie's face in her hands, then looked her over from head to toe. Nickie closed her eyes and shook her head. Gloria was the one making sure *she* was okay?

"Are you sure this is the last time?" Posing butt naked was become increasingly embarrassing, not the other way around. "What are we doing with this anyway?"

"You said, 'we.'"

She was supposed to have a sultry look, and now she couldn't help but smile. "Last time *we* weren't engaged."

He stared at the canvas, then set down his brush and pulled out a band from the pocket of his slacks. He tied his hair in a quick, short tail, then changed brushes. "Just a few finishing touches. I'm nearly done."

"You said that last time." She wasn't really complaining. Posing for his paintings always made her feel special. It wasn't so much that she was posing, but the deeply intense way he studied her. The way he saw her.

"And we can do with it whatever you'd like."

"No art shows?"

The comment jarred him enough for him to turn his focus and frown at her, but only until he realized she was joking.

The silver rings from her necklace lay warm down her neck. Her hair was soft over her shoulders. But that's not what made her embarrassed. "I think you should have to be naked, too."

A single brow lifted. The comment didn't do enough to make him glare at her or even lose his stride, but at least she changed his expression.

"I think we should sell the town house." That ought to get him.

And it did. He stopped and sighed, then continued working.

But he didn't answer. It completely backfired and made her more self-conscious than ever. It was what he wanted. It had to be. He'd been picking at her about it for months, hadn't he? They were engaged. She had the ring to prove it.

"Who do you think is the mole?" he asked. The change in subject didn't make her forget his reaction.

"I don't want to think about it tonight. Jun Zheng is in custody along with two of his cronies. We are on the way to finding the other groups of girls. I have a new police-issued unmarked. No wait, that's not a good thing. A Camry? It's like abuse to a police officer."

The corner of his mouth lifted once more, making currents of warmth run through her. She was getting married. She was in love and getting married to the best thing she'd ever had.

He walked to the fridge and pulled out a Diet Coke. On his way back, he grabbed the pile of clothes she'd left on the floor.

"You're done?" she asked, sitting up.

"I am."

Yanking on her jeans, she left them undone and pulled the shirt over her head. She'd seen it before. Thought he was done three sittings ago, but she was still curious.

When she walked around to the back of the easel, she wasn't sure how she felt. It looked like a photograph. All of his paintings did. "You made me look prettier than I am. I suppose I should thank you."

He took her face in his hands and dropped their foreheads together. "I could never do justice to your beauty."

She shivered. "I guess you're forgiven, then."

"Hmm?" he questioned as he kissed the top of her head.

"You never answered me about selling my place. You know how I am about all of this stuff, and you didn't say anything."

His thumbs traced her cheeks. The stubble on his face was longer than usual, giving him a deeper, more menacing appearance. "I'm not going to live with you until we're married."

Throwing her head back, she roared. She stepped away and held her hands to her chest as she laughed some more.

He wasn't smiling.

"Come on, Duncan. I already live here. I sleep here every night."

"Except when I'm out of town."

"Is that wrong?"

"No, no, it's not wrong."

She grabbed the side of her hair and growled. "I'll never get relationships. You want me to have a drawer. You want me to share the closet. You want to marry me. You don't want me to move in."

He nodded as he answered. "It may seem trivial to you, but I don't want us to officially live together until we are husband and wife. Laugh if you want. I'm firm on this."

Why did that flatter her?

The doorbell rang. She'd been taken in the moment and needed to check and make sure she was dressed. No bra. That was a problem. "I'd better finish getting dressed. You get it. It's your place anyway."

He grunted and headed for the stairs. So, they weren't going to live together? It did make her laugh. She had kale in the fridge and nearly her entire wardrobe in his closet and dressers. Shrugging, she finished dressing and made her way after him.

He wished he'd installed an elevator. She hated elevators. It made her think as she jogged down the stairs. He drank coffee. She drank soda. He ate donuts. She ate yogurt. Yet, she was sure this was going to work. More sure than she had ever been about anything in her life.

The door shut and there was quiet. A box sat at Duncan's feet. "Who was it?" Nickie asked.

The box made noise. Her feet froze on the stairs and her mouth gaped open. "You didn't."

"Maybe I did. You should come find out."

Her feet sped double time down to the foyer. She practically slid next to the box, ready to tear it open when she realized the size and stepped away.

"It's a small box," she said flatly and clutched both her hands close to her body.

"Yes," he said slow and condescendingly.

"We were going to get a dog."

"Yes." He did it again.

The thing scratched the box. She heard whining. Puppy whining. "That doesn't sound like a dog."

"Those are definitely dog sounds."

"I said 'dog.' There is a puppy in there." She backed

up to the first stair.

One of the largest smiles Nickie had ever seen come from Duncan spread across his face. "You're scared of a puppy."

"I'm not scared. And stop smiling. This is not funny." She stepped up to the next stair. "I don't know what to do with a puppy. Take it back."

He reached down for the lid.

"No!" she yelled and heard the thing yelp and squeal like she'd stepped on its foot. "See? I scared it. I'm going to ruin it. Take it back," she repeated as he opened the box. "Take it back and get a bigger one."

A tiny, timid, black and brown Rottweiler cowered in the corner. Both Nickie's hands stuck out in front of her like stop signs.

It took a few moments for the thing to analyze the situation. Maybe it was a smart puppy. Except, then decided it was safe. Which made it a stupid puppy. It crept closer to her and sniffed before its tail went berserk and its body waved and flailed.

"What the freaking hell would I do with a puppy?"

Duncan picked it up and walked toward her.

"No, no, no. Put it down. Put it back. Take it—"

Duncan placed it against her chest and let go. "I'm going to drop it. I'm going to drop it." Its fur was silk and it smelled like...puppy. She held on tight as it licked her shirt, then bit her buttons. "What do you feed it? It's going to pee on the floor. I don't know how to train it not to pee on the floor."

It sniffed her again, then started the tail-wagging squirming again. "It's biting me. It has needles for teeth."

"Scratch its belly."

"Do what?" She looked down at its belly. It was a she. Nickie moved her fingers over its belly like she was plucking her cello. The puppy's eyes rolled to the back of her head and her four legs stilled, falling outward like she had no bones in her legs and exposing her silky underside. The little girl made purring noises like a cat and craned her head so her tongue could reach Nickie's shirt.

"It's a she," Nickie said and sat on the stairs. "She's a she." Nickie looked to Duncan.

The smile on his face was large and beautiful, and for the first time she could remember, he had to share the spotlight of prettiest thing in the room.

Turn the page for an

excerpt from

SAVAGE

DISCLOSURE

The Nickie Savage Series
Book Three

R.T. Wolfe

———◆ ◆ ◆ ◀———

Juggling both the take-out bag from Mikey's Bar and Grill and the yogurt she snatched from home, Nickie stepped into the elevator and pushed the button to the top floor. Except, this was Northridge, New York, which meant the top floor to the tallest downtown building was a whopping four floors. And yet the man the local newspapers called *The Taste of L.A.* stayed for her. Here. And bought the top floor of the tallest building to serve as an office he used only part-time.

The doors opened and she stepped into the hallway, her mind still rolling through the roadblocks of her frustrating new case. She understood the reluctance rape victims had to pointing fingers at their assailants, but the college dean? As she spotted his morning receptionist's empty chair, Nickie realized how late it was for lunch. Luckily the bag from Mickey's was heavy.

It wasn't like her to walk into anyone's office unannounced, especially when the door was closed. With the absence of his receptionist, Nickie attempted to raise her full hands to knock. The door opened before she had the chance.

Duncan greeted her with a half smile. He took the

Mikey's bag from her, then wrapped his free hand around hers. Twirling her wedding ring between his thumb and forefinger—the habit he'd picked up since their marriage—he leaned in and kissed her softly. The familiar scent of him dove into her lungs and settled next to her heart.

"There you are," he said just as softly. She blinked three times in order to regain her composure.

Turning, he headed back for his desk with his bag, opening it as he walked.

"Am I so late that you waited by the door for your lunch?" she asked as she sunk into the guest chair on the opposite side of his enormous desk. She lifted a boot, ready to plop it on the top before noticing the polish of the glass and letting it fall to the floor.

Pulling out the over-sized tenderloin from the bag, he gestured to the monitor at the side of his desk. "I saw you on the security cameras."

Of course.

"Sorry for leaving you hungry. And for the hectic past few days. It doesn't look like the next few will be any better."

"Hmm," he said as he swallowed bites of the French fries, never one to talk with his mouth full. "That it a shame since I haven't seen you naked in seventy-two hours."

Opening her half-empty yogurt container, she considered. "What about the other night?" On the stairs. Yum.

"You weren't naked."

She smiled. It couldn't be helped, but it was followed by the frown created from her predicament with her recent case.

"Would you like to talk about it?"

"Hmm? Oh." She shrugged and dunked some of the blueberries she'd thrown in the container on her way out of the house. "Roadblock on a case. Alleged college rape."

"You use the word 'alleged' often. I know better, but others view this as assumed innocence."

Another shrug. "Innocent until proven guilty and all that. The girl sounds legit, but no need to throw some bloke under the bus until I have proof. Which is where we come to my roadblock. Statistically, these things don't come in isolated cases. I've got the alleged victim." Oops. There was that word again. "I've got the dude's ID." She dug in the pocket of her blouse and pulled out the photo she'd downloaded of him. Waving it around with her free hand, she took another bite before continuing. "I can't exactly stand in front of his Drama Club practice and show his picture to girls as they leave, making accusations. I'm a NPD detective."

Duncan set down the burger that so ironically mismatched everything about him and walked around to her. Would the reaction of her heart rate to this kind of simple gesture ever wane? He reached down and placed his hand beneath one of her calves, lifting her leg and setting her boot on top of his desk. Before repeating the process with the other leg, he snatched the photo from between her fingers. "I, however, am not a cop and would enjoy an afternoon on the beautiful Heritage Junior College campus."

● ◆ ◆ ●

SAVAGE DISCLOSURE

**available in
print and ebook**

THE NICKIE SAVAGE SERIES

MEET THE AUTHOR

R.T. was born and raised in the beautiful Midwest, the youngest of six ornery children. She married at a young age and began her family shortly after. With three amazing small boys, life was a whirlwind of flipping houses and working two jobs in between swim lessons and games of Candyland.

Now that her boys are nearly grown, R.T. spends much of her time on the road, traveling from one sporting event to another, serving as mom and cheerleader.

When she isn't writing or traveling, she works with several non-profit organizations, promoting the work they do for those who cannot help themselves.

R.T. enjoys hearing from readers. You can contact R.T. through her website: www.rtwolfe.com